Recent Books by Anthony Gilbert

No Dust in the Attic
Ring for a Noose
The Fingerprint
The Voice
Passenger to Nowhere
The Looking Glass Murder
The Visitor
Murder Anonymous
Missing from Her Home
Mr. Crook Lifts the Mask
Tenant for the Tomb
Murder's a Waiting Game
A Nice Little Killing

A Nice Little Killing

A Nice Little Killing

Anthony Gilbert

Random House: New York

Library of Congress Cataloging in Publication Data

Gilbert, Anthony, 1899–
   A nice little killing.

   I. Title.
PZ3.M2943Nhb3   [PR6025.A438]   823'.9'12
ISBN 0-394-48991-8   73-15566

Manufactured in the United States of America
9 8 7 6 5 4 3 2
First Edition

A Nice Little Killing

One

The clock in the public bar of the Bee and Honeysuckle was always kept five minutes fast so that laggard drinkers shouldn't get Jim Severn, the licensee, into trouble with the authorities. At five minutes to three he started calling "Time, gentlemen, please. Drink up. All glasses, please." By three o'clock by the bar clock everyone had departed, except a stout, sturdy patron in bright brown clothes that would have set a connoisseur's teeth on edge. This man snapped the locks on what was probably the shabbiest briefcase in London and was oiling towards the door when Jim came in from the private bar.

"Mr. Crook!" he said. "There's something . . ." He looked distressed, an unlikely expression on the face of a licensee when not threatened by the police.

"Don't be bashful!" beamed Mr. Crook. "Maybe we could drop into your back room and talk things over. Don't want the rozzers dropping on you for flouting the regulations, wouldn't do my reputation any good either."

"It's not that, Mr. Crook. It's the young lady in the saloon."

"What's a young lady doing there?" demanded Crook, pleasurably anticipating an unexpected development.

"She's been there an hour, Mr. Crook, and all on one small sherry."

"All on her owney-oh?"

"That's about the size of it."

"Been stood up, would you say?"

"Doesn't seem like it, Mr. Crook. Never once looked at the door. Just sitting there, going right through the ads."

"Probably hunting for digs. Does she look like a country cousin?"

"I can tell you one thing, Mr. Crook. She doesn't look right in my saloon. As for country, I wouldn't know. She doesn't seem to comprenny the Queen's English. Not when it comes to leaving, anyway."

"What do you expect me to do?" demanded Crook. "English is my only tongue."

"She'd understand you," murmured Jim. "You have a way with you, Mr. Crook."

"Flattery will get you nowhere," Crook admonished him, but he'd known him for quite a while, knew, too, that the police come down like the Assyrian on the fold on these slightly suspect pubs in Earl's Court and its purlieus, where you can spot practically every nationality under heaven.

Mind you, he wasn't blaming them, he knew they had their reasons, a lot of funny stuff went on barely under cover in these streets.

"If she's foreign she mightn't understand about closing hours," he encouraged Jim. "Stay open day and night, as I understand it, on the Continong." He sighed. "The only good thing I know about going into the Common Market, they might extend the licensing laws." He followed Jim into the saloon bar.

The girl sat at a wall table, an empty sherry glass before her; she looked as if she had been there for a long time, and was prepared to stay indefinitely. She wore an absurd little fur hat, more like a trapper's cap, thought Crook, but perhaps the latest thing. She had the right figure for a trouser suit, with its big patch pockets, and her hair bobbed in a pony-tail. Someone's nice cup of tea, thought Crook, though not his. Well, he didn't go much for tea at any time. She was too pale for his approval, but those violet eyes, under short, thick eyelashes that matched her hair, wouldn't pass unnoticed in most company.

4

Crook's characteristic reflection was that he'd as soon find himself saddled with a hand grenade with a wobbling pin.

"She shall make trouble wherever she goes," he paraphrased under his breath, moving towards her with the deceptively light step of a man as solidly built as a bull.

"Make with the feet, Sugar," he offered. "You're embarrassing Jim. Time his place closed."

The girl looked down at the watch on her wrist, a small gold watch on a chain as fine as a hair. And that never came from Woolly's, reflected Mr. Crook shrewdly.

"Three o'clock," he amplified, speaking in the slow careful voice he might have used towards a Hottentot who couldn't be expected to know the lingo. "Place shuts down."

"At three o'clock?" He got the idea she really didn't know—or perhaps she was in such a daze she didn't realize the time or where she was.

"Drinking hours," explained Mr. Crook patiently.

"I have finished my drink."

"Lucky for you. Come, Sugar, you don't want to get Jim into trouble, to say nothing of having to appear before the beak."

"The—beak?" She frowned.

Crook got the idea she did this rather too often. Though she was as slender as a rail, with long narrow hands and feet, and was probably less than twenty years old, he saw she was as immovable as the Rock of Gibraltar and possibly quite a bit more dangerous. He recalled a news story of a girl who had boarded a plane with a hand grenade strapped to her stocking. He found himself looking down at this girl's legs, but there was no suspicious bulge there, and she only carried a small handbag that would hardly have accommodated even one grenade.

"The magistrate. Come outside and I'll explain."

She looked stubborn. "Why may I not wait here? I do not drink."

"Because Jim might lose his job if the rozzers found a customer on the premises after the magic hour. Don't ask me

5

why. I don't make the laws. They'd be very different if I did."

He didn't lay a finger on her, but somehow she found herself standing in the street, while the door of the Bee and Honeysuckle closed instantly behind her.

"Didn't you really know about the place shutting at three?" he asked her.

She put up her small aggressive head. "At three o'clock I am not sitting in bars," she assured him. "I have my work."

"Well, that's British law for you. Why not find a nice coffee bar and settle down there?"

"I do not like coffee bars," the girl told him haughtily. "There is not real coffee in them."

"Then why not go home?" She seemed pretty difficult to please.

She looked amazed rather than indignant. "How can I go home? There is no one but an aunt, and she finds me *de trop*. That is why I am here."

"Meaning you've run away?" Suddenly he slapped his thigh . . . well, nearly. "I've got it. Where are my wandering wits tonight? You're an *au pair* girl."

"That is what they call us." Her voice was full of disdain.

If they think we're all such muck, why do they leave their own country? Crook wondered.

"I'm still not with you," he acknowledged. "You must have slept somewhere last night, so why not go back to wherever that was? Or have you been shopped? They can't do that, you know, not without you've committed a crime." Still, perhaps that was what she had done. "Not in Dutch with the police, are you?" he wheedled.

"I do not wish to talk to the police."

"Shows your good sense. Well, then, this household where you're working—who is there besides Lady Himuckamuck and her ever-loving?"

"There are two little girls. I have brought them to London today to spend a holiday with their aunt. An aunt."

"What's wrong with aunts?"

She stretched her neck till he thought she must suppose she was an ostrich. He remembered a shade too late that she had an aunt and there didn't seem much love lost between them.

"I shall never be an aunt."

"Might be bad luck for someone," said the diplomatic lawyer. "Brought them to London, you said. From . . ."

"A place called Buzzard Minor. A buzzard is an English bird."

"I gather they get around a lot," Mr. Crook assured her. "Well, you've handed 'em over, so why not go back? Or don't you plan to go back? According to Jim, you were rubbernecking through the local rag. Looking for some place to kip?"

"No one will think of looking for me here."

"Running out, are you? I hate to throw cold water on your plans, Sugar, but if that little satchel's all you've got in the way of luggage, you won't find any respectable landlady to let you a room. Luggage is sort of an insurance for a landlady. Then if you find you're a bit short in the morning, she can hang on to your bits and pieces . . ."

The girl looked more haughty than before. "Naturally I have luggage."

"Pardon me for breathing," apologized Mr. Crook. This girl puzzled him, and whatever puzzled him aroused his interest. Besides, under her surface stone-walledness he doubted whether she'd really be much of a hand at looking after herself. Her English was good enough to get by—must have been fooling Jim if she'd persuaded him she didn't understand the lingo—but a kid of three could have told you she wasn't born this side of the Channel.

"Quite sure you don't mean to go back?" he urged. "I mean, if I had a daughter your age, there are better parts of London I'd as lief see her hived up in. You want to play it clever, you know, or you might find yourself pushed back into Auntie's arms. You don't have a visa to play fast and loose in a strange land."

"She would not wish me," the girl assured him, disregarding his final remark. They were walking along the pavement and now Crook could see the Old Superb, his notorious aged yellow Rolls, in the cul-de-sac where he had contrived to park it. "She has a husband," the girl continued. "She was forty." Her voice suggested that Methusalah was a babe in arms by comparison. "And when one has waited so long for a man . . ."

"You ain't going to risk losing him to a girl who looks like this one," agreed Mr. Crook, prudently keeping the comment to himself. Not likely the fellow had wed for love alone. He paused to wonder why she should have made such an impression on him, seeing she wasn't strictly speaking beautiful, and any charm she had she was reserving for a more worthy audience. Still, he didn't go so much for beauty—handsome is as handsome does and it does a lot of people, he was wont to quote. "What is it, Sugar?" For the girl was staring incredulously at the astounding old car.

She pointed a finger at it. "What is that?"

"Beauty, ain't she?" said the beauty's owner proudly.

"You make a joke?"

"You try chasing her, and find out if she's a joke or not. Where's this luggage of yours?"

The girl—Jan Van Damm was her name—hesitated.

"Oh, come, Sugar," protested Crook, "you say you have luggage, brought it up this morning. O.K. Now, luggage ain't a bird of prey. It don't have wings. Or can't you remember where you put it?"

She said sullenly, "It is at Victoria Station."

"So what are you doing in Earl's Court?"

"The aunt meets us at Victoria. The children have each a case and a little purse, and a present their mother tells them to give their aunt. We will take one each, says the aunt, the children can carry their own satchels—she meant purses—then if you leave your luggage at Victoria in the office we can go by underground. The children must learn thrift." Her voice changed

8

comically, becoming a suburban matron's voice, finicky and managing.

"How old are these kids?" asked Crook curiously.

"They are six and eight. Dawn is eight and Coral . . ."

"Don't give me that," Crook pleaded. "No one hates their kids enough to saddle 'em with monikers like that."

"The Bankses are heathen people," retorted Jan scornfully. "They know nothing of Christian names." She rolled her r's like a music-hall comic. "Dawn and Coral are what they are called."

"Wonder the local parson stood for it. So—you parked your bag. Couldn't you tell the aunt you were going from the terminal too?"

"She say, 'My sister tell me you stay at Eastbourne with a friend who has married an Englishman, so your bag will be at the right station.' "

"Well, ain't that true?" asked Mr. Crook.

She gave him a scornful dismissing glance from those great violet eyes. "I am not bound to tell Mrs. Banks where I go," she announced. "Well, I put my bag with the left luggage, it is a zipper, striped, new—I do not travel like a snail with my house on my back."

"So why ain't you back at Victoria?" asked Mr. Crook reasonably.

"I have a holiday until Wednesday." Mr. Crook recalled with surprise that this was an annual holiday weekend; holidays didn't mean a thing to him. "Mr. and Mrs. Banks go to friends in Holland, Dawn and Coral go to their aunt— Oh, they do not wish it, they will stay here with Jan, they say, but Mrs. Banks says, 'Perhaps you will wish to see your family . . .' "

"Offer you an air ticket?" murmured Mr. Crook politely. "No? Well, it shows you believers in miracles ain't dead yet. Don't suppose you save much from your pocket money for weekend air fares."

Under his eyes she seemed to turn into a tigress. "This is the big laugh for you," she told him. "I am to go to Greece with my friend Nikki. Nikki says I must meet his father and mother. He says his father and mother do not like foreign girls, but they will like me. He will buy the tickets, book the seats . . ."

"I can believe a lot of things," Crook warned her, "but Greece for a long weekend—ain't that what it's called?—not that. He must be well-heeled, this chap."

She said demurely, "I think perhaps I stay, if his father and mother like me."

"And how about those kids, those whiz kids, Dawn and Coral. Going to sell them down the river to Auntie?"

Her face softened. "Those poor children. But they will forget. To children life is new every morning. And when I have children of my own," she added explosively, "I will not let them have heathen names."

"So," suggested Mr. Crook, feeling as though he were plodding down a rutted lane and pretty hard going at that, "you came up here. Where were you meeting Nikki?"

"At the terminal." Her voice was impatient. "Where else would we meet?"

"So why is the bag still at Victoria and you in Jim's pub in Earl's Court? Let me guess. Nikki wasn't there."

"I wait where he is to meet me. There will be time to fetch my case, we will take a taxi. But he is not there. I think, Perhaps some other bar, some other floor . . ."

"In short, you searched the terminal from end to end, but the bird has flown."

"I ask at the desk," she said. "Flight to Athens. But there is no flight to Athens. This morning. Tomorrow. But not today. He was not booked on this morning flight, he is not booked for tomorrow. The clerk rings up Heathrow. No sign of Nikki."

"Could have used another moniker," offered Mr. Crook. "Pay in advance?"

"Nikki says he will get the tickets, he can get them at a special price, he works in a travel agency. And he will get me currency, too. Easier here than there, because of the pound."

And she lapped it all up like a kitty with a saucer of milk, reflected Crook. "Where did you meet this paragon?" he inquired.

They had met at a pop festival held at Buzzard Major. They had danced together, met in coffee bars.

"How long?" asked Mr. Crook.

About two months.

Quite long enough for her to lose her head over the fellow, he supposed. He didn't know much about Greeks, except the sort you find in Soho. Pudgy little fellows on the whole, he thought, though in mythology they were represented as high, wide and handsome enough to bedazzle any girl. Maybe Nikki had reverted to type.

"Spika da Englische?" he asked, and she stared and said "Of course" in offended tones. Wonder if he knew any more Greek than I do, reflected Mr. Crook. "Never tried talking to you in his own lingo, I suppose? No, I thought not." Probably didn't have a job either. Just opened his big mouth and little Miss Jan had walked straight in. There should be a trade union for abandoned females, one overt betrayal being enough to ensure membership. Biggest union in the country at that, he wouldn't be surprised. Of course, till her eyes had been opened, Little Miss Tigress wouldn't have believed her chap was a no-gooder, not if she'd seen him taking the money out of a blind man's tin. Oh well, it was one way of buying experience, and like everything else, the price had gone up.

"So," he said, "why here?"

"I think perhaps I find a room . . ."

"Know the Metrop?"

She shook her head. "You want to be a bit careful sorting through some of those ads," warned Mr. Crook tactfully. "Don't know anyone in London?"

Of course she didn't.

"In that case, and seeing that Greece is off, how about going home to the family residence? Or is that shut up till Wednesday?"

Jan shrugged. "Mrs. Brown is there."

"Mrs. Brown being the caretaker?"

"She is the housekeeper—she says the chatelaine." Jan pursed her lips and spaced the syllables with extreme care. "She is an old virgin . . ."

"With a name like that?"

"Oh, perhaps she once has a man," Jan allowed grudgingly, "but she is old—old . . ."

Old like Methuselah? Probably to a girl of her age anyone past his or her thirty-fifth birthday was right over the hill.

"Forty-five, perhaps forty-six. How do I know? But old, old. She stay to look after the silver, because Mr. Banks won it playing games with little balls. And it is a remote house . . ."

"Staying there alone, is she?"

"I could not go back there. Suppose she has a friend, she would not want me. And Mrs. Banks . . ."

"Mrs. Banks 'ud feel a lot more comfortable to think of you cheek by jowl with an ogress than rollicking round the parts of London where you'd be likely to find a room on your own. Nikki clean you out?" he added conversationally.

He saw that was a mistake. "I do not beg."

"Quite right. Just as a matter of interest, what did you tell Mrs. B. about the pal at Eastbourne?"

"I say I meet her at the conversation classes and she tell me if ever I have a few days, come down to stay with her. She have two little girls."

"And Mrs. B. swallowed that?"

"She say, 'That is a busman's holiday.' What is a busman's holiday?"

"Sort of out of the frying pan into the fire. No, I wouldn't expect Mrs. B. to be very enthusiastic." It was hard enough, he'd been told, to get a reliable girl anyhow, either they thought they were the cat's whiskers—baroness's daughters was their way of putting it—and menial jobs are for menials, or they turned out to be pushers and slappers, or stayed out half the night and then stopped on to have the consequences of their adventures on the National Health. So, naturally, if you got anyone passable, you hung on to her like grim death.

"You can't hang around about London on your own on a holiday weekend," he protested, thinking that one of these days he'd wake up and find himself in a mobcap and apron. "Mrs. Brown 'ud be better than that. Anyway, London's creaking at the seams. Unless you know of some hostel specially for girls who've been led up the garden." He wished she wasn't so young, he was far more at home with plain stolid women of mature age who talked his language. These flibbertigibbets of girls had him stoned. "Give you a lift to Victoria," he offered, "to get the bag back. Only I wouldn't count on getting into a billet there. Buzzard Minor might be better than that."

"So Mrs. Brown shall laugh at me?"

"Oh, come, Sugar, you don't do yourself justice. You rang your friend at Eastbourne to say which train to meet—well, you couldn't know beforehand because you didn't know how long Auntie would keep you hanging around—and you found she'd been trying to get you on the blower. One of the kids started measles, so you can't go there, because of your kids, see? Oh, you can tell it nice enough."

"It is not true," she protested, and he could hardly believe his ears.

"Hark who's talking. Seeing the lady don't exist. Well, then, how about the truth for a change? Not that I advise it here. Truth's wasted on the Mrs. Browns of this world. Half the time they don't believe you, anyway. Talk about a liberty!" He realized that under her disdainful air she was probably all burned up with humiliation at having fallen into the oldest trap in the world. She might even have cared for the wop—still did, for all he knew, women were unaccountable.

"I might go to Eastbourne," she suggested thoughtfully.

"To stay with a dream woman? Or sleep under the pier? You'll find all those berths booked, Sugar, and I don't think you'd care to double up with the hippie band. Didn't give up your passport, I take it? Well, that's something. No, you listen to your Uncle Arthur, pocket your pride and go back to Buzzard Minor. And I'll see you on your way, as far as Victoria. Now, now, soothe your troubled feathers, you'd do as much for me." She clearly thought he was talking claptrap. "You've taken the knock, we can't afford to let you lose all your faith in human nature."

He only stayed long enough at Victoria to see her join a sizable queue at the Left Luggage Office. The station seemed, as usual, full of people who had no particular reason for being there. They crowded the public seats but showed no interest in train arrivals. Many of them had no luggage; about half of them seemed quite alone. He would have liked to wait and make sure that no further mishap befell this bird of travel, but the Superb was too conspicuous for even the regulation traffic warden to pass over for more than a few seconds. He had a passing desire to fill the empty cars with the empty-minded people thronging the platform, and leave some clear area for those whose lives held some purpose, but having an innate mistrust of the fantastic, he got back into his car and drove away. Without mentioning the fact, because, as he said later, two eyes is what nature gave me and two eyes is what I hope to retain, he had slipped one of his famous (some said infamous) business cards into the pocket of Jan's suit before they parted. Bid adieu but not farewell, he reminded himself, and shot out of sight.

The queue at the Left Luggage Office wound as slowly as the notorious wounded Alexandrine snake dragging its slow length along. The instant she appeared, violet eyes flashing, half a dozen voices warned Jan where the queue ended, one or two adding superfluously, "These foreigners, they don't know about fair do's. With them it's looking after Number One, and the rest of the world nowhere." Jan shook her head so that the ponytail jumped between her shoulders, but affected not to understand the insult. The man at the desk seemed to take a relish in being as slow as possible. Sometimes he didn't seem to realize whether luggage was being deposited or retrieved; some of the passengers hardly seemed quite sure themselves. Jan heard herself say, "But I have a train to catch," and all around her voices reminded her that she wasn't the only one. The man at the desk said tranquilly, "This is British Rail, always at your service. If you should miss your train, we'll find some way of getting you to your destination, a later train, maybe." A voice from the queue inquired acidly, "Today or tomorrow," and he laughed.

At last only one passenger stood between Jan and the smart striped bag she had bought for her Greek adventure. It bore a plain label—"I'll get the air labels and give them to you when we meet," Nikki had said. Jan could see the bag now, standing perkily on a side shelf. The elderly, rather shabby woman in front of her saw it too. She was having trouble finding her receipt docket, talking garrulously to herself and to the clerk while she rootled through an untidy handbag and dug into deep coat pockets.

"I know I had it," she said. "I mean, I must have, mustn't I, if you gave it to me?" She dropped a wad of Kleenex on the platform. "Perhaps you forgot," she added brilliantly.

"You wouldn't have let me get away with that, lady," the man said. He was the only untroubled character in this small piece of by-play. "P'raps you put it in your pocket and it's got a hole in it."

A perfectly audible voice behind Jan said, "Put it in a hole in her head most like. At this rate we'll never get a cuppa before the train comes in."

The man with her said humorously, "Only let her out at weekends, I daresay. Everyone needs a bit of fun."

The desperate passenger dropped a soiled powder compact and cried, "Oh, I hope I haven't broken the mirror. That means seven years' bad luck."

"We're getting that," said someone else.

"Sure you left it at this station?" suggested the clerk. "Not Paddington?"

The woman scuffled down and picked up the compact. "Paddington's the name of a bear. Anyway, it doesn't matter because I can see it. That striped bag there."

Jan almost jumped off the ground. "Do not give her that," she cried. "That is mine. I have the ticket here. It contains all my treasures."

"Cheeky monkey," grumbled the older woman. "Don't own the only zip bag in London, I s'pose. Maguire," she added to the clerk. "That's the name. Isobel Maguire. If it's got my name on it, it shows it's mine, doesn't it, even if I can't find the docket."

"I can't give you nothing without you give me a docket," the man explained. "Not even if the address was Buckingham Palace."

"You cannot give her what is mine," insisted Jan. "I tell you, it is valuable."

"Wonder you trusted it with us at all," said the clerk unemotionally. "Now, missis, if you can't find your ticket, you'd best have a word with the constable there. He'll tell you the same as me."

"Will he make you give me my luggage?"

"If it's yours, it won't be given to anyone else. Maybe he can think of something. Me, I have to go by the rules."

"I don't wish to get mixed up with the police," the maddening passenger declared. Most people by now had decided she wasn't more than ninepence in the shilling, as they said in pre-decimal days. "How old are you? What is your church affiliation? Were your mother and father married? What is your job? Questions, questions . . ."

"You seem to know the ropes," said the man.

The crowd's irritation had melted for a moment at this stab at the police, who were fair game and good for a laugh at any time. Still complaining, the woman retreated. Jan put down her docket and was given her case.

Where next? Eastbourne? Naturally not. She knew no one there. So—back to Buzzard Minor, possibly to interrupt a sedate middle-aged idyll on the part of Mrs. Brown? Perhaps she really had invited someone for the weekend. In six years she must have made friends locally. There was the bingo crowd and the people she met at a singing class she attended.

A woman of secrets, reflected Jan, remembering an afternoon when she had been out with the children and had seen Mrs. Brown come out of a little paper and sweet shop rather off the beaten track, carrying a letter in her hand. There had been a notice in the shop window: *Letters May Be Left Here.* Presumably Mrs. Brown had her own private life and intended to maintain it.

"Is it a post office?" Dawn had asked. "Why doesn't the postman bring her letters?"

"Not all letters go by post," Jan had explained airily. "Sometimes it's more convenient to call for them yourself."

"I should have thought it was less trouble to let Postie bring it," insisted Dawn.

"This way Mother won't know," explained Coral.

The insight of the young sometimes shattered Jan, but the children weren't really interested. They plunged forward into the shop, demanding ice lollies. A youngish woman came in to inquire if there were any letters in the name of Black, but there weren't. A lover? wondered Jan. The young woman wore a wedding ring. There couldn't be any question of a lover surely where Mrs. Brown was concerned. Sending for beauty hints perhaps, they never got past that; for a horoscope, even for news of a dirty book. Or perhaps—Jan's imagination had widened like the ripples on a stream when you toss a pebble in—she wasn't really a widow, had a husband in prison or hiding from the authorities. The possibilities were endless.

Still, it wasn't often that she had the house to herself. She'd insisted on staying for the weekend. It got around in country districts if a house was left unguarded, and though Mrs. Brown might not think much of the silver cups and salvers Roy had won by hitting little balls around greens and over tennis nets, or even the Battersea enamels that were Kay's pride and joy, rogues would know their value. Oh, she wouldn't be lonely, she had assured Kay, there was bingo on Thursday and a whist drive on Friday, Saturday the choir rehearsed—no, let the Bankses go to Amsterdam, let Aunt Lolly take the children, let little Miss Au Pair go to Eastbourne or wherever, she, Felicia Brown, would hold the fort.

No, it wasn't very likely she'd give Jan a very warm welcome.

But if she didn't return to Buzzard Minor, then where? Find a room for the weekend, of course, explore the city. Something was bound to be happening in London over the holiday weekend. In the meantime, nature had just reminded her that that small sherry was all she'd had in the way of lunch. She decided to go to the refreshment room and buy herself a sandwich and a glass of milk. When she had had that, she would go out and hunt for a room. This part of London was honeycombed with apartment houses, somewhere she'd find a place.

The room seemed as crowded as the platform benches. She wondered if homeless people took a seat there for the night. At the refreshment room also, there was a queue. You took a tray, walked past a series of glass-fronted receptacles, abstracting whatever took your fancy—a cheese sandwich, a hamburger, a doughnut—and set them on the tray you'd already collected. At the head of the queue there was the inevitable delay while patrons chose drinks, watched them being poured out and then stopped at the checking-out desk to fumble for change. But the

18

far-sighted ones made certain they had somewhere to put their trays down when at last they'd collected their provender. Jan's brilliant eyes darted over the crowded eating space. Near her a couple leisurely collected their trays and began to move. In a flash the girl had left the queue and dumped the striped bag on the table. The solid-looking couple, who might have come out of an Arnold Bennett novel, were exchanging secrets—at all events, they were whispering.

Jan banged down her case. "I come back," she announced.

An elderly woman with bird's-nest white hair, wearing a bright blue coat, looked up from an adjacent table. "That'll be all right, dear," she said.

Jan stalked off in the direction of the queue, which had lengthened even during the last minute, and took up her place behind a mother with four young children, all of whom were playing a secret game that involved snatching open the various glass lids, plucking out the contents and returning them to the wrong compartment.

"You'll 'ave the policeman after you," the mother said wearily.

Each child had insisted on taking a separate tray, all were demanding fish and chips, which were not available at this counter, and whined "Want a Coke" when Mother said milk was best.

Jan found herself butted in the chest by an imperfectly wrapped sausage roll that shook crumbs all over her suit. She caught the waving wrist. "You put that on the tray," she commanded.

The mother—another tigress at bay, the station seemed full of them—flew to her offspring's defense. "News to me he's your kid. What are you doing with that sausage roll, Morry? I told you . . ." She caught the fat hand and slapped it. Morry roared and dropped the sausage roll on the floor, where it was promptly stepped on.

"I'm not paying for that," the mother announced. She

dragged her brood after her, ordered a cup of tea and changed it for coffee, ordered two milks and two Cokes and changed those for four Cokes, held everyone up by arguing the toss with the lady at the checking-out desk—"Six new pence for a glass of milk and then British Rail says it can't pay its way. No, I know I'm not having the milk, but what difference does that make?"—and finally withdrew.

Jan bought a glass of milk and a sandwich. She collected these quickly and returned to the other side of the glass partition, looking for the table where she had left her bag.

But though the table was there, the striped bag was not.

Two

The woman who had been refused luggage because she couldn't produce a docket was called Rita Gould, who had for some years been on the stage, but only just on it. She had walking-on parts, occasionally a dozen words; she danced in crowd scenes and shouted with rebels, but the modern play called for fewer supers and the going was hard. So for the past year or two she had been getting her living in a less conventional way. She watched Jan move towards the refreshment bar, saw her deposit her case on a convenient table. She pattered into the room after her and began to walk up and down between the tables, searching for an invisible face. Then, apparently resigning herself to the inevitable, she dropped down into the empty place at Jan's table. The Arnold Bennett couple were beginning fussily to collect their things, bickering like two sharp-beaked birds, the man protesting, the woman insistent.

"Train won't even be in for another twenty minutes," he asserted.

"Won't stop the queue from assembling, and you well know I can't sit with my back to the engine. I should have thought it was worth a little extra trouble."

Still nagging, they began to move away. A party of four came noisily into the room and stood looking around.

"There's two here," said one, indicating the chairs the fussy couple had just left.

Rita came suddenly to her feet. "Why, there she is all the

time," she exclaimed. "And me waiting." She snatched up the striped bag and fled. No one tried to stop her. The other members of the party took the two empty chairs, and thus it was that Jan came upon them.

"Where is it?" she demanded fiercely, of no one in particular but holding the attention of practically everyone in the room. "My case. I left it there."

Someone anonymous muttered, "The more fool you." And in an aside, "These bitches don't know they're born."

"You saw it," declared the girl to the woman with the bird's-nest hair and the bright blue coat, who was busily writing an airmail letter and sipping milk, which she had chosen because, having never been hot, it couldn't get cold.

The woman looked up, startled. "You've been such a long time," she said accusingly. "But there, look at the queue. I always say it's one way of learning patience. Why, where's your bag? Such a pretty one. I noticed it specially."

"I ask you," said the girl ominously. "It was here, with the two people who went out."

"Well, they've gone, haven't they?" said Bright-Eyes cheerfully. "Perhaps they picked your bag up by mistake. It's easily done."

"There is no mistake, they know it is mine. They are here when I leave it. I say I come back . . ."

"I did hear that," the woman admitted.

"You see them go?"

"Well, not really, dear. You see, I was busy writing to this friend of mine in Kenya. But no—they had only one piece each, I noticed particularly. I'm sure they wouldn't have taken yours. What you want to do, dear, is talk to the constable in the station. There's always a constable in a station. He'll tell you what to do."

"You think he will notice one person carrying a bag as though of right."

"Well, dear, it was a very *striking* bag."

Jan drank the milk, set down the sandwich and marched out. No one here was going to be the least use to her. She could see that. As for the policeman, he wouldn't help either. She remembered tearing the label off the bag when she got it back from the clerk. It was just possible—possible though not probable—that the words "Passenger to Greece" might attract attention, but an unlabled bag . . . She ran out of the refreshment room, almost bowling over an incoming passenger. The thief might just conceivably be waiting in a train queue or buying a ticket at the office, and label or no label, once she saw her bag, she would regain possession. But, of course, there was no sign of it anywhere. Whoever had stolen it wasn't that kind of a fool.

In any case, the policeman was already engaged by a tearful elderly woman who was telling him "I only left it for one minute, less than one minute, then I realized I hadn't got it, I must have left my bag in the phone box, I thought, but when I went back it wasn't there."

"What did you expect, madam?" asked the policeman rather wearily.

"I thought perhaps some honest person would find it and give it to you."

"That would be most unusual, madam."

"It's what I should do in her shoes."

He didn't doubt it. You found these pillars of honesty, outdated as dinosaurs, particularly among women of her generation. "Why don't you go along to the station and give them a description . . . ?"

"The police station?"

"That was the idea, madam."

"And will they find it for me?"

Jan moved away; the same advice would doubtless be given her, and she would be expected to uncover the whole humiliating story of Nikki and her deception of her employers. Now she knew she had no choice. Buzzard Minor it must be and Mrs. Brown must make the best of it.

Consulting the Train Departure Board, she discovered she had just missed the last quick train, and must make the journey by the slow one, which involved a change at Bantock Green, where there was a twenty-minute wait for a connection. The train was like one of those paths that seem to travel all round the county; by the time she reached Manor House, Mrs. Brown would doubtless be back with her anonymous friend. Meanwhile, she must concoct some credible story to explain her sudden return. She thought of Mr. Crook's ingenious suggestion about the child with measles, but perhaps the plain truth would be better. Fictitious friends, while starting as a convenience, often become difficult to explain away. All she need say was that her luggage had been stolen—yes, of course she had seen the railway police constable. If Mrs. Brown chose to assume that she had also spoken to him, that was her affair. Jan examined the money in her purse. When she had paid for her ticket she would have just enough cash in hand to pay for a taxi from the station to Buzzard Minor. There could be no question of having a meal on the train, and in any case, you could be dead sure there wouldn't be a buffet car. She'd have to make herself a scratch supper on her return.

Meantime, Rita Gould had walked briskly through the station yard into a small shopping arcade just outside the station, where a tall dark man loitered outside a jeweler's shop. She lined up beside him and unobtrusively he took the bag from her hand.

"The girl said it contains all her treasures, whatever they may amount to."

"Brand-new case. Pity, really, but you know our rule. Never keep containers. It doesn't pay to be too greedy, that's how you choke yourself. Best not go back to the station, girl may be on the rampage. And make it Paddington tomorrow. Sylvie can

24

work Victoria." He began to laugh. "Remember that bag you got this morning? One of these fancy-work spectacle cases in it, jammed with the old dear's treasures—diamond ring, diamond brooch, eardrops, string of pearls. Probably thought no one would look in it."

"It was a nice bag," said Rita wistfully.

"Won't look so nice when they find it on the garbage dump. See you tonight, usual place."

That was how he kept the gang together, kept them in close contact, paid them fair and square. Only a small business, of course, but a thriving one; you couldn't take time out, though, you never knew when you might recruit a fool who'd sell you up the river. He'd picked Rita up a couple of years back at Euston, when she'd just helped herself to someone else's handbag . . . well, purse really.

"It was on the floor, I was going to give it in at the office," she had pleaded.

"I'll come with you," said Terry, "if that's what you really want."

"I've never done anything like this before," she protested.

"Must be a natural for it," he told her, though as a matter of fact her statement was true.

She proved quite an acquisition; the airs and graces she'd picked up on the stage came in very handy. Someone had once remarked in Terry's hearing that most elderly women tend to be depressingly alike. That was Rita's strength. Line her up with twenty like her, and even the police might be at a loss. He watched her stroll away, then walked over to where his car was parked, a car as unobtrusive and unshowy as Rita herself. He opened the boot and dropped the case in; there was already a handbag, a pair of fur gloves, a pair of binoculars some benighted idiot had left on a table while he went to fetch some beer. No need to cultivate the delicate touch of the pickpocket and take a pickpocket's chances—the poor sodding British public met you more than halfway. "The best things in life are free," caroled Terry, unlocking the car and climbing into the driver's seat. Millie had done quite nicely at Charing Cross and the light-fingered Dolores had gone through Waterloo like a knife through butter. Some chaps came hurrying past, their eyes on the station clock. These were the daily-breaders, earning— what? £25? £30? £40? maybe. Nose to grindstone all through the bright day, no fun, no adventure, no pitting your wits against the stupid blundering majority—not that it was much of a contest, of course. They deserved as little as they got. He put in the clutch and drove off.

Jan's train started ten minutes behind time, but that didn't really matter, since a nasal voice at the connecting station was announcing a further delay of twenty-five minutes, due to an engine breakdown. This evening train was known irreverently as the Commuters' Nightmare, but British Rail courteously explained there wasn't the money to improve the service. Anyway, only the mugs traveled by this train. Tonight it proceeded even more deliberately than usual; shadows lay deep over the countryside as it stuttered and hesitated and drew up at each station on the line. Anonymous figures dropped off the train and were engulfed in darker shadows still. Two stations before Buzzard Minor an apathetic collector came through to take the tickets, which he retained. The train was almost empty when Jan alighted, and stood a moment watching the train move languidly round the curve and disappear. Leaving the world to darkness and to me, reflected Jan. Gray's "Elegy in a Country Churchyard" was one of the poems Dawn was reading, a gospel of depressed meritocracy, Roy Banks called it. She wasn't quite certain what he meant but the tone had been derogatory.

Buzzard Minor could never be called a lively station. Locals used it, but the plutocracy, what there was of it, went into the big market town of Buzzard Major, driving their own cars or being ferried by wives or chauffeurs. Even the boy who normally collected tickets had gone home. The waiting room, no better than a shed, was locked, and doubtless the same held good of the Ladies. At the foot of a flight of steps a faded-blue wooden door led to the indifferent world. There was no sign of a taxi, no car from whose driver she might have hitched a ride; a little office card read Car Hire Day and Night, but the window was dark and no battering on the door or ringing the bell had any result.

Nothing for it, she thought dismally, but shanks' mare. It was two miles to the Manor, two countryman's miles, Roy said, and the road was rough and very poorly lighted. Fortunately, she had learned never to be without a small torch, and she lugged this out of her bag and started on the slow walk home. She had no driver's license—where she came from girls of eighteen didn't run their own cars, they cycled and they tramped like little ponies. Since coming to England she had picked up a lot of knowledge, and shocked Kay sometimes by riding pillion on madmen's motorbikes, or squeezing six into a car where there was only room for three.

This morning she had dressed carefully, putting on high-heeled shoes because Nikki didn't like girls in loafers, and the additional inch or so they gave her improved her self-confidence. One thing was certain, though, they weren't the right shoes for walking by night on a stony uneven road. Passing a telephone box at a crossroads, it occurred to her that she might ring Mrs. Brown and warn her of her impending arrival. Then, if she was planning some orgy—though you might as easily suspect Queen Victoria making whoopee while Albert was away—she would receive due warning. But though she could hear the bell shrilling away, ringing its head off, in fact, there was no reply. Prolonged holiday bingo presumably; or perhaps they were putting in overtime at the Lord Charles, where they retired at the end of the evening to enjoy themselves in a refined way.

She looked at the gold watch Mr. Crook had admired. Time

seemed to have rushed on like a mad horse. Already it was past eight-thirty. The wait for the connection had eaten up the evening, and the train had drooped along as though it had lost all heart to arrive at its destination. If Mrs. Brown was keeping her word to Kay about not neglecting the house, she'd be back any time now; or perhaps she hadn't gone to bingo, after all. She could be entertaining in the room Roy coveted for his photographic experiments. But Kay told him sharply that you couldn't expect top class domestic help without making sacrifices, and did he fancy wearing a HIS apron and standing at the sink six nights out of seven? (The seventh night they presumably fasted or went out for a meal.)

But she must have gone to bingo, Jan thought, remembering that unanswered phone. Not even for an orgy on the sofa would Mrs. Brown let a telephone ring itself into silence.

The road seemed twice as long and twice as hard as ever it had done by daylight. But then, she'd never done the walk alone before, always there had been the children or what Kay described as your raffish friends. At the end of a mile of weary trudging Jan happened on a signpost that indicated a short cut to Buzzard Minor; the path looked overgrown and thorny, but it seemed to offer a better prospect than the endless stony road. It had, after all, been a long day. She hesitated a minute or two on the chance of a lift from some late traveler, but practically no cars had passed her. Like the lorries and heavy tractors, most of them now used the by-pass.

The woodland through which she now began to move seemed abysmally dark, and she was glad of her little pencil torch. Now and again a rustling close at hand betokened the movement of some night creature, a bird stirring perhaps or a hedgehog shuffling through the leaves. Once an owl hooted and derisively she hooted back. Later she almost stumbled over a dark mass in her path, and for a moment she thought it was a man dead or drunk, but it was only one of the forest ponies that had chosen this path to lie down for a kip. It lifted its head and looked at her with its wild incurious eyes.

"That's no place to be lying," she told it severely, while her heart beat with relief. Presently she became aware that she must have strayed off the path somewhere, for she found herself plunged into a morass of ferns rising almost as high as her waist. The children loved these ferny enclosures where it was possible to hide and remain invisible, but there were marshy places here, too, and she didn't want to stumble into one of them. She lifted her torch and played it on the distance in the hope that she might see a lighted window or even a roof, but it was Housman over again.

In all the secret roads you tread/There's nothing but the night.

At last she heard wheels in the distance, so knew she must be nearing a main road. But before she reached it she had stumbled on a little alehouse called the Huntsman. A good deal of noise came through the doors. It was a meeting place for what Kay called the hippie element; someone was playing a jukebox, someone was singing. Jan didn't think it noisy, just friendly and alive. However, what held her attention was a motor scooter leaning against a tree and looking as out of place as a pterodactyl in these days of crashing motorbikes and cars that from their appearance were built up out of a couple of biscuit tins. In its own way this was as distinctive as Crook's Rolls.

Her eyes sparkled, some of the weariness dropped from her. She recognized the scooter, there couldn't be two like it in the county, and she knew the owner, a wild boy according to the local sobersides, a self-confessed revolutionary. His name was Hugh Wheeler, known affectionately (or derisively) as Hugh the Wheel. She'd met him several weeks before when he was trying to drum up volunteers for one of the demos he supported so ardently. "If you won't come for the others, come for yourself," he'd urge. "No man is an island, what happens to one affects us all." That went for the aged, the shipyard workers, the students, armies fighting overseas, and all the underpaid slaves of capital. Chap was born on a soapbox, someone had observed. He'd been in trouble with the police on two occasions. "One law for the civil service and another for the underdogs," he declared. "They may hustle me but I mustn't hustle them."

Except among his own generation he didn't attract much sympathy. You paid for the welfare state, you paid for pensions, whether the recipients had contributed or no, you paid for education, free orange juice and free milk, and still these pestilential young men came round to your door, shaking their collecting boxes, and like the horse-leech's daughters of old, crying for more. He got off with a caution, probably due to the fact that no one could accuse him of living on the dole provided by harder-working citizens. It seemed odd that such a fiery young man should have such a tame job. He worked for Mr. Pringle at the big nursery beyond the crossroads. Green fingers he had, according to Mr. Pringle. Red hands, said his opposers. "I wonder you work for a capitalist," Jan had taunted him, but he said that if all capitalists treated the man in the street with the devotion old Mr. P. gave to his plants, you could stop demos tomorrow, because you'd have done away with the cause of them. "Let the Health and Security wallahs look after their charges as he does, digs them, waters them, separates them so that they don't choke each other to death, sits up with 'em all night if need be. No, he's all right."

He had run into Jan and the children one day as he was coming away from the Manor House, where he was delivering, in his lunch hour, some plants Kay wanted in a particular hurry. Delivering plants wasn't his job, there was a boy for that and a lorry for the big stuff, but the lorry was in dry dock and the boy couldn't be expected to do everything, so he'd come up with two pots on the back of his scooter.

"Can I have a ride on your bicycle?" Dawn had demanded.

"Against trade-union regulations," he told her.

"What's trade unions?"

"Bodies of chaps out to see you keep the rules."

Jan and the children began to laugh.

"It's true," Hugh assured them.

"Does the trade union let you bring the flowers?"

"The trade union's at lunch," said Hugh.

"Were you collecting for something?" asked Jan innocently.

"I wasn't very successful."

"Mrs. Banks is out and Mrs. Brown does not give at the door."

"I saw a female equivalent of the saber-toothed tiger. Was that Mrs. Brown?"

"That would be her."

"What time does *he* come back? I might have better luck with him. After all, he'll be one of the aged himself one day."

Dawn said clearly, "My mother says we can only just make two ends meet."

"Then you'll have to pull in your belts, won't you?" He smiled encouragingly, "Or take a blanket off the bed."

"Then Mother might be cold."

"That's the idea," said Hugh. "If you're cold, it makes you sorry for other people who're cold. D'you know what I'm talking about?"

"Oh yes." Dawn nodded her head. "You are begging."

"So I am. Would you give me anything if you had it? For some poor old lady, say?"

"As old as Mummy?"

"Older than Mummy."

Dawn looked scandalized. "An old lady couldn't wear my coat. And Mummy would be cross."

"O.K." agreed Hugh. He turned to Jan. "How about you? Do you get Sunday off?"

"To go to church."

"What about the rest of the day. Come on the demo. You

can ride on the back of my scooter. She's safer than she looks."

"I have ridden on scooters in Holland. But this Sunday I cannot. Mrs. Brown will be out, and I must stay with the children."

"You should join a union and learn your rights. Or bring them with you. I'll fix transport, and you can't start too young."

Coral let out a roar and stamped her foot. "Jan belongs to us."

"She belongs to the community."

Coral looked helplessly at her sister. Dawn was not so easily silenced. "We are the community," she said.

"You win," said Hugh. "Don't forget, though, we're always glad of an extra pair of feet."

When they got in, Mrs. Brown was in the hall. "I saw you talking to that tearaway," she said severely. "You don't want to encourage him."

"Oh, Dawn disposed of him," said Jan airily.

But she met him again in the bar of the Red Chestnut in Buzzard Major and then in a coffee bar, and presently at his place of work, where she was sent by Mrs. Banks to inquire about some seedlings. In a small community the young insensibly drew together. And now, just when she needed a helping hand, here was his scooter, unpadlocked, free, inviting her to help herself.

She hesitated by the inn door, but the sounds from within discouraged her. She reminded herself she wasn't anxious to advertise her return at the very start of the holiday. Secrecy was the order of the day. And wasn't it Sir Philip Sidney who had said "Thy need is greater, friend"? Noiselessly she wheeled the scooter off the path and a few steps along the road. A minute later she was speeding joyously in the direction of Manor House. Her spirits continued to soar as she rode in and out of the patches of moonlight, for the moon seemed as reckless as she, now blazing forth like a beacon, then vanishing behind a bank of cloud, as though retiring for the night. Her exhilaration made her careless. She knew she had almost reached her goal, and she took the final bend at breakneck speed. As she swerved round the corner she found herself vis-à-vis with a red car, whose driver appeared to be as startled as herself by this apparition on what he had supposed to be an empty road. He shouted something violent, but the wind carried the words away. Then he shot out of sight round the bend.

Not so much as a scratch on his paintwork, thought Jan disdainfully. She herself had come off less well. In an endeavor to avoid the car, she had turned the wheel of the scooter sharply and collided with a tree growing by the roadside for no purpose any ordinary mortal could guess. Into this tree the scooter cannoned, throwing its rider; there was a crash of glass and the headlight went out. Jan disentangled herself, more annoyed than hurt, and called a belated reply to the motorist in her own tongue. She wasn't hurt, just a cut on one hand where it had come in contact with a piece of glass. She licked the blood off impatiently. She waited a moment but there wasn't another sound but the wind among the trees, so she righted the cycle, intending to wheel it a few yards and leave it propped against the hedge. But though it looked all right, it had sustained worse injuries than she. The front wheel was a bit buckled—I hope Hugh is insured, she thought.

She half pushed, half carried it to the roadside to where a lot of bushes overgrew what had once been the entry to a right of way. It was so overgrown now no one used it, and the farmer at the further end had put up a PRIVATE notice, and though it might be possible to compel him to remove this in law, the rumor was that he grazed a free-range bull in the field, and accepted no responsibility. Jan didn't believe this; no farmer worth his salt risked anything as valuable as a bull; a good many hikers were an untutored lot who thought nothing of leaving gates open, plowing through growing corn and depositing their rubbish on the land. Still, the cul-de-sac, which was virtually what it had become, would prove a useful hideaway for the scooter. Tomorrow she could await her opportunity and let Hugh know where it was. She wasn't afraid of retribution. Borrowing a car for a joy ride wasn't a crime, and borrowing a scooter should be even less of one. She didn't worry, either, about Hugh having to walk home. He'll get a lift, she told herself comfortably, or he will enjoy the walk. He is as strong as a pony.

Her own plans were nebulous; she intended to stay at Manor House as short a time as possible. If Mrs. Brown was not back, she might even be able to creep up to her room—the housekeeper never came to that floor—and early morning, before Mrs. Brown was astir, she could steal away again, taking the shabby bag she had arrived with, packed with the clothes she hadn't thought good enough for Greece. It was a pity about the accident, she had intended to ride the scooter back to the Huntsman and leave it where she had found it, realizing that anyone would know it was Hugh's, there couldn't be another like it within fifty miles, but she couldn't move it in its present condition.

A few more minutes and Jan was standing at the gates of Manor House; the wind had risen considerably during the past half-hour; the clouds blew about like clothes on a line, and there was rain in the air. It was like walking over a chessboard, first a white square when the moon beamed, then a black when she vanished again. The house itself stood out like a cardboard erection against the harlequin sky. Jan opened her bag for the key to the front door. Everything here was quiet and dark—so Mrs. Brown hadn't been able to resist the call of bingo, after all.

Jan drew her hand out of her bag; the key wasn't there. And then she remembered putting it in the zipper pocket of the striped bag—for safety's sake. She went on rummaging in her pockets in the way of women who expect a miracle to be performed for them, but all she found was a largish squarish card she'd never seen before. By the light of the little pencil torch she read:

> Arthur G. Crook. Your Trouble, Our Opportunity.
> And We Never Close.

and two addresses, complete with telephone numbers, and remembered him for the first time since their parting. He sounds like a plumber, she thought, and was about to throw the card away when some impulse made her return it to her pocket. In any case, she didn't want Mrs. Brown smelling over it, and Kay once said she believed the woman dusted the very plants under the window.

She rang the bell again, without much hope, again remembering the unanswered telephone call. Mrs. Brown's room was at the front of the house, and unless she was dead drunk, a delightful prospect as improbable as that Judgment Day would dawn tomorrow, she wasn't at home. She went round to the side of the house, but the door there was fastened as tight as a drum, and careful Mrs. Brown wouldn't leave a key under a stone.

So I have to wait for her return, thought Jan furiously, and she will not be pleased when it is known she did not come back as promised. There seemed no alternative. Even if she walked the mile or so into Buzzard Major, there was only the Lord Charles, and suppose Mrs. B. wasn't there, after all. Besides, she'd be furious at being tracked down among all her friends. Beyond Buzzard Major was Firlmere, with its inn, the Pumpkin and Pie, but that was off the bingo players' route. In any case, someone might bring Mrs. Brown back by car. I shall have to wait, thought Jan, remembering the fairy tales of her childhood in which a large convenient tree, usually a walnut, grew against the wall, giving the interloper access to one of the upper windows. She knew there was no such tree here, nor would careful Mrs. Brown have left any window ajar, but she walked round to the back of the house.

She was pondering on the possible character of the late Mr. Brown, if indeed the housekeeper was a widow and not that sad creature the deserted wife, when she heard the telephone ringing inside the house. So someone else besides herself believed Mrs. Brown would be here tonight. The house was, Kay had once declared, honeycombed with instruments, one in the back hall, one in Roy's study, one in the big upstairs bedroom. Jan wondered why no one put telephones in a bathroom, it was the only place where you could be assured of privacy and be permitted to recline behind a locked door, but perhaps there was some safety regulations governing this. The old, thought Jan, were security-mad. If they weren't, Mrs. Brown would have left a key under a stone by the back door.

There are few sounds more eerie and compelling than the crying of a telephone in an empty house. Its summons is so imperative, its patience endless.

"Oh, don't go on," cried Jan. "Can't you understand? There's no one there."

But the telephone reasonably took no notice of her. Jan shivered. The wind hadn't abated a jot, and she was dressed, not for a cool British evening with the inevitable rain beginning to fall, but for the balmy airs of Greece. The phone stopped and she drew a deep breath. But an instant later it began again.

"Give them one more ring," she could imagine the caller saying.

The thought came to her that it might be Aunt Lolly ringing up with news of the children. Could there have been an accident? Had they run off? But they'd never do that. Where on earth would they run to? Still, for a moment she felt that if she could lift off the receiver, she wouldn't be surprised to hear their bright voices—"Jan, come back and fetch us." She dismissed the notion as folly. They'd be coming home next week when their aunt brought them. The phone call was for Mrs. Brown, only she hadn't come back from the bingo. Her own window was dark, and though there were shutters over the ground floor, except for the drawing room whose French windows were

36

protected by heavy tapestry curtains, upstairs there were none. A light would be seen from outside.

She went again to the back door, tugging absurdly at the lock, as if sheer will power and rage could make it yield. But she might as well have tried to break into Parkhurst Prison. She knew those bolts.

"You would think they kept the Crown Jewels here," she once said scornfully to Mrs. Brown.

"Better be safe than sorry" came the inevitable retort.

The moon, as if disturbed by that incessant ringing sound, came leaping through a bank of cloud, swamping the garden in silver. Hitherto invisible flowers took shape, bushes waved frantic arms; it was like a light being turned on. In the orchard the wind rustled importantly among the trees. It seemed fantastic, so much life outside the house but everything motionless within. As she thought this, even the bell stopped.

Desperate, she walked round the house lest the careful Mrs. Brown should, for once, have left some window ajar. It happened often enough in books, but, naturally, not here.

"I wouldn't give much for a woman like that," Mrs. Brown had been heard to say, turning scornfully from the television screen. "No sense of responsibility."

No, when she locked up a house, a mouse couldn't get into it.

Jan reached the French windows, their dark panes reflecting the moonlight. The thick curtains were drawn. This was the most beautiful room in the house and the least used. More like a museum than a room, Jan thought. Here was housed Kay Banks' collection of Battersea enamels, which had been inspected and approved by an official of the Victoria and Albert; here hung the silk Chinese scrolls and some miniatures, also approved by the V. and A.

Why can I not be like Aladdin and cry Open Sesame?

wondered Jan, confusing one fairy-tale character with another. She ran at the windows, beating on the dark panes. They were locked from within by a special lock and couldn't be opened from the outside. Yet now, to her incredulous surprise, the door moved under her hand.

Three

In Amsterdam, Roy and Katherine Banks, having bidden their hosts an early goodnight, walked slowly towards their hotel along the banks of the canal. Here couples or small parties of three to five persons were gathered around tables, drinking coffee or schnapps. The water was dazzled by the reflection of stars among the small gold lights.

"Like fairyland," Roy suggested. "Let's sit down and have something, shall we? We can't very well go to bed at this hour. You know"—he drew back a chair—"this might be a place to bring the kids."

"What on earth would you do with them here?" Kay demanded. "There's only the canal, and the shops, and Bournemouth is better at both. Better altogether, really, because they can swim at Bournemouth."

"There's that child's town we stopped at—Madurodam—I'd like to show them that." He laughed with inward pleasure. "Fancy a local council whose members were thirty boys and girls of your own age. It really is something, Kay."

"They copied the idea from Beaconsfield," said his wife, who was imprudent enough to know all the answers. "If you want to amuse the children, take them there. There's a model railway and several churches all playing different tunes, and a fox hunt—there's even a burglar, a fat chap running off with a bag marked SWAG over his shoulder. My grandmother took me there once—on the whole, I think she enjoyed it more than I did."

"For someone who didn't enjoy it, you remember it pretty well," Roy teased her. "Well, we might make a start there, but seeing they'll be expected to grow up little Europeans— Besides, we can't leave their leisure entirely to your sister and the *au pair*. She's rather a daisy by the way."

"You tell Mrs. Brown that and she'll tell you daisies are all right but not on her lawn. It's a good thing she had this invitation to go to Eastbourne—Jan, I mean—if that's where she really has gone."

Roy was up in arms at once. "Why should you think otherwise?"

"Going to stay with a married friend with two kids of her own? It doesn't sound much of a holiday to me."

"If you weren't sure, you should have checked. We're responsible for the girl. Didn't you get an address or anything?"

Kay laughed. "What an old worrywart you are. Always worrying about something—immigrants or the children's education or some injustice on the other side of the world."

"She's here on a daughter's status, remember."

"You try asking a daughter of eighteen how she proposes to spend the weekend. She'll tell you to get lost."

"But this girl's a foreigner," Roy urged. "Where can she go to?"

"Oh, she's made a lot of friends at the language classes. It's all they go for, I think. We certainly shan't keep her long if we cross-examine her on every detail. Well, suppose it is a boyfriend? That's what you're afraid of, isn't it? Girls of eighteen know how to look after themselves these days. Anyway, I want to keep her as much as you do. The children are devoted to her. As a matter of fact, I'm glad they are off for a few days with Lolly. We don't want them getting too devoted. To hear them talk, you'd sometimes think they hadn't a mother or an aunt."

"I daresay Jan is a nice change from your sister and Mrs. Brown."

"Mrs. Brown's a housekeeper, not an *au pair* girl. I must say," easily changing the subject, "it was a relief when she offered to stop on while we were away. There have been too many of these country-house burglaries lately—word gets round that the place 'ull be empty."

"And up comes a fat white man carrying a sack marked SWAG." Roy grinned.

"There's no need to joke about her. We should be grateful to have got her at all. You wouldn't like it if she left. She runs the house like a computer."

"That's an interesting thought. Do you suppose that's what she really is? The bit that worries me about those machines is that when they make a mistake, they can't go back and correct it. You're stuck with it for life. Who was Mr. Brown, by the way? Or don't you know?"

"Mrs. Brown's husband, presumably."

"Poor devil. Or perhaps he was a computer too."

"When we get back to the hotel," reflected Kay, "I think I'll ring her."

"Mrs. Brown? You must be crazy. What on earth for?"

"She'll probably be tickled pink, a call from Europe. I shall say you're anxious to know she's all right."

"And if you don't get any answer?"

"Then she'll still be at bingo. But she said she'd come back early and perhaps ask a friend in for supper."

"It's an awe-inspiring thought," murmured Roy. "Mrs. B. and friend in the housekeeper's room—shades of Anthony Trollope. Take my tip, Kay, forget about that phone call. (A) she may take offense, think you don't trust her . . ."

"She wouldn't believe that of Almighty God," said Kay.

"(B) she won't thank you if she's shacked up on couch with said friend . . ."

41

"You've a disgusting mind," said Kay coldly.

"It does take some imagination, doesn't it? Perhaps she's regaling the minister with coffee and cakes."

"He's a married man with seven children . . ."

"Then he may be glad of a change. Still, you've made your point. I'm glad she offered to stay on. It 'ud be a courageous burglar who tried to outface her. And I wouldn't like to lose my collection." He brooded fondly on the shelves of silver cups and salvers he had won through his skill at hitting little balls around greens and over tennis nets. At thirty-five he had a physique a man ten years his junior might have envied.

"You and your cups." Kay said. "And speaking of cups, is that one empty?" She refilled it from the tall coffeepot.

But her kindly thoughts for the housekeeper went unrewarded, for when she got through with remarkably little delay (good old Holland, up the Common Market, she said), there was no reply.

Standing just inside the dark room, hearing the rain patter against the glass, the moon once again obscured, Jan became conscious that something was wrong. Mrs. Brown, that pillar of perfection, would never leave the French windows unfastened even while she went to the post, let alone to a bingo session. Wild and irreverent thoughts poured into the girl's mind.

Perhaps she is in league with a gang? she thought. Perhaps that is why she said she would stay. (The idea had its humor.) Perhaps it is not the first time. But no one will ever catch her. St. Felicia Brown, with an alibi all wool and a yard wide, as Hugh says.

She moved, like a beam, through the darkness, avoiding the chairs, and switched on the light. The lovely Venetian chandelier seemed more brilliant than the moon itself, filling the room with a silver glow. Jan turned instinctively towards the fireplace, where the two Chinese scrolls hung, the man in a boat and the

42

sacred bird—then stood transfixed. In their place was nothing to be seen but a slightly brighter oblong of gold-colored wall, marking the places where they had been. A further alarmed glance showed her the glass-fronted case of Battersea enamels with the lock broken, the glass cracked, the case, of course, empty.

"It is not true," she said aloud. "How could she explain?"

But if Mrs. Brown were truly part of the plot, she would simply assure her employers and the police that she had closed and barred the French windows when she went out, and closed and barred they would certainly be before she raised the alarm, and leave it for the authorities to discover how the intruders had made an entry. Or perhaps she would break a pane of glass to make it seem more realistic. She had been standing there for more than a minute when it occurred to Jan that her own unexpected arrival would be a godsend to the real criminal. She had a key—who was likely to believe she had packed it in her case and the case had been stolen?—she knew Mrs. Brown would be out till late, she had no alibi for her movements, the stolen case could have been part of the plot, she had refused to report the theft, she could have caught the earlier fast train, no one was likely to notice either her or her absence, and come down to admit the thieves.

No one knows I have come, she reminded herself. The sensible thing would be to insure that nobody ever did know. But where would she spend the night? And what would she do for luggage?

When she was able to move and look through the rest of the house, she found other treasures were missing. Some handsome miniatures were gone from the wall, some pieces of jade from a glass cabinet, a pair of heavy antique silver candlesticks from the mantelshelf. If not Mrs. Brown, thought the girl, then who? Automatically she erased her own name from the list of suspects, which left only Mrs. Jelf the charwoman, but she'd told everyone her two sons were off with their doxies to the

Continong and she intended to go down with her gentleman friend to Brighton. No doubt she could produce an alibi. And anyway, Mrs. Brown was so respectable, she should surely be the police's ideal suspect.

"That's a woman's argument," Crook would have said.

Leaving the drawing room, she crossed into the hall, but when she pressed the switch no light came on. By the gleam of her little torch she found her way to the door of Mr. Banks's study and flung it open. No need for speculation here; the shelves were swept clean of silver trophies, nothing else had been touched.

Is it possible, Jan wondered, that Mrs. Brown came back early, a headache perhaps—and going straight to bed, heard nothing of the thieves? Or perhaps she is lying on her bed, bound and gagged? She could not restrain a faint grin at the thought. She had modern youth's contempt for property. Silver plates and cups can be replaced, Battersea enamels may be beautiful, but their right place is a museum. Lithe as a cat, she darted up the stairs to the housekeeper's room. This was on the next floor, at the end of a short passage culminating in four steps separating her from the other bedrooms on that level—the Bankses' communal room, Roy's dressing room, the guest room, the bathroom. The Bankses had their own bath. Mrs. Brown shared the visitor's, or rather, had sole use of it except when people were staying; then she went up one flight and used the bathroom allotted to the children and their mentor of the moment. There had been a governess before Jan, but she had been unappreciated and short-lived.

Jan stopped outside Mrs. Brown's room; there was no sound of struggle, no scuffling or panting, no movement at all. Jan tapped on the panel.

"Mrs. Brown!" she called. "Mrs. Brown, are you there?"

She felt rather silly talking to a nonexistent ghost, probably at this moment sipping port-and-lemon in the Lord Charles. She opened the door softly; no voice called out, no one stirred. She pressed the button on her little torch, and the light streamed on the neat bed on which a coat lay folded. Assuming this was the one Mrs. Brown had worn to attend the bingo, that meant she had returned. But it was a light coat and she might have changed her mind about wearing it. And if she was in league with the thieves, she would take care to stay late and establish her alibi. The coat meant nothing. Softly Jan closed the door and came back down the four stairs.

What now? The obvious thing was to telephone the police and report the robbery. Or was it a burglary if it took place after dark? She imagined herself with the receiver at her ear: "This is Manor House. There has been a burglary. Many things are missing. No, this is not Mrs. Brown; Mrs. Brown is not here. No, not Mrs. Banks either, she is in Holland. This is the *au pair* girl." Wouldn't they wonder what she was doing in the house by herself over a holiday weekend? Someone would probably know (and tell them) that she was expected to be at Eastbourne. Uncomfortable questions would be asked, the story of Nikki and her betrayal would become public property. The story would go all round the village, it would be impossible for her to stay. And everyone knew what people said about *au pair* girls. They wanted money for jam, didn't expect to earn their keep, were finicky about the jobs they would do, stayed out at night, got themselves with child, which they subsequently loaded onto the National Health.

As if it was necessary to come over to England for that, thought Jan scornfully. Plenty of sturdy Dutch youths ready to oblige. And the police were like everyone else, expecting foreigners to be stupid, ignorant, not knowing how to queue for buses, helping themselves to goods in shops without paying for them. The police, Roy had once said, normally suspect an inside job in circumstances like these, and the more she thought of her own position, the less she liked it. You couldn't really believe they'd suspect high-nosed, high-principled Mrs. Brown before a flibbertigibbet of a girl from abroad. Probably no better than she should be, they'd say, look at the manner she went around with all sorts of queer types; promiscuous, they wouldn't wonder. Why, they might think Nikki was part of the plot—a very enterprising body, the British police force.

Still hesitating, she went along to the Bankses' room, but here nothing seemed to have been touched; the marauders hadn't gone further than the ground floor; you could be sure they'd have worn gloves and left no fingerprints; and magic men in a way to be able to open the French windows. In Mrs. Banks's room the silver table appointments shone as always; the Wedgwood candlesticks with their dull blue candles sat sedately on either side of the little Regency looking glass. A white-leather jewelbox stood on a night table, but this was locked and the key had been removed.

That lock could be broken with a hairpin, Jan reflected, but it wouldn't be worth anyone's while. Kay didn't have much jewelry and anything of any value was lodged at the bank; for all the use it was to her, the burglars might as well have taken it. Yet Kay had taken the key with her. Natural caution? Or didn't she really trust Mrs. Brown even after six years?

It is like a house of the dead, Jan thought, coming softly down the stairs again, as though even now she feared to disturb some invisible intruder. She hadn't bothered to mount to the third floor, which was apportioned to the children—bedrooms, playroom, which Kay thought should be called the schoolroom now, bath, attics, where Dawn and Coral loved to play with the rolls of old wallpaper, tattered rugs, a broken chair, ancient trunks with domed lids, never used but never parted with, a decrepit sweeper, all the flotsam and jetsam of a normal household. They played desert islands on the bare patches of floor, climbing, diving, making believe to swim. It was a far better playground than the official amusement park in Buzzard Major Recreation ground, which provided swings and roundabouts but nothing personal at all.

"So long as you do not disturb the household, you should play what you like," decreed Jan.

Now she stood at the head of the stairway considering pros and cons. Her employers' loss didn't concern her. Now she must decide whether to telephone the police, which everyone would agree was the sensible or at all events the right thing to do, or steal out again like a shadow, leaving no trace of her coming. Only—where to go? Her purse was woefully thin, tomorrow perhaps she could sell her small pieces of jewelry and find a room, after which she could get a temporary job. Her young crowd always knew where there was something to be picked up, if it was only dishwashing, or baby-sitting. She would take the shabby case with which she'd arrived and what she'd left in her bureau drawers. Whatever she did, she wasn't going to need much in the way of clothes.

No, tonight was the real problem, and she came back to her original notion of spending it quietly, silent as a mouse, in her own room, and stealing away at dawn. She was accustomed to early rising, the children were often up at break of day. If she went by the French windows and crossed the lawn, she would remain invisible. Even the milkman didn't come so early. And if Mrs. Brown should wake, her window looked over the front. There were cheap early-morning tickets; her money might just cover the cost of one, though no more. She could be sorry now that she hadn't paid more attention to Kay when she advised her to save a percentage of her pocket money each month.

"Then you will have a nestegg," she had pointed out.

"But I am not a robin, I do not want an egg," protested Jan. "Not till I have a mate to care for me."

Still, she would scrape through. She had left two pounds in the pocket of the old case, to be sure of having something in her purse if and when she returned from Greece. As though she feared Mrs. Brown was still on the premises, she came very softly down the stairs, closed the door of Roy's den and turned to do the same to the door of the drawing room. But on the threshold she trod on something that rolled under her tread. She picked it up, incredulous. No doubt what that was. Mrs. Brown's great pride, in addition to her knowledge of her own integrity, was a handsome and very unusual necklace of large crystal and jade beads. She only wore this on state occasions, of which bingo night was presumably one.

Swinging her torch in a wider radius, Jan saw other beads scattered on the floor and at the corner of the staircase. Automatically she began to collect them, remembering Roy's heartless joke about his housekeeper's piece of finery. "Each bead a thought, each thought a tear, my rosary, my rosary," he used to say. And Kay would scowl and warn him, "One of these days she'll hear you and give notice. It probably belonged to her grandmother." "Or was a personal gift from the Shah of Persia," riposted Roy. And here it was, broken, scattered, disregarded, lying all about the hall. Chains do break, of course, and Mrs. Brown had rather a habit of caressing it "telling her beads," said Roy—pulling it unconsciously, but surely if it had broken, she wouldn't have left the beads sprawling on the floor. Even the children knew enough to respect that chain.

"Like the Lord Mayor?" asked Dawn.

"Just like the Lord Mayor," said Jan.

Suddenly Jan felt faint. The situation was becoming more complicated than she had supposed. But perhaps the indomitable Mrs. Brown had also felt faint, had clutched at the chain and broken the string. Or she might have been violently embraced— but common sense rejected that. All the same, the problem remained. Where was she now? Perhaps she had staggered as far as the kitchen and was lying there in a swoon. Perhaps she had celebrated too heartily at the Lord Charles. But for her, Jan's, unexpected return, she might have remained there till Wednesday. Still, Jan could hardly believe Providence would go to these lengths to insure her own reluctant revisitation of Manor House.

The kitchen was at the end of a passage behind the hall. Turning abruptly, one found oneself confronted by three doors, the china cupboard on the left, the broom cupboard on the right, the kitchen door straight ahead. She opened the kitchen door, kicking one or two more beads out of her path. But the kitchen was as bare as Mother Hubbard's cupboard. Neat, uncluttered, the floor spotless—Mrs. Jelf might gossip but she was a good cleaner—but no sign of human habitation. So—Mrs. B. hadn't expected anyone tonight.

Then Jan espied an unusual feature. Standing on the dresser was a wrapped bottle. Jan pulled the paper back. To her surprise it was whiskey, surprise because Mrs. Brown let everyone know she never touched spirits. Presumably this was in honor of the expected guest. Who hadn't yet arrived? Or perhaps they'd decided to eat out and come back for a nightcap. Or she had left the whiskey behind when she went to bingo, had accidentally broken the beads but decided she couldn't wait to collect them till her return. Turning, Jan stepped on yet another bead and fell against the china cupboard door, bruising her shoulder; the door swung slowly open to reveal the glasses and china gleaming in a reviving shaft of moonlight, coming through the narrow slit of the window.

"So you're not hiding there," she addressed the invisible Mrs. Brown. "But perhaps you have put yourself in the umbrella stand among the sticks and all." And very like a stick she looked, at that. Kay insisted on umbrellas being kept in this cupboard, saying they made the front hall untidy. No wonder she does not care to walk in the country, reflected Jan. All those untidy flowers coming up in bunches, no neat borders . . .

Chuckling a little, she turned the latch of the broom cupboard—it had a catch fastening, not a key—and stood transfixed, disbelieving, too shocked for the moment for fear. For there she was, after all.

Mrs. Felicia Brown—after so much looking and speculation, and she'd been here all the time, Felicia Georgina Brown, that was her improbable name—more wooden, less human than she had ever seemed before, pushed down among the brooms and polishers, her bingo finery tumbled, her open purse beside her. But her head was no longer upright and defiant. "Look the world in the eye," she used to tell the children. Another favorite quotation was "Give to the world the best you have, and the best will come back to you." But she'd never say that again; her face, no longer sallow, was a queer reddish-purple, her head crooked on the thin neck might have been made from papier-mâché.

"I knew at heart," whispered the girl, "I knew always she would not conspire to rob."

So—she had stayed behind expecting a friend, and in the friend's place had come whoever was responsible for this nightmare. Or perhaps he had been another Nikki—it wasn't only the young girls who were deceived. No chance visitor could be anticipated at this hour of night, with the Bankses away and the children gone. And the marauder had challenged, or perhaps this was how he had always meant it to end—he had taken his spoils, and fearful of a chance passer-by, had left the house by the French windows and gone through the garden and out of the gate in the wall, over the bridge that spanned the little stream at the orchard's foot and so on to the common, where he might have a car or an accomplice. No one would notice a car on such a night, or if anyone did, it would be put down as a courting couple making the most of their chances.

What is that expression of Mr. Banks? Jan wondered. Riding in front of the hounds. I am so far in front, the hounds are out of sight. After all, it wasn't for her to solve the mystery of Mrs. Brown's death. Let the police do their own stint. The criminal or criminals could be miles away by now, coming and going unperceived. "You could stand at a window and not see a soul," Kay used to boast. Roy said you could say the same thing in the condemned cell.

"Why must you stare so?" she whispered to that thing, moving abruptly. "I don't know who it was, I don't know."

She struck against an electric polisher, which moved an inch or two on the bare floor, touching the dead woman, so that the body moved, too, dropped down a little and settled into its uneasy perpetual sleep.

"Now I *must* get the police," cried Jan defiantly, slamming the door shut and refastening the catch, as though she feared the thing inside would follow her up the hall. And as she reached the wall instrument at the foot of the stairs, once again the bell began to ring.

She stood, aghast. This, of course, was her opportunity. Pick up the receiver. "This is Manor House." Perhaps it would be a wrong number, but she couldn't believe that. Most likely it would be someone for Mrs. Brown. "Yes," she might say, "of course she's on the premises. No, she won't run off, I can promise you that."

An extraordinary sound, something between a hoot and a giggle, broke through the monotonous ringing.

I can't answer it, she thought, I can't. I will let it ring itself out and then I will call the police.

"I hope nothing's wrong," said Kay uneasily, setting down the telephone for the second time. "I'm sure she said she'd be in tonight . . ."

Roy had a fleeting vision of the errant Mrs. Brown lying dead drunk under the kitchen table. "I wouldn't worry," he soothed. "It's not often she has a chance to let her hair down. Ring her in the morning when she'll be her usual metallic self, and blow the expense."

Four

The telephone had stopped. Now there was nothing to prevent Jan from calling the police station. Since the authorities must be informed sooner or later, surely the sooner the better. Buzzard Minor still boasted a village constable who had probably never been connected with a major crime in his life. He was as much a part of the landscape as the common and the village church. Buzzard Minor didn't go in for law-breaking on a big scale; they left that to Buzzard Major, with its new factory and planning areas and its tall blocks of flats where anyone but a bird 'ud be bound to feel dizzy. Probably the case would be passed on to them. The longer she lingered, the less promising did her own situation appear. They would look for a suspect, and perhaps they would look no further than herself. They will say, "All these aliens are bent." Here she was quoting Roy, who could be very irreverent about his National Force. And they will ask for proof. Proof that she was dead when I came; proof that I traveled on the slow train—there'd been no one on the station, I had met no one en route—discount the car, that driver wouldn't want any limelight; proof that my case was stolen. The one thing they could prove easily was that the friend in Eastbourne was nonexistent. And if they believed in Nikki's existence, they might think it was a put-up job between the pair of them.

Her head began to swim, it had been a long day. She, Jan, could tell the police nothing relevant to Mrs. Brown's death. But for the chance of her case being stolen, she wouldn't have come back before Wednesday morning, and surely, surely someone would have found the body before then. So—she would cling to her original plan, spend the night here, leave early by the French windows, cross the common and join the trail of commuters setting forth on a new day's work, catch the London train.

I shall find a room and work for a week. She knew all about picking up these short-term engagements. In what Kay called her raffish set, there were several who alternated between short-time working and national assistance.

Her room at the top of the house seemed smaller than usual, neat as the proverbial new pin—in case, for some inexplicable reason, Kay came upstairs before leaving. It had an unoccupied feeling. Just so had Mrs. Brown's body seemed unoccupied, as though no one had lived in it. Just before she got into bed Jan locked her door, though, if that dreadful ghost could break out of its prison, it would have no difficulty melting through a slab of wood. She struggled with the key, stiff because it was so seldom used. One of the children might have a bad dream or want a drink, in any case, both must feel she was instantly available.

"Don't tell Mummy," Coral would say, creeping into Jan's bed, "but there was a tiger on the stair. But it won't come in here, will it?"

Dawn was a more matter-of-fact child. If she thought she heard a tiger outside she'd go out and let it in. "Not many people," she would explain, "have tigers in their bedrooms."

Jan lay awake, thinking about the house. How dark, silent, innocent it must seem to any passer-by. How long would it be before Mrs. Brown was discovered?

She fell asleep suddenly, dreamlessly, and slept right through the trilling of the third telephone call.

Hugh Wheeler was a young man of communist principles

who lost no opportunity for preaching his red-hot gospel to anyone who would listen. Tonight he'd been at it hammer and tongs in the Huntsman, though for the most part he was preaching to the converted. Now and again, though, a dissenter arose in the group. There was one such tonight.

"Chuck it, Hugh," he admonished his neighbor. "You're all gas and no flame. If you believe in true equality, why don't you break into one of the stately homes and help yourself?"

"And get myself torn to pieces by a guard dog? Besides, that's not what it's all about. I don't want the bits and bobs of decorative trash. What I want is equality of opportunity, and that's what the Old Gang has resolved we shan't have."

The Huntsman clock began to strike and the landlord instantly threw all his remaining clientele off the premises. All gas and gaiters, he thought disgustedly, but you can't refuse the trade. The Huntsman was a paltry enough place that might have found it hard to keep going if all these young revolutionaries, talking through their nonexistent hats, didn't patronize it. He supposed they'd been thrown out of the more high-class drinking shops.

They emerged into a windy silvery night, a little rain still blew about half-heartedly. Hugh was still talking, but he broke off in the middle of his speech, looking round as if he expected a witch to fall out of a tree.

"My scooter!" he exclaimed. "I leaned her against the palings when I arrived, and she's gone."

"That old bone-shaker!" said the candid friend.

"Gets me from A to B, which is all I ask of her," retorted Hugh sturdily.

"Padlocked?" asked a knowing friend.

The candid one laughed. "Gertcha! Who'd want to steal a scooter?"

"Someone who couldn't drive a car," said someone else, with more truth than he realized.

"A minute ago you were all on about equality of opportunity," said a fourth man slyly. "Opportunity to get home on a dark night. Now someone's taken you up on it."

To their surprise Hugh broke into a gust of laughter. "I always wondered what a petard was. Now I'm hoist on my own."

"Teenagers, that's who it'll be," a wiseacre observed sagely. "A regular chap wouldn't want to be seen tinkling about on that. They'd think he'd borrowed it from his kid sister."

"Everyone hasn't got a kid sister who looks as if she came from St. Trinian's."

For a minute it looked as though a roughhouse might be going to develop, but the landlord, standing at the front door, his hand on the bolt, opened it a crack to call out, "If you're going to indulge in murder, don't do it on my doorstep. Apart from that, you can all cut each other's throats for all I care."

"Surly old devil!" someone said.

"Anyone 'ud be surly on the beer he sells. Don't know why we go on coming."

"They wouldn't have Hugh on respectable premises. Just try going into the Tory Chairman . . ."

"Wouldn't even let you leave your scooter outside there. By the way, you're sure you did leave it? I didn't see it when I came in."

"Because it wasn't here, you clot. I was over at Huntsden looking for old Wenham to produce the leaflets for Sunday's demo. How was I to guess he'd close down for the long weekend whether he'd fulfilled his obligations or no? Closed till Tuesday —that's all he did. Left a notice on the door, and the place as fast locked as the Tower. I tracked him half round Huntsden, his favorite pub included, but even his house was dark. Gone off for the weekend, I suppose. One thing we haven't paid for—the leaflets, though it's not going to be very easy to manage without them. Thank heaven for the banners, and you'll all have to be more vocal than usual."

"What about the leaflets, if and when he does deliver them?"

"They'll do for some other demo," said Hugh airily. "Facts are facts whatever the cause. All the same, it shakes my faith in human nature, a printer closing down for a public holiday—he knew we wanted these things for Sunday. Oh well." He shook himself like a dog. "If I've got to walk two miles, I may as well get started."

"Not going to the police?" someone jeered. "You have your rights."

"That'll be the day," said Hugh. "As Len says, it's only some kid. It'll turn up. If it doesn't, I can go hunting for it. I don't belong to the classes that expect the fuzz to do their work for them."

"It's a funny thing," said a youth called Chris, watching Hugh stride away, "but that chap really would give you the shirt off his back if he felt you needed it."

"And get picked up for indecent exposure. Just the same, I wouldn't want to be the mug who pinched his scooter. He thinks more of that than my mum thinks of our dog, and everyone knows she thinks more of Hammy than she does of my old man. Short for Hamish," he added politely.

They broke up and quiet fell on the area. "I've half a mind not to serve 'em again," said a surly voice, hearing those other voices die away. "That young Wheeler may never have been in real trouble, but some of those other chaps are proper tear-aways, and you get known by the company you keep. You mark my words, one of these days there'll be blood flowing."

But his wife, after the disappointing manner of wives, only said, "Just you make sure it isn't yours. I've enough to do as it is."

Although she hadn't believed she would need it, Jan had wound her alarm, and it was the sound of its cheerfully insistent bell that aroused her very early next day. For a moment, still not wholly awake, she thought it was an echo of the telephone, then realized she was in her own bed in her own room in a silent house. Then it all came back to her—last night's return, the open windows, Mrs. Brown . . . Mrs. Brown. And the telephone pealing through the dark.

I must go, she thought, panic-stricken, or it may ring again.

She knew she was alone in the house, but she moved soundlessly. The bathroom she shared with the children had been left spotless, fresh towels hanging, she was almost afraid to turn on a tap. But at last she was ready, case in hand, anxious eyes searching the room for any possible clue to her presence here last night. Then down, down, resist the temptation to open the cupboard door and make certain it wasn't all a hideous dream—but the beads were still scattered, the shelves of the study (she peeped in) and the case for the Battersea enamels still empty.

Of course I could not imagine anything like that, she told herself scornfully. She stole through the shadowy drawing room, its blank spaces making it seem unfamiliar, through the French windows, which she drew close behind her, over the dark dewy lawn and through the orchard. There was a pear tree where the children could sit on a long branch side by side, pretending they were at sea. Fallen apples lay in the long grass; she saw a plum with a gold bead on its head.

She pushed through the gate at the orchard's foot and struck out across the common. I have forgotten nothing, she told herself reassuringly. Nothing. Nothing.

But in fact she had forgotten two things that were to prove important. She didn't give a thought to the scooter stuffed into the hedge, and she had forgotten Arthur Crook.

No one had seen her enter or leave the house; she had melted into the pedestrian traffic from the common. But there was something else she had forgotten—the Christian dictum that no sparrow shall fall to the ground but the Heavenly Father seeth it. And though the cynic might argue that the sparrow was still on the ground, the fact remained that it hadn't fallen unobserved.

Mrs. Brown had died on a Thursday. Well-to-do couples like the Bankses started their weekends on that day so as to avoid the inevitable Friday crush. Her absense was noted by Mr. Bates, the milkman, on Saturday morning. He was the house's first visitor, outrunning even the postman or the paper boy. A note on the Friday morning said: 1 Pint Please. Family away, Mr. Bates recalled, putting down a bottle and collecting the empties. A little later the paper boy whistled his way up the front path and shied a rolled-up copy of the *Record* at the front door. No *Times* or *Guardian* before Wednesday; he'd know better than to roll them up. Mr. Banks 'ud have my blood, he thought. Postie brought a few envelopes that he pushed through the letter flap. No parcels, no registered letters, nothing to bring anyone to the door. Last of all came the baker. No note for him, but leave a small white to be on the safe side. Like the rest of the village, he knew the Bankses were away and Mrs. Brown was in charge. Having a nice lie-in, he thought, and who's to blame her. None of the locals had any illusions about Kay Banks being an easy employer. So far as could be ascertained, no one else called, and if the phone rang, no one heard it. No second postal delivery, so no one noticed the uncollected provender and mail.

No one collected the scooter either, but that was more securely hidden. Whoever had lost it wouldn't think of looking for it there. Hugh went back to the Huntsman on Friday night in case it had been surreptitiously returned, but his hopes couldn't have been very high. Kids (assuming it was a kid) don't do things that way. He hadn't bothered to insure it against theft, and he still didn't go to the police. Sooner or later it was bound to turn up, and not even the fuzz could prosecute you for having your own property stolen and not notifying the authorities.

Joe Bates, calling next morning, and finding yesterday's milk untouched, was the first to raise the alarm. If Mrs. Brown had been in her normal health she'd have taken the milk in and left a note about today's supply. Or a note to say: No Milk Required. That's how they all worked round here. Besides, there was the bread. Tentatively he rang the bell, but still nothing happened. He went round to the front and saw the paper and the post. He went back to the other door in case of a miracle, but the two pints and the loaf were still *in situ*. Scratching his head, he continued his round of the house, in case Mrs. Brown might have been overcome while watering a lilac bush or something. And so it was that he in his turn discovered that the French windows were ajar. The wind had blown them wider still since Jan's departure.

She'd never go out and leave them like that, the milkman decided. He stepped over the threshold, and saw at once that something was wrong. Case broken open, patches on the walls where pictures or something had hung. His mind moved slowly but along logical lines. Someone had been helping himself. And Mrs. Brown didn't know, which was unusual to say the least of it—she normally knew about things before they happened, or so they said in the village. If Mrs. Brown had discovered the theft the place 'ud be crawling with bluebottles. The fact that yesterday's milk, yesterday's bread, yesterday's paper hadn't been touched suggested she hadn't come home. But she'd been at the bingo that his wife also attended. And if she had a mortal sickness and lay abed, well, she knew her rights, none better, she'd have a doctor, the place crawled with telephones. Reluctantly he crossed the carpet and came into the hall. Nothing missing here, so far as he could tell. It was a light hall in the daytime, so he didn't need to press the switch. Not for him to examine further. Unto each man his destiny, unto each his crown—in a word, his job was to deliver the milk on time and it was the job of the police to track down evildoers. He kicked aside a scattered bead without noticing it, and picked up the telephone at the end of the hall. He rang up P. C. Trubshawe. (The local police force was represented by P. C. Trubshawe. "A yokel," snorted Kay. "I suppose they think he's good enough for us. Shows what a high opinion they have of our moral probity." But Buzzard Minor wouldn't have exchanged him for the head of the C.I.D.)

"Best come, Ted," he said. "Intruders at Manor House. No sign of Mrs. Brown. But French windows opened. That's how I got in."

"What's happened to her?" Trubshawe wondered. "Take much?"

"Well, I don't know what was there, do I?" said Mr. Bates reasonably. "Lot of empty showcases, though. Being held for ransom, p'raps."

"That'll be enough from you, Joe Bates. You stay where you are, and I'll come right round. Had some nice stuff there, I heard."

Buzzard Major 'ud get the jam, of course. Big fine new station they'd got there, and needed it, too. Place crawling like an ant hill, bound to be a few villains in that lot. Trubshawe remembered the biblical story of Dives and Lazarus, between whom was a great gulf fixed. No more than any other countryman did he like townees intruding on his territory.

"You haven't touched anything, Joe?" was his first question.

"Only the phone. Had to touch that. If you don't want me any longer, I'll be on my way."

His customers were used to finding their milk on the doorstep early of a morning. No one wants to drink yesterday's milk for breakfast. And here was Ted, portly as an elephant, telling him he'd got to stay. Chief witness, first on the scene of the crime. Oh well, he'd get a free pardon when the facts became known. Good for quite a lot of free beer, he shouldn't wonder, grinning slightly at the thought. But then he became grave again. Good stories and good beer were all very well in their way, but where the deuce was Mrs. Brown?

"One thing's for sure," said Trubshawe. "Those windows were opened from the inside. They've got a special locking device; if there'd been any attempt to force them, there'd be traces. How come you happened to notice them?" he added.

"I found them because they were there," said Joe, puzzled. "Ask a silly question."

"One thing, if the villains didn't come in through the French windows, that's the way they left. And Mrs. Brown would never have left them open all night. Easy to go through the garden, had a car parked on the common maybe. Good thing you came right round the house, as it happens."

"Well, I had to think of Mrs. Brown, didn't I? She might have had a heart attack or something. There was that case in Alton Barnard the other day, old chap found dead in a deck chair in his own garden, heart they thought, might have been dead four days. Shows all this independence is a mistake. Have the milk delivered and there's someone to keep an eye on you."

"Best make sure she's not on the premises," said Ted. "Could be tied up or something. Villains would know the Bankses were away, Mrs. Brown at the bingo . . ."

In Mrs. Brown's room they found the coat on the bed, everything else in apple-pie order. It didn't make sense.

"Best ring Buzzard Major," said Trubshawe. "More their line of country than ours. Got a C.I.D. too, might come in handy."

"You're never thinking what I think you're thinking," exclaimed Mr. Bates.

"Mrs. Brown's disappeared along of a lot of valuable stuff, that's enough for me. Mind how you go," he added sharply. "Stepped on something, then."

They had reached the hall. The day had swelled into full

light, and both men could see them clearly—one, two, three beads scattered on the polished floor.

"She'd never leave those lying there," said Ted.

They followed the trail into the kitchen. The unwrapped bottle was further proof she'd come back last night. Expecting company, maybe. Plenty of food in the fridge, but nothing prepared specially. The two men looked through the kitchen window into the garden. If she'd left the house that way, it 'ud explain the open windows. But believing in doing a job without scamping, Trubshawe knew a minute later they wouldn't have to bother themselves with spades and sacks. And knew, too, why Mrs. Brown hadn't taken in the milk or opened Friday's newspaper.

"Buzzard Major can take this," said Trubshawe simply and picked up the phone.

Detective-Inspector Moon wasn't available, but Detective-Sergeant Finney, accompanied by D. C. Kite, was round in a twinkling, shiny new car, all energy and go.

Finney took instant brisk command, alerted the doctor, the ambulance, all the routine crowd who play their part when a violent crime has been committed. "Lady alone in the house?" he asked.

"Well, not when she was killed, naturally," said Trubshawe innocently. "Expecting someone, though. Unopened bottle of whiskey in the kitchen, and home early from the bingo."

"Any proof she went to the bingo?" snapped Finney.

"The wife saw her there," put in Mr. Bates. "Left early, though. Mrs. Banks doesn't like the house being left empty over a public holiday."

"Any sign of breaking and entering?"

Trubshawe told him no, and there'd be signs with the sort of locks they had on the Manor House doors.

"Inside job?" wondered Kite to his superior.

"Could be," Finney agreed. It often was.

"Not Mrs. Brown," said Trubshawe. "Could have let them in, of course, thinking it was whoever she expected."

"Anyone know who that was?"

"She kept herself to herself, did Mrs. Brown. A very quiet woman."

"Anyone else in the house?"

"Not Thursday, there wouldn't be. Mr. and Mrs. Banks gone to Amsterdam . . ."

"Anyone have the address?"

"Could have given it to Mrs. Brown, I suppose. No letters being forwarded, Mrs. Banks told Miss Papworth." Miss P. was the local sub postmistress.

"No milk till Wednesday, not the regular order, that is," put in Bates. "Just what Mrs. Brown ordered. It was finding Friday's milk . . ."

They took him through his story and let him go on with his rounds. He'd be wanted to sign a written statement later.

"Buzzard Major?" Like all the other locals, he'd sooner have Ted Trubshawe than the head of London's C.I.D.

"Well, of course. This is murder."

Detective-Inspector Moon arrived and summed up the situation within a couple of minutes. He addressed his questions to Trubshawe, realizing he'd get more out of him than half a dozen sergeants, for all he looked like an elderly chaperon hovering on the verge of the party. He heard about Jan—off to friends, not likely she'd leave an address with Mrs. B.; kiddies gone off with their auntie till Thursday; missing articles. Well, all Mr. Banks' trophies were missing and the villains had made a killing in the drawing room too, from the appearance of the place. Nothing else disturbed so far as anyone could tell.

But when it came to Mrs. Brown, he couldn't help much. Been in Buzzard Minor nearly six years, kept herself to herself, no special friends, the bingo lot, of course, maybe the members of the weekly choir get-together.

"According to Postie, she doesn't get much in the way of letters, local notes mostly being left by hand. Never spoke of any family that I heard tell."

"We'll have to hope the Bankses will be a bit more forthcoming. When are they due back? Wednesday? Staying with friends, do you happen to know?"

"Hotel," said Trubshawe. "Mr. Banks let on."

"Dutch police might be able to help. Sooner they're back the better. We don't even know what's missing. Funny thing, if she was expecting someone, why didn't he raise the alarm when he couldn't get in?"

The answer to that seemed to be that he was part of the setup.

"Mrs. Brown wouldn't open the door of a night, not to a stranger," Trubshawe volunteered.

"Motorist wanting to use the phone? Car broken down."

"Like on the telly last week," agreed Kite.

But Ted reckoned she wouldn't fall for that. There was a box on the Green and another near the church, and there wouldn't be any queues for either that hour of the night.

"Jug of water for a boiling radiator," suggested Finney.

"She'd send him round to the side door, nearer the tap, see. Only the chain was broken in the front hall."

The Recording Angel wouldn't have much on this chap on the last day, reflected Moon.

"And I wouldn't count too much on Mrs. Banks," Trubshawe continued. "I don't say she'd buy a pig in a poke, but if you can find someone respectable and honest who's ready to live in the country and knows her job, as by all accounts Mrs. Brown knew hers, you're not going to be too fussy."

"Wonder why she stayed so long," murmured Kite.

"Well, a woman on her own, not too nice. This place was like home to her, had her own sitting room, more or less in charge, six years is a long time. Major Harrison might know something," he added. Major Harrison was in charge of the bingo. "Or there's that woman works at Maurice." Maurice, accent on the second syllable, did the hair of Buzzard Minor's elite, clients even came in from Buzzard Major. Still, not likely Mrs. B. would confide in her.

Trubshawe was right; the bingo crowd knew nothing of her personal life; not likely she'd confide in the young girl (Jan). Anyway, she was always with the children. Nothing in her scanty personal papers threw much light on the past. Her bedroom revealed two yellowing photographs, assumed to be her parents, no record of any husband, no marriage lines, no passport. Trubshawe felt uneasy. It wasn't natural to have no past. Still, six years was a long time. The barmaid at the Lord Charles knew nothing about the whiskey. Mrs. Brown never touched the hard stuff, even when someone else was paying. Port and lemon, maybe a Dubonnet or a medium sherry—spirits, never. So the bottle had been bought for the intended visitor. And someone had clearly turned up. Only—was it the same chap?

Five

Buzzard Minor didn't need a newspaper. Its inhabitants, all hundred of them, knew that the proper study of mankind is man, and they studied with application. Of course, if you wanted news farther afield, you relied on the press or the television or even the radio. Midday editions might be O.K. for racing fans but they reached even Buzzard Major too late to be much use. There was a new betting shop in Buzzard High, and if your credit was good, you could place your bets by phone. If you hadn't got a line, there were the public call boxes.

The news of Mrs. Brown's melodramatic death went the rounds by word of mouth. Joe Bates made his excuses—trouble up at Manor House—the whisper spread from lip to lip. And even if you're a deaf-mute, you can't disguise the presence of the police or misinterpret it. The police spelled trouble with a capital T. Anything less would have been dealt with by Ted Trubshawe. Mrs. Brown was more popular than she'd been during the past six years. The outlying villages, who held themselves aloof from the new town of Buzzard Major, got the news on the Saturday night or even Sunday morning. Elsie Farmer, the barmaid at the Pumpkin and Pie at Firlmere, one of the more exclusive villages, heard on Sunday morning in her own bar, her informant being a disconsolate commercial traveler complaining at finding himself isolated at the Back of Nowhere for the weekend.

"No wife to go home to?" asked Elsie briskly. But most likely he'd been stood up by a popsie. If he'd really wanted to get home, he'd have grown wings if need be. Elsie gave the human race credit for more enterprise than it normally showed.

"Same again," said the traveler mournfully. "And what's yours? And how about that old girl they've found in a cupboard at Buzzard Minor?"

"How about her?" asked Elsie, pricking invisible ears. It wasn't the done thing to be curious about goings-on outside your immediate purview, but the situation would seem to have possibilities.

"Didn't know her, then?"

"We keep ourselves to ourselves in these parts. This old girl—you didn't mention her name—she belongs to Buzzard Minor."

"Isn't it marvelous?" reflected the commercial traveler. "Here's the world growing smaller every minute, already we're getting trips to the moon, and Venus and Mars will be on the map before you can say knife . . ."

"Then don't say it," Elsie counseled him. "We've trouble enough with one planet without adopting a couple more."

"And you don't know about a woman who's been found murdered practically on your own doorstep."

"Who says she's murdered?"

"You don't choke yourself and then get into a boot cupboard. Here, don't you see the papers?"

"In them, is it? George—that's my husband—gets the papers first thing Sunday, not that they come much before opening time. I see them when we close after lunch. Big headlines, is it?"

"This is the national press," rebuked the traveler. "Most of the papers give their front pages to this psychopath who got out of Avondale New Gaol and is said to be roaming the Downs. You remember him? Killed two little girls four years ago, and 'ull kill two more if they don't find him double-quick."

"Awful." Elsie shivered. She and George had never had kids. "What's about the housekeeper?"

"Mrs. Brown, Manor House, Buzzard Minor. Ring a bell?"

"I've heard the name," acknowledged Elsie. "Excuse me." She moved down the bar to serve two newcomers. Her hands shook as she pushed the tankards across. Would you believe it? Mrs. Brown. Still, asking for trouble the capers she got up to at her age. And in this very bar no later than Thursday night. Might have known there was something queer, seeing it was a Thursday and Friday was her night. George isn't going to like this.

"Wake up, lovey," taunted a voice, and she found she was being asked for a double Scotch and a gin and orange. When she was free again, she saw to her relief that the commercial traveler had gone, gone to spread his glad tidings at the Blue Lion, no doubt, pick up a free drink or so, she shouldn't wonder.

As soon as the bar closed, which on Sunday meant peace till you started getting ready for the seven o'clock opening, she approached her husband, who lay surrounded by newspapers.

"See about the news from Ireland?" he said.

"Never you mind about Ireland. I've got to go along to Buzzard Major, might as well go now."

"What's with them?" he asked, flabbergasted. "You haven't stuck a knife in one of the customers."

"Not me. And I don't know about a knife. It's this Mrs. Brown from Buzzard Minor. Found murdered in a boot cupboard. Don't ask me why. Bankses are away till Wednesday, that's all I know."

"Silly old cow!" said George. "I daresay she asked for it."

"If so, she's got it. No, listen, she was in this bar on Thursday. It's in the papers."

"She didn't die here, did she? Why do you want to get mixed up with the police, Elsie? You know it doesn't do a house any good to have the fuzz rubbernecking on the premises."

"Anyone could see she was set for trouble, but you can't tell that sort. Wonder why he did it?"

"Why who . . . ?" Words seemed to fail him.

"That's what I've got to tell the police; they can carry on from there. Yes, of course I must go, George. You said yourself we don't want them on the premises, and you know how tongues wag."

"Like a dog's tail," he agreed. "Can't you keep yours still for once, Elsie?"

But he might have saved his breath. She went, as she'd meant to all along.

"We must hope the Bankses can tell us something helpful," Moon was remarking to Finney. "So far as this woman was concerned, she might have been born the day she came to Buzzard Minor. I don't say I go along with this Common Market lark, but these countries that keep fingerprint records and make their citizens carry identity papers have got something." Still, the Bankses would be back tonight. The Dutch police had turned up trumps, identified the wanted pair and booked them back on a late evening flight. And then a constable came in to say there was a lady with information about Mrs. Brown.

"Sure it's the right one?" muttered Finney, but they saw her just the same. Died Thursday night so far as anyone could tell. Sunday afternoon and they were still in the dark.

Elsie came straight to the point. "This Mrs. Brown you're asking about she was in the bar of the Pumpkin and Pie, Thursday night. Thought you ought to know."

"Sure it's the same one?"

"There won't be two Mrs. Felicia Browns in this neck of the woods. Besides, she's the Bankses' housekeeper. Talked about them being away— Well, she's generally at the bingo, and then the Lord Charles of a Thursday, but she'd left early. 'Houses get lonely, too,' she said. 'You should have a dog,' I told her. 'It's funny how burglars are scared of even a little dog. Like elephants. Go mad if a little dog yaps at their heels.' But she said dogs brought in dirt, and she had enough to do as it was, with that girl encouraging the children to roll in the woods and bring back mud on their shoes. To tell you the truth, I was a bit surprised to see her, seeing Friday was her usual night, though not regular."

Finney reminded himself that patience is a virtue. "Did she come on her own?"

"She always came alone."

"And met her friend in the bar?"

"If that's what you call him."

"Was he a regular?" Finney wondered, doodling. He drew a school of fish with ferocious fins on the pad in front of him.

"Not from these parts at all," Elsie said. "A townee, you might say. A snappy dresser, though. Might be from Stainton or Waterlow Cross. A lot younger than her."

"A son perhaps?" suggested Finney smoothly.

Elsie shook her head. "Not him. But I'll tell you one thing. He was there for what he could get."

"Ever hear what they talked about?"

"I was never near enough to hear. She used to come in first and buy a short, and take it over to one of the little tables. She'd sit watching the clock till he came, usually about ten minutes later. He always had the same thing, a large whiskey, and you can take it from me he never paid for that out of his own pocket. Sometimes he'd come over for a refill—for himself, mark you, never for her."

"No names mentioned?"

Elsie shook her head again. "I never heard her call him a thing. And, like I said, he was a foreigner to us. Dark-haired fellow," she added vaguely.

"Know him again?"

Elsie looked dubious. "Well, if he was put up with the rector and the sexton and that little fellow who works for the stonemason who has only the one leg, I'd know him then, but these young chaps look so alike. Wore a very fancy ring," she recalled, "but they're all dandies these days. Came in a car, of course. I'd hear it rev up the minute he was out of the door."

"Know that again?"

"Well, he wouldn't bring that into the bar, would he?"

"How long had she been coming?"

Elsie considered. "Say three months, give or take a week. But like I said, not regular."

"But always on a Friday?"

"That's what I said."

"But last week it was Thursday."

"She wasn't expecting him, if that's what you mean. Just ordered her usual short and sat up at the bar, never looked at her watch or nothing. I wondered why she'd come till she asked for the whiskey. 'Do you sell whiskey here by the bottle?' she said. 'It's one of the things we're here for,' I told her. Then I saw why she'd come. I mean, she wouldn't ask for it at the Lord Charles, seeing they knew her there and knew she never touched the stuff. And if you don't, you won't be buying a bottle for yourself."

Finney added a muffler to a frail-looking fish. "This Mrs. Brown—you didn't know her well?"

"No one knew her well."

"Would you say she was a woman of substance?"

Elsie sniffed. "She'd not grow rich on what Mrs. Banks paid her. Close as a semidetached, that one is."

Finney nodded. "Happen to notice if she was wearing her chain?"

"The one she got from the Shah of Persia?" Elsie grinned faintly. "Well, but she was wearing her coat. I wouldn't know."

"And she didn't stay long?"

"Just had the one short and bought the whiskey. Told me about the house, going back early because everyone was away but her—not that she missed them, I'd guess."

"And this young chap—did he turn up?"

Elsie stared. "What? On Thursday? I told you he never . . ."

"Come the next night perhaps?"

"There wouldn't be much sense in that, would there? She wouldn't be there."

"But would he know that?"

"Well, but I don't know if he was coming that Friday, anyway. Sometimes it 'ud be two, once it was three, weeks."

"You noticed?"

"Well, she was a woman of mystery, wasn't she? I mean, six years and no one knew anything about her, not even in Buzzard Minor, if you can believe what you hear."

"That girl they had . . . ?"

"Jan? She never came into the bar. Besides, she always had the kids with her."

"Never came of an evening?"

"Her lot don't come here. Anyway, half the time they go to coffee bars, drink Coke. And if she had come, not likely she'd have talked to me."

No, she said, she hadn't noticed any strangers specially, though naturally you always got a percentage of new faces. No, she'd no notion what the link between this young chap and Mrs. Brown had been, she wasn't keeping anything back, that was the $64,000 question, wasn't it? If she thought of anything else, she'd let him know, and Mr. Farmer 'ud be wanting his tea.

One more bit of information came in. An anonymous woman telephoned to say she had noticed a woman walking in the direction of Buzzard Minor on Thursday evening; she was carrying what looked like a wrapped bottle. No, she couldn't say who she was, nothing to do with this Mrs. Brown perhaps, but the police always wanted to know everything. Walking alone—around eight, give or take a few minutes. Don't ask her why she noticed her, except that there weren't many people around, it was the bottle that caught her attention—it was funny the way details struck you. No, her own name wasn't important and her husband wouldn't like her getting mixed up with the police.

And she rang off.

"Doesn't get us much further except that it bears out Elsie Farmer's story, and we knew that was right because we found the bottle at Manor House."

No young chap had come forward to say he'd had a date with Mrs. Brown for Thursday night and hadn't got in. It would help a lot if they could identify the young fellow who used to meet her at the Pumpkin and Pie. But whether he knew anything about her death or not, he showed his sense by staying underground.

"You know, murder may not have figured in the original setup," Finney told Moon. "Trouble with situations like this is they outrun the constable. Whoever had come hadn't seemed prepared for violence—no gunshot wound, no stabbing, no assault with a blunt instrument. Just hands, which left few clues. We may learn something from the Bankses. At least we'll know what's missing."

"I felt in my bones something was wrong when she didn't answer the phone," said Kay after the Dutch police had told her the house had been broken into and the housekeeper assaulted. They were playing their cards very close to the chest, let the English police finish the story.

"Wonder how bad she is," brooded Roy. "She's the sort that 'ud fight, but I'd say she was taken off her guard. I mean, talk about lèse majesté."

"Mrs. Brown of all people. The soul of caution."

But Roy only reminded her that care killed the cat, and they moved on to wonder what had been taken.

"Easy to say we're insured!" exploded Kay. "You can't insure adequately against the irreplaceable. If they've got my

Battersea enamels . . . But of course they would have." She brooded.

"Unless it's a personal vendetta against Ma Brown."

That was the first time it occurred to either of them that their housekeeper might have come to serious harm.

The Bankses were getting the VIP treatment. A car met them at the airport and whirled them back to Buzzard Minor.

"Have they taken everything?" demanded Kay.

"Is Mrs. Brown badly hurt?" asked Roy.

When they were told the truth they found difficulty in accepting it. Kay found herself thinking it was vulgar and conspicuous to get yourself killed in such a fashion. Probably the place would be swarming with the press. Roy thought, Thank God the kids are away, reflecting an instant later that if they'd been at Manor House, with Jan in attendance, this would probably never have happened.

As Kay had anticipated, everything—well, practically everything—of value was missing. "They won't be in this country any more," she said accusingly to Moon, who was in charge of the situation. "Why, you didn't find her till—till— When did you find her?"

"Milkman noticed on Saturday that Friday's milk and bread hadn't been taken in. Then he noticed the French windows were ajar . . ."

"Mrs. Brown would never have left them open. Anyway, you must know that."

"We don't know anything about Mrs. Brown, or virtually nothing," said Moon. "We thought you might be able to help us. I understand she's been with you for several years."

"Nearly six," agreed Kay. "She's not the sort of woman who makes friends or gives confidences. There's the bingo crowd, of course, and she sings with a weekly choir."

But the police knew that and it hadn't got them anywhere. "We were thinking of the time before she came to you," Moon explained. "You must have had some sort of reference with her, and in the course of years she'd have dropped some hints . . ."

"Mrs. Brown no more dropped hints than she dropped pins," said Kay scornfully. "I'll tell you what I know, but it won't get you very far. She'd been working in Harrogate as housekeeper-companion—that's how she put it—to a Mrs. Arnold, who'd gone to California to join a married daughter. She gave Mrs. Brown an excellent written reference, not that you can put much reliance in them. You have to use your own judgment. She'd got that job through a local agency, but it had closed down from lack of custom. Domestic service is a dying industry. This Mrs. Arnold was a widow, and I don't suppose Harrogate is any livelier than most of these spas. Practically everyone is ninety. Mrs. Brown got the impression that Mrs. Arnold would like to be married again and there might be better chances in the States. A go-ahead woman, she called her."

"And how did you hear of her?"

"We advertised. Of course, you either get no replies at all or you get a succession of creeps, so when we found someone who looked presentable and wasn't likely to get into trouble locally, we took a chance. After all, Buzzard Minor isn't exactly a riot of activity, you have to take what you can get. We did our best to make her comfortable and she asked rather more wages than I had in mind, but if you can get a sensible woman, you're getting something as rare as a white rhinoceros, and my daughter assures me you can't be much rarer than that." She laughed abruptly. "There were difficulties, of course. She wasn't a good mixer, couldn't hit it off with the woman who came to do the rough twice a week, and they're hard to come by, too. And before we had the *au pair* girl we had a governess for the children, and she didn't stay."

"She didn't have visitors, so far as you know?"

"She could. We gave her the room beyond the kitchen for her sitting room, and her friends would naturally come in at the side door."

None of this helped the police much. The world's full of solitary women: only daughters, spinsters who, so far as can be ascertained, never even had parents, living in bed-sitters and hostels, somehow always apart from the world. It was natural to suppose that in the course of six years Mrs. Brown would say, "That was the year we went to Margate" or "that was about the time Mr. Brown died . . ."

"Perhaps," suggested Roy thoughtfully, "she isn't a widow, after all. Perhaps she clung to the refuge of our roof because she thought he wouldn't dare follow her here."

Finney dropped his little bomb. "Never spoke of this young chap she used to meet at the Pumpkin and Pie?"

"Oh no," expostulated Roy. "That's too much. Who was it who could believe six impossible things before breakfast? I'm the same, but even I can't accept the idea of Mrs. Brown with a boyfriend."

"We don't know that he was a friend." Finney's tone was sober. "But we have evidence that she used to meet a young man at the Pumpkin and Pie . . ."

"But that's Firlmere. Right off her beat."

"I suppose that's why," said Kay crossly. "Really, it seems impossible to trust anyone. And after six years."

"Everyone's got a right to a private life," protested Roy.

It was like being a dormouse going round on its wheel; you seemed to end just where you'd started.

"You can't know any more about these people than they choose to tell you," Kay pointed out, and Roy startled them all by quoting:

> "The shroud is done, Death muttered, toe to chin.
> He snapped the ends and tucked the needles in."

"That's a layman's point of view," said the police dryly. "About this girl you had here?"

"She left the house before we did, going to stay with a friend in Eastbourne."

"Do you know the friend's name, madam?"

"I didn't think to ask. Someone she'd met at the English conversation classes, I think she said. She used to go into Buzzard Major for those."

"If the lady lived at Eastbourne, what was she doing attending classes in Buzzard Major?"

"I didn't think to ask," admitted Kay. "Wait a minute, I don't think she said this woman lived at Eastbourne, she was going to be there for the holiday. Married an Englishman and has two little girls. Bit of a busman's holiday, I thought."

"No postcard from Eastbourne?"

"Oh, come on," said Roy. "Who would she send one to? Not Mrs. B., and everyone else was away."

"She had a label—*Passenger to Eastbourne*—on her case. She'd bought a new one for the purpose. She left the old one on top of the wardrobe. That's the one she brought with her from Holland." Kay frowned. "I ought to have smelled a rat. Why should she buy a new case just to stay with a friend?"

"Wanted to impress her friend, perhaps. Didn't she leave an address, Kay?"

"Well, of course not. I didn't ask her. She's due back on Wednesday. And I shouldn't have been any wiser if she had. And if she was planning a weekend with one of her raudy friends, you don't seriously think she'd admit it to me?"

"All we ask of Jan is to look after the children, and the Lord Chief Justice couldn't fault her on that. They're crazy about her. I'm only surprised they agreed to trail off with your sister."

Kay snorted. "You can't go by children's likes and dislikes," she snapped. "Dawn and Coral are just at the impressionable age."

Moon with some difficulty concealed his amazement at the names of the Bankses' children. All the locals knew that, of course, and thought them, as names, vastly inferior to the Sheila and Maureen that their wives preferred.

They asked Kay if she'd go over the house and indicate what

was missing. "Well, my enamels for one thing," said Kay. "The Victoria and Albert were positively respectful when they saw that collection when it was Aunt Arabella's, and there have been additions since then." She was rather prone to hang over the smashed case. "I suppose I'm never likely to see those again."

No one disagreed with her. She listed other missing objects.

Roy stood in the doorway of his den, ruefully surveying the empty shelves. "Clean sweep!" he said. "They'll have to melt 'em down, of course. They were all inscribed."

Up they went to the main bedroom, but nothing had been disturbed there. No sense, said Kay, going to Jan's room or the children's, even an amateur wouldn't take the trouble to climb the stairs. The police were adamant. Jan might have left some trace.

"If you think girls leave notes these days, Inspector . . ." But she went just the same. The room was very quiet and unnaturally tidy.

"All present and correct?" suggested Roy.

But Kay had stiffened, like a hound at scent. "No," she said. "It isn't all right. The case has gone."

"Case?"

"I told you, I saw the case on the top of the wardrobe *after the girl had left the house*. I came up here to make sure she'd bolted the windows and not left a tap running in the children's bathroom—it's just what girls do do. And while I was here . . ." She moved swiftly across the room and flashed open the drawers of the little bureau. "Empty!" she cried in a dramatic and satisfied tone. "Oh, she hadn't left much behind, but there were a few things, and they've all gone. Don't you see what that means?"

"You tell us," suggested Roy.

"She came back later, after we'd gone." They'd hired Benson's car to the airport. About three o'clock that had been."

"Do you always go through her drawers?" asked Roy.

"I'm supposed to stand *in loco parentis* to her while she's under this roof—more than most *au pairs,* really, if this mysterious aunt is her only relative. She never gets any letters from abroad . . ."

Moon looked surprised. "You're sure of that?"

"Dead sure," agreed Roy. "Because of the stamps, see? My children are great collectors—Dawn collects stamps, Coral prefers slugs. No foreign stamp would pass unnoticed, just as it would be a very wary slug who could elude my younger daughter."

"If you'd only put down that stuff, we shouldn't have slugs at all," snapped Kay.

"And Coral wouldn't have a collection. Besides, how do I explain to her that it's all right for me to poison her protégés, but if she tries to dunk weed-killer in Mrs. Brown's porridge, well—just an example—anyone's porridge, she'll have the whole police force after her?"

"Oh, never mind about the slugs," cried his wife. "Don't you see what this means? It means *Jan isn't coming back.*"

"Because she's involved in the plot?" wondered Roy. "Doesn't seem very intelligent to me, to leave such obvious proofs that she returned. I suppose we're sure she did?"

"Who else do you suppose would want her old clothes?"

"Might be part of a setup, what you call a frame." Roy turned hopefully to the police.

"You think Mrs. Brown removed her things?" shrilled Kay. "Before or after she was murdered?"

"She wasn't the only person on the premises on Thursday night. And it's drawing a bow at a venture to suppose the other one was Jan. Personally, it seems to me too silly to make sense."

"Did the young lady have a door key?" asked Finney.

"Well, of course," said Kay. "Mrs. Brown wasn't going to open the door every time Jan came in with the children. I nearly took it back for the holidays, these girls are so careless. I wish now I had." A new thought struck her. "Dawn and Coral might know of any special friends she had. They follow her around like Mary's little lamb."

Roy turned white. "I will not have my children dragged into this. At all events, wait till Wednesday, give her a chance to get back and offer her own explanation."

"You're so sure she'll be back on Wednesday? I should have expected any girl of good feeling to come back as soon as she saw the news. I suppose it's been in the papers?"

"She was only found yesterday," expostulated Roy.

"Don't tell me the Sundays are going to miss that?"

"Depends on the competition," her husband pointed out. "Anyway, she may have the good sense not to read the papers when she's on holiday."

"If she does come back, she's got a lot of explaining to do," said Kay grimly, with more truth than she knew.

"Oh, she'll come back," prophesied Roy. "Poor little devil, where else has she got to go?"

Six

Mrs. Brown's bizarre death might thrill Buzzard Minor to the bone, but it left the world in general unmoved. Interest continued to focus on the psychopath who hadn't been recaptured. It wasn't only families with young children in the vicinity of the Downs who were worried, but mothers of young children everywhere. Psychopaths look like other people—don't they?—can travel by train and talk as sensibly when they've a mind to as you or me. Mrs. Brown might be more popular locally than she'd been in the past six years, but apart from that, she remained a paragraph on page 2.

Jan read about her on Sunday in the top room of a sleazy house near Victoria Station. This part of the world was crowded with rooming houses, and since she wasn't likely to be staying long, she took the first that offered.

"Week in advance, that's my terms," said Miss Lucas, who seemed to have spent her life keeping a hungry wolf from the door. She looked at the girl speculatively. Foreigner, but then London was alight with them. In trouble? Could be, it didn't show at the start. Not much luggage, so her story of coming for the holiday weekend could be true.

"No men visitors after ten o'clock," said Miss Lucas sternly. "Front door locked at eleven-thirty."

Jan paid her week in advance and went out again. She had disposed of her jewelry at a little place near the station, and was shocked and wounded, as aren't we all, at the smallness of the amount offered. In the event, she had had to throw in the little gold watch that Mr. Crook had admired. Now she made a survey of the streets. Small cafés abounded in this part of London for people who went to work early and hadn't the inclination or possibly the facilities for getting their own breakfast. Come nine or so, the tables filled up again with workmen having a tea break, drivers, milkmen who left their floats outside for ten minutes and chanced the traffic warden. There were a lot of these caffs, and the surprising thing was how well they all did. When they wanted fresh staff they didn't bother the Labour, they put a written notice in the window. Mrs. Luigi was the British-born widow of an Italian lay-about, who had finally managed to lie under a tram, apparently under the impression he was going to bed. One of her best girls, Annie, hadn't turned up this weekend. Mrs. Luigi didn't ramp and roar; these things were a part of life. Girls got a chance of a bright weekend or took up with a feller or just found something they preferred. Annie was strong and quick, but likely she'd come back; if not, there'd be someone else. Her clientele worked hard for their money and they'd no time to fool around with the waitresses, but they treated them human, which was more than you could say in some of the big places.

"Done this kind of thing before?" asked Mrs. Luigi. The girl was a foreigner, her dad might keep a café somewhere on the continent.

"I am a student," returned Jan. "I teach. [And so she did. "You must never leave us, Jan," said Dawn. "We never learned anything till you came."] But there are no classes and my pupils have gone away until next week. So I come to London."

And what you do out of hours is your own affair, reflected Mrs. Luigi. "Anything the customers give you is yours," she said. "No helping yourself behind the scenes, I say this to all the girls and then they can't say they weren't warned, any trouble over a bill come to me. Pay by the day, it's what the temporaries prefer."

84

A Nice Little Killing

She wasn't sure how much of Jan's story she believed, but she didn't seem to mind the idea of serving in the café, so it wasn't likely she was on the run from the police, and with London bursting at the seams, you'd hire a dog if it could walk on its hind legs and carry a tray.

For the rest of the day—Mrs. Luigi was of one mind with Dickens' famous Mr. Mell: there's no time like the present—Jan hurried from kitchen to café with plates of sausages, spaghetti, ham and eggs, scrambled ditto, all served with chips, brought substantial mugs of tea and coffee without spilling, cleared tables, made out bills.

"New, yes?" one client murmured to Mrs. Luigi. "Quick as a kingfisher, that one."

"Just temporary." Mrs. Luigi smiled. "Student—they don't get much change from their grants, they say." Though when she was a girl no one paid you to learn your job. It occurred to her there might have been trouble with a father of one of the children she claimed to teach. Legs like those, thought Mrs. Luigi dispassionately, hard to blame the chap, seeing what men were, talk about a flamingo. Still, her clientele worked too hard to start trouble with a girl who brought them their bangers and chips, if trouble was what they wanted, they'd go further afield.

Mrs. Brown made the papers on Sunday, but in quite a small way. It wasn't till Monday that the police let it be known they were anxious to interview a girl called Jan Van Damm, employed by the Bankses as an *au pair*; it was thought she might be able to assist the police in their inquiries.

The Café Luigi opened very early, Mrs. L. herself always being on the premises by six o'clock. The girls came a bit later, but none of them had time to see a newspaper before starting work. One of the customers left a *Morning Sun* on his chair and Jan collected it. Her first impulse was one of satisfaction that she had had the wit to use her mother's name, both at Miss

Lucas's apartment house and at the café. Jan Van Dyck she'd called herself, but the British public weren't fools, and certainly the two women with whom she was most concerned were not. Pretty soon they'd start adding two and two together, and the sum total in each case would be four. She looked askance at Mrs. Luigi after the lunch break, but Mrs. Luigi never had time to look at the paper until the evening. Jan could safely finish the day's work and draw the day's pay. About five-thirty things slackened off for the day. The pubs opened then and the café itself closed at six. Jan helped to wash china, sort cutlery and wring out sodden dishcloths. She would get a final edition on her way back and discover if there had been any fresh development. She had no intention of returning earlier to Buzzard Minor than Wednesday—it had all happened before I arrived, I can tell them nothing, she assured herself stubbornly.

The jeweler to whom Jan had sold her treasures also read the account and recalled a girl resembling the description of this Miss Van Damm, bringing in some bits and pieces on the Friday morning. True, the name hadn't been the same, but the accent had been foreign, and girls up a gum tree frequently adopted pseudonyms. Being of those who believe in keeping their noses clean, he stepped round to the local police station in his lunch hour. No reason to doubt her story, he urged, student from the Continent forced to sell her few treasures because of a remittance held up. The address she had given proved to be false, but none of the articles was on the police list of wanted goods. The watch, far the most interesting of the items, had been sold almost immediately, but since it was a cash transaction, naturally he couldn't supply the purchaser's name or address.

"Would you recognize the young lady if you were shown a photograph?" he was asked, and at once he became evasive. Everyone looked so like everyone else these days. Often difficult to tell the sexes apart. Look at their feet, he was advised. Men still tend to have larger feet than women.

He had to give up the articles belonging to Jan that he hadn't sold and was given a receipt. The pieces were then shown to Kay, who claimed to recognize a brooch and a chain with a medallion on it, schoolgirl stuff, she called it. The watch was a different affair. When they described it, she remembered it very well.

"I'd have said it was a twenty-first-birthday present," she explained. "Only, the girl wasn't more than eighteen, or so she told us. Seventeen when she arrived and she had a birthday since she came here. It was a bit conspicuous among the other costume stuff she wore."

"Presented by the new uncle on his wedding day perhaps," suggested Roy. But though he sounded flippant, he was much more concerned about the girl than was his wife. Why on earth had she needed to raise money on her small possessions? It sounded as though she didn't intend to come back. And that secret return on the Thursday night to collect her few clothes— it must all add up but he couldn't as yet foresee the total. All he could do was wait—wait till Wednesday.

That was Monday. To date there'd been no mention of the scooter.

Jan had decided not to go to the café on Tuesday. She was due to finish that night, in any case, and she didn't want to be picked up openly by the police, presumably in uniform. Besides, it wouldn't do Mrs. Luigi any good. When she didn't turn up, Mrs. Luigi nodded to herself as if to confirm a well-founded suspicion. She read her papers of an evening and she hadn't missed the paragraph about a Dutch *au pair* wanted by the police, though so far only as a witness. Still, big oaks from little acorns grow, and it doesn't do little cafés any good to have the police loitering in and out. Also, there'd been a card in the morning post, addressed to the café, from Annie explaining that unexpected family matters had caused her to take leave of absence for a few days but she'd be back on Wednesday. It was all working out very conveniently, reflected Mrs. Luigi. It simply meant that for one day they'd all have to put their shoulders even more firmly to the wheel.

Jan left the house early as usual; it was a benign sort of morning, the kind when London looks her best. She put on a short-skirted frock instead of her usual trouser suit and yellow Swedish sandals that looked like sabots. The streets were as empty as usual when she let herself out, and Miss Lucas, who watched her own interests like a cat at a mouse hole drew back a few inches of flowered curtain to watch her go. She also had seen the evening papers, and an embittered life had taught her you can't afford to take chances when you're not young any more and are on your own.

Jan made her way to the river. During her few days in London she had had little opportunity of discovering the city. It wasn't like being at the docks and seeing ships of every nation come up the tide, but she walked up to Westminster, where she bought a newspaper and sat down on a seat to read it. Almost the first thing she saw was a picture of herself. Roy had taken some very good snapshots of them all, and this was part of one of the children and their *au pair* in the garden. It wouldn't attract particular attention, thought Jan, unless you were looking out for this particular girl. A paragraph a little lower down said the police had found a motor scooter concealed in bushes near Manor House; its owner had been identified and was assisting the police in their inquiries.

A foreign vessel with a striped orange and black funnel sailed by, but Jan didn't see it. She didn't see anything but Hugh's dumbfounded face when he found himself in the hands of the police on a possible charge of being involved in Mrs. Brown's death. How could she, Jan, have forgotten about the scooter for so long? Finding it so close to the house, it was probably inevitable to try and tie it up with the murder.

"But he didn't put it there," she said aloud. She moved her feet restlessly, so that a covey of pigeons, looking like Victorian (or Edwardian?) ladies with feather boas on their necks were disturbed and flew away with a clatter of wings that were iridescent in the sunlight. "I put it there," Jan continued. But no one knew that except herself and no one would guess it—how should they?—unless she came forward with the truth. She knew how hotheaded Hugh could be, how indiscriminate of speech when his passions were roused, as who wouldn't be, given the same circumstances. I must go back today, she decided. After all, she'd always intended to return on the Wednesday. As Roy had said, where else had she to go. Walking back, she wondered who had found the scooter.

The scooter had been found by a Mr. John Aslett, a citified type recently retired from an office existence to one of the hideous new bungalows that stood in clumps in Buzzard Major. He lived alone with a West Highland bitch and it was due to her that the scooter was found. Every day Mr. Aslett walked her to Buzzard Minor, following the path Jan had taken on her return journey. Near Manor House the little dog gave a sudden yelp and ran towards her master, limping on three legs. He saw that she had cut one pad quite deeply, presumably on broken glass.

"Motorists!" he snarled, with the hatred of one who is both a pedestrian and a dog lover. "At least if they have to smash up their cars, they could clear up the mess."

He found the offending piece of glass and hurled it with considerable violence in the direction of some bushes and shrubs, blocking what had once been apparently a right of way. To his surprise, he heard a clinking noise, as if it had collided with more glass or metal, and pulling the shrubs aside, he found Hugh's scooter where it had been thrust into the bushes. It hadn't been abandoned, because it still carried number plates. A careful type, Mr. Aslett copied them into his notebook. He explored no further. Motor scooters don't run themselves off the road, there was always the possibility the driver was concealed somewhere also. After all, the place was close by Manor House, where one violent death had already taken place. His little dog, one paw lifted, was staring at him in an imploring fashion, and he stooped and dressed the cut with a bandage recklessly torn from his handkerchief. It didn't occur to him that this might be no concern of his, and therefore he could let the matter slide. He had all a townsman's sense of dependence on authority. The cul-de-sac was in P. C. Trubshawe's manor, but he was anxious to get Bridie to the vet in Buzzard Major, and the police there could deal with his discovery.

To his chagrin, not much interest was taken in his report by the young policeman behind the desk.

"That's Buzzard Minor," he said.

"Of course I know it's Buzzard Minor," said Mr. Aslett. "Only, seeing where I found it, I thought you might be interested." He went out, wondering why anybody bothered to help the police.

"See if P. C. Trubshawe recognizes the number," said the inspector. "I shouldn't think much gets past him. Did that chap say he took his dog that road every day? Glass can't have been there long, surely."

Ted Trubshawe recognized the number immediately. "Belongs to a young chap called Wheeler," he said. "Motor scooter. Wonder how long that's been there. He thinks the world of his scooter, does Mr. Wheeler. Don't know how he's managed to get on without it."

"He hasn't reported it as missing?"

"Well, no," allowed Trubshawe, "but then he wouldn't. A great one for do-it-yourself is Mr. Wheeler."

"Perhaps he'll be able to explain what it's doing near Manor House, then."

"I'll have a word," Trubshawe promised. "He'll explain, all right, if only to say he doesn't know."

Buzzard Major suggested they might ask the questions, but Trubshawe thought that until some connection was established between the missing scooter and the dead woman, it might be better to treat it as a run-of-the-mill affair.

He got out his old second-hand car—the village bobby didn't rate a panda, and he'd given up going around on his sturdy old bike because a car, however small, is quicker, and even minor criminals move fast these days. One thing, he was convinced Hugh hadn't hidden his own machine. Wouldn't have been able to get it round to Mr. Benson fast enough if he'd known there was anything wrong. He found the scooter easily enough, but no body with it, as that fellow, Aslett, had melodramatically feared. The next step was to see Hugh.

Mr. Pringle kept his market garden open on public holidays until four P.M. He said it was one of the best days for customers, who stopped their cars to buy a plant for Mum or Dad or old Nanny. People got tired of chocolates, and cut flowers don't last. Hugh, whose attitude towards holidays approximated Crook's, and who had spent the previous Sunday organizing a not very successful demo had volunteered to come in. It was a busy morning. Hugh had sold two plants to an old dame who hadn't believed she wanted more than one, when he saw the familiar figure of P. C. Trubshawe marching stolidly down the path.

"Looking for us?" he asked. "Mr. Pringle's in the office."

"It was you I came to see, Mr. Wheeler," said Trubshawe in his slow stately way. "Wondered if you'd been missing anything lately."

Hugh caught on at once. "You mean you've found her? I knew she was bound to turn up sooner or later. Still, I was beginning to wonder."

"When did you miss her, Mr. Wheeler?"

"Thursday night. Pinched from in front of the Huntsman sometime after nine. I've been traveling around on a pedal bike these last few days. Who had her?"

"Well, Mr. Wheeler, that's what Mr. Moon—Inspector Moon, I should say—would like to find out."

Hugh looked surprised. "Where does he come in? Oh no, you can't be trying to link her up with Mrs. B.'s death."

"Seeing she was found in that sort of cul-de-sac near Manor House, hidden, if you want my opinion . . ."

Hugh interrupted him. "What a daft place to put her. She might never have been found. Anyway, why leave her on the scene of the crime, as I daresay the inspector would put it."

"She's been damaged, Mr. Wheeler."

Hugh looked concerned. "That is overdoing it," he said. "I supposed some chap had seen her outside the Huntsman and the rain was coming on, so decided to borrow her. But in that case, why not leave her where she could easily be found? But of course, if she's been knocked about— What's the extent of the damage?"

"Headlamp broken, a piece of the glass cut the foot of a gentleman's little dog—that's really how she was found—and something amiss with the steering."

"No blood?" murmured Hugh, and Trubshawe couldn't be certain how serious he was.

"You didn't report it," the constable pointed out.

"I didn't want to make a case of it. I argued that no one but me would want her for good, and if she didn't turn up tomorrow, she'd turn up the day after. Anyone round here would recognize her—oh, I really had no fear of not getting her back."

"You didn't padlock her?"

"Not at the Huntsman, I'm known there. Besides, I was so late. I'd told the chaps I'd meet them at eight at latest, we had to fix the final details about Sunday's demo. I'd gone in to Huntsden to collect some leaflets old Wenham was getting out for us, a rush job—he said, 'So leave it as late as you can.' Anyway, we were fairly busy here. But when I arrived the place was shut down and as black as night. I thought Wenham might be in his favorite pub, so I dropped in there. According to him, he has a quick one or two at the Pheasant every evening before rejoining Mrs. Wenham, but though the place was pretty crowded, there was no sign of him."

"Did you ask the man at the bar? I mean, he might just have gone out."

"I didn't get near him, they were too thick on the ground. A lot of firms these days pay out on Thursdays. And it's not my line of country, they were all strangers to me, and they might have thought it rum me asking for old Wenham. After the Pheasant I went round to his house, he lives near his premises, but the whole place was shut up and a note for the milkman, no milk till today. Coming back tonight, I suppose. Pretty sickening for us. The leaflets make a lot of difference. Even if a chap leaves it on a bus, it can be picked up by someone who may have more intelligence. It was too late, of course, to get anything done elsewhere. I came back to the Huntsman and told the chaps and we decided we'd have to have a few more posters—and when I came out at closing time the scooter was gone. Where is she? I'll pick her up in my lunch break and get her round to Benson first thing in the morning."

"I'll have to make my report to Inspector Moon," Trubshawe explained. "He was the one who put me on to it in the first place, and they'll want you to identify it, and I expect make a statement like the one you've just made to me."

"Lot of red tape," muttered Hugh.

Mr. Pringle came out of his office and walked down the path. "Hope we've got what you want, Constable," he said. He was very formal in his business dealings. "Hugh, there's a Citroën just stopped at the top, chaps like that don't like being kept waiting."

"Ted's been telling me they've found my motor scooter," Hugh explained. "Want me to go along and identify it or something."

"Yes, well, you can do that in your lunch break. It's twelve-thirty now." The garden closed between one and two.

Still complaining about red tape, Hugh went along to the station at Buzzard Major, where he repeated his story to Finney.

Finney looked puzzled. "You say you got to Huntsden—what time?"

Hugh thought it would be about seven. The works might be closed but Mr. Wenham stayed on the premises, doing accounts and checking on this and that. Then he popped into the Pheasant—"If you don't find me at the works, you know where to look," Wenham had told him once—then he'd gone round to the house before giving up hope of getting his leaflets.

"And that's the lot?" said Finney. "Didn't go back to the Pheasant and get a sandwich or anything?"

He knew the Huntsman didn't do "eats," and if it had, no man in his senses would have bought them.

"I stopped at that mobile coffee bar or whatever it calls itself at Bransdown Cross," acknowledged Hugh. "Got a sandwich and their version of coffee. Still, it was hot and wet. If you're going to ask me if I saw anyone I knew there, it's not my stamping ground."

"Didn't talk to anyone?"

"I was in a hurry. I just took my stuff and paid and went. Got to the Huntsman round about nine . . ."

"If you came on the direct road," suggested Finney, "wouldn't that bring you past Manor House."

"Of course it would." Hugh sounded impatient. "But seeing the place was empty . . ."

"How can you be so sure of that?"

"Black as night. Anyway, no one answered the bell."

Finney's head came up with a jerk. "You mean, you actually opened the gate and went in?"

"I actually opened the gate and tried both doors, front for visitors, back for followers, or don't you read Cranford? There wasn't a light to be seen, there wasn't a sound to be heard."

"You didn't mention this to Constable Trubshawe."

"Well, no. What conceivable bearing could it have on the case?"

"What was your reason for trying to effect an entry?"

"I wasn't trying to effect an entry. It occurred to me that Jan, the *au pair*, might just conceivably be able to lend us a hand on Sunday. Public holidays are difficult, a lot of chaps go away, and we can always do with an extra pair of hands and feet. I knew Mr. and Mrs. Banks had gone abroad, leaving the place in the housekeeper's hands . . ."

"Who told you that?"

Hugh looked vague. "I don't remember. But I thought even a demo would be more amusing for Jan than spending the weekend with Mrs. B."

"You didn't know she'd gone off to stay with friends?"

"You can't have been listening," said Hugh. "If I'd known that, I wouldn't have bothered to open the gate."

Finney doodled. "What made you go to the back door?"

"If Mrs. B. was in, she might have been in the kitchen, that's at the side, and she's got a sitting room of sorts where she entertains her friends. So Jan told me."

"You know Miss Van Damm well?"

Hugh looked surprised. "She's not a special girl friend, if that's what you're driving at."

"But she talked to you, perhaps, about the setup at Manor House?"

"She wasn't much concerned with the house, only the children."

"She never asked you to visit her there?"

"The *au pair* girl doesn't rate a sitting room. And I've only once been inside the house. I took some plants in after hours and he—Mr. Banks—was at home and asked me in for a drink, which I wouldn't have got if she'd been there."

"So you'd see his cups and so forth?"

Hugh laughed. "It gave him a lot of pleasure to win them, I expect. I wonder if Mrs. B. or Jan kept them clean."

"And how long did you wait at the back door?"

"I didn't wait at all. There wasn't a light to be seen, I decided they were all off, so I came on to the Huntsman."

"You happen to mention there that you'd called at Manor House?"

"I don't remember. I didn't make an issue of it, and I don't quite see why you are."

"I don't understand why you didn't mention it to P. C. Trubshawe."

"Oh, I suppose I didn't think of it," cried Hugh impatiently. "If I've answered all your questions, can I identify my own property and then Mr. Benson will collect her, if I can't wheel her back."

But Finney said they'd like the statement in writing first, and went away leaving him with a detective constable. He came back before the statement was finished. He'd just been talking to Mr. Wenham, he said, who'd arrived home about an hour earlier. Mr. Wenham recalled that he'd warned Hugh the leaflets might not be done in time, as he had another rush job on and was closing on Thursday. He had waited till five o'clock on the Thursday—as it happened, the leaflets were done by putting men on to overtime to get them finished—and he'd waited till just after five o'clock. Then he'd closed the place down, all the other men had gone, and departed with his wife on an evening flight to Boulogne. He still had the leaflets and Hugh could collect them or send for them whenever he pleased. The theme was a fairly usual one, starvation among the underfavored nations; the leaflets would do for the next demo if they were too late for this.

"He's bonkers," said Hugh simply. "He told me he'd have to

make a rush job of it, but nothing about closing down the place on Thursday. I thought they'd be working through to Friday teatime certainly. And he knows I can only go there of an evening because of my job with Mr. Pringle."

"Someone seems to have got confused," Finney agreed. "Of course, if you could remember anyone you saw in Huntsden . . ."

"I've told you," cried Hugh, more exasperated every moment, "it's not my manor. And I can't explain how my scooter got into the cul-de-sac, but I expect if you hunt around a little, you'll be able to solve the mystery for yourselves."

That was bad enough—never tangle with the fuzz, Crook warned all his clients—but worse was to come. He was invited to identify the scooter, which had been collected from its place of concealment, and instantly laid possessive hands upon it. His notion was to depart pronto, plus scooter. The fuzz said they couldn't let it go as easily as that. When the constable tried to lay hands on it in his turn, Hugh lost his temper and a bit of a dust-up ensued. This was quite a blessing to Finney, because now he could detain a possible suspect on the ground of obstructing the police in the execution of their duties and showing violence towards a member of the force.

It wouldn't do him any harm to cool off for twenty-four hours, and a lot of things can happen in that time. So far they hadn't even got anyone who remembered seeing Hugh park the scooter outside the Huntsman—or even see the scooter, come to that. And on Wednesday the girl should be back and she might be able to help. Young girls are mines of curiosity, she probably knew more about Mrs. Brown and her affairs than the two Bankses put together.

Seven

It never occurred to Jan that she should not immediately return to Buzzard Minor. She rehearsed the story she would tell Kay as she folded her few belongings and put them into her shabby case. Miss Lucas had met her in the hall on her return and Jan had said at once that she would be going back that night." My work starts again tomorrow," she explained, though the children weren't due back till Thursday morning, and surely even an unimaginative woman like their Aunt Lolly would keep them a bit longer, away from the limelight. Children and animals are said to be irresistible on the stage; they also show up very well in the press.

She took off the cotton dress and put on the trouser suit in which she'd traveled to London.

"My luggage was stolen," she would tell Kay. "I came back for the other case. I have been working in London . . ."

Why hadn't she gone to Eastbourne? Kay would ask. Wouldn't the friend have advanced her a few pounds? You could be sure Kay would turn the situation inside out, and the story of Nikki would emerge. Undependable, Kay would call her, but it wouldn't stop there. Deceitful, totally unsuited to look after small children. I shall get the sack, reflected Jan. It was a comfort to realize that Roy was human, he wouldn't let her be turned adrift with only a five-pound note in her purse. It even went through her mind that the press might ask for her story—"Life inside the Manor House. Do *au pairs* get a square deal?" Still, that would be no temptation to her. The less she had to talk about herself, the better.

She snapped the case and pulled on the coat of her suit. Shoving a handkerchief into her pocket, her hand encountered a bit of paper—well, pasteboard, really, probably one of the innumerable cards advertising a new restaurant, an antique market, a discotheque, that get pushed into your hands as you go through the London streets. She pulled it out and looked at it without much interest.

Arthur G. Crook, she read. *Your Trouble, Our Opportunity. And We Never Close.* And two addresses and two phone numbers.

She stood like a lay figure, the card clenched in her hand. Of course. The Gingerbread Man she'd met in a public house in Earl's Court. What was it he had said? She couldn't recall. But he must have slipped the card into her pocket, knowing the time might come when she'd be able to use it. Her aunt had once said that only a fool went into a business transaction without consulting a lawyer; this might perhaps fall into that category. She put the card back into her pocket, picked up the case and was down the stair and into the street, wily as a little cat, before Miss Lucas realized she was on her way.

Mr. Crook worked in an office that was grossly over-crowded and hideously uncomfortable, but he seemed aware of neither fact. When Bill Parsons, his A.D.C., brought in his latest client, he looked up like an amiable alligator and said, "So you've surfaced, Sugar. I wondered how much longer you'd be."

Jan was breathing rather fast, a fact that didn't escape his notice. He didn't put it down to the flights of stairs she'd climbed, he didn't give them a second thought himself, and even his official age was more than twice hers.

Anyway, he knew apprehension when he saw it. "Find

yourself a pew," he offered hospitably. "You haven't brought the fuzz with you, I take it."

"I found your card in the pocket of my coat," Jan explained. "Why did you put it there?"

"Never any harm having a friend at court," said Mr. Crook. "And it's always as well to get legal advice before tangling with the fuzz."

"The police do not know where I am."

"You don't do them justice. They may not know as of this minute, but they'll soon find out. Some Nosey Parker will tell them. Well, be your age, Sugar. You are Jan Van Damm, aren't you? And you can read the newspapers."

"Why did you give me the card?" the girl persisted.

"There didn't seem much sense us having such a long interesting conversation if there wasn't going to be any follow-up, and there wasn't any harm me giving providence a bit of a nudge." He looked at her thoughtfully. "Taken your time, haven't you? I mean, this Mrs. Brown—poor lady!—she was found on Saturday and the Sunday papers carried the news, but you stayed in your little hidey-hole."

"What could I tell them?" demanded Jan warmly. "I did not put her there. Is it my fault my bag was stolen?"

"I hadn't heard that bit," confessed Mr. Crook. "Which bag was this?"

She explained the circumstances. "And you didn't report it to the police?"

"The police ask too much questions."

Mr. Crook looked astonished. "Well, what had you got to hide? Being robbed is a misfortune, not a crime. And if you're bothering about Nikki, they hear that story every day of the week. Come on, Sugar, give. Where have you been since we parted?"

"I have been in London. I have a job—and a room."

"Without luggage?"

"I have luggage." She indicated the shabby bag leaning against her chair.

"Where did you get that from?" asked Mr. Crook. "I thought Nikki had practically cleaned you out."

"I left it at Manor House." The police had managed to keep this fact to themselves.

"Meaning you went back for it?"

"On Thursday night."

"Proposing to spend the weekend there. So—what stopped you?"

"There had been a burglary."

"Who told you?"

"The French window was open, I came in, I could see."

"So—why didn't you tell the police?"

"What could I tell them? Let Mrs. Brown telephone. How was I to know that she . . . ?"

"Well, no, you couldn't. And anyway—what time was this?"

"It is not for Mrs. Brown that I am here," protested Jan. "How do I know who attacked her? It is because of the scooter. The police think Hugh Wheeler left it where it was found, and they are holding him. But he knows nothing, nothing. I did not even remember about the scooter . . ."

"Don't draw too long a bow," Crook advised her. "You ain't in the habit of removing scooters every day of the week."

"After I found Mrs. Brown I forgot everything else. I only wished to get away fast, fast."

It wasn't often that Mr. Crook's clients succeeded in dumbfounding him, but he really did start asking himself if he could have heard right. "You mean you knew she was there?" he said at last. "And you just got out as quick as light."

"There was nothing I could do. She was dead."

"Never heard of the duty of the citizen?"

"I am not a citizen," insisted Jan.

"Well, if not, you're takin' advantage of our hospitality. You've put up a black there, Sugar. You're going to be asked why you didn't pick up a phone—the house rattles with them—and get the police round."

"You do not understand. The house has been burgled. It is known that Mr. and Mrs. Banks are away. Mrs. Brown is out at bingo. The house contains treasures, it is a good time to come in and take them."

"No sign of any violent break-in," reflected Mr. Crook.

"So they say— Who has a key?"

"And you had a key?"

"It was in my case."

"The one that was stolen?"

"How can I prove that? If I tell them about Nikki, they ask for an address, some proof—and I have no proof. Perhaps I make him up. They ask about my friend at Eastbourne, but there is no friend at Eastbourne. They think perhaps I come back from London, let in the friend, they take the treasures, and then Mrs. Brown spoils it all by coming down the stairs."

"And starts raisin' objections and gets her light put out for her trouble. Could be that way, Sugar, but just the same, you'd have done better for yourself by ringing the police. You'll have to tell them now."

"Only because of the scooter," she reiterated.

"It's a pretty thing," murmured Mr. Crook, "unless they're holding him for something else. Well, Sugar, maybe we should be getting down there. Of course I'm coming with you. You've made me accessory after the act, haven't you?"

"I have done nothing wrong," she insisted.

"Withholding information vital to the police. I'm coming with you to make sure you know your rights. If there's any question you shouldn't answer, I'll tip you the wink."

"Mrs. Banks will be expecting me in the morning," reflected Jan.

"I wouldn't be too sure of that," said Crook. He thought if she really believed that, she'd believe anything. "And if you're expectin' her to welcome you with open arms, I should think again. This ain't Central Europe or the Far East. I don't say Mrs. B. would ever have been my favorite woman, but you can't go round strangling even pushy housekeepers with impunity." He thought perhaps it was fortunate for her that she didn't realize the enormity of the story she was going to tell.

All the same, faced with Moon, she told her story with a composure that startled Mr. Crook. "Tell the inspector same as you told me," he warned her on the way down. "No frills, no opinions. Save those for drinks in the bar later on. The facts on their own are enough to put his eye out, in any case."

"I could not come before," Jan told the inspector. "I have heard Mr. Banks say that all the police want is proof, and I have no proof."

"You don't think Mrs. Brown's body was sufficient proof?" Moon was staggered as Crook had been, though he concealed it better.

"What could I prove? That she was dead. That you could see for yourself. I could not prove who had killed her, I could not prove who had opened the French windows. I could not prove my luggage had been stolen—I had told Mrs. Banks I was going to Eastbourne, why should I tell her my secrets? She is not my mother. I cannot even prove that my friend had to go abroad at the eleventh hour—all that I can prove is that Hugh Wheeler did not leave the scooter in the cul-de-sac. I did not guess Mrs. Banks would search my room . . ."

"This is a murder case, Miss Van Damm," exclaimed the outraged inspector.

"And perhaps you think I know more than I say."

"If you'd rung us at once, there might have been clues."

"Any clues there were would be there when you found her."

"Suppose she hadn't been found?"

"Someone would notice the milk and the papers. They are not fools in the country. If I had not come back, nothing would have been different except that the scooter would have stayed outside the Huntsman. I do not know who she was expecting . . ."

"Or if she was expecting anyone."

"There was the whiskey bottle. She never drank whiskey. She said it was a man's drink."

"She didn't speak of any friend . . ."

"She never spoke to me at all. My work was with the children. And she would not expect me back. I could tell you nothing, nothing. I cannot even prove there was a driver who knocked me off the motor scooter."

"Didn't touch him, did you, Sugar?" suggested Crook. "No? Not much sense circulating the local garages for a touch-up."

No, Jan agreed, she hadn't seen the driver's face, the car was a sports variety, it looked dark, but there hadn't been time to register the actual color. "I was saving my life, I could not take down the number of a car," she explained. "He sounded . . ." She paused.

"Angry?"

"Frightened. He shouted at me, something about damn teenagers. He must have heard the scooter go into the tree, but he never stopped."

"Well, there's a clue for you," said Crook heartily to Moon.

"Too bad there weren't any witnesses," Moon said.

"They are all indoors watching the TV or drinking in the bars," Jan told him.

"And that's the only sign of life you saw?"

"Yes. But I cannot prove it. I cannot prove anything. Oh, I can prove where I have been working and sleeping. Mrs. Luigi would remember me, and Miss Lucas. But how does that help?"

"Where do you propose to go now?" Moon wanted to know.

"I go back to Manor House. The children return on Thursday."

"Been in touch with Mrs. Banks yet?"

"Mr. Crook says I should come here first."

"Occur to you that Mrs. Banks may not be too keen to have you back? Well, work it out for yourself, Miss Van Damm. Once this story breaks, and we shan't be able to keep it out of the press, she'll have the reporters coming down the chimney for a statement."

"I have made my statement to you. I cannot make it any different."

"It won't be very pleasant for you."

"It was not pleasant having my bag stolen and then finding Mrs. Brown," Jan reminded him.

Spirited as a bottle of Scotch, reflected an admiring Mr. Crook. He left her to it, pro tem, while he went into Buzzard Minor to have a word with Mrs. Banks. It 'ud be a bit too much to expect the girl to tell her story three times in the twenty-four hours, and if Mrs. B. was the harridan he rather thought she might be, more concerned with losing an ace housekeeper than with the feelings of the girl who had found her—after dark and in an empty house, mark you!—it 'ud give her a chance to let off a bit of steam. Make things easier for the ever-loving too, reflected Mr. Crook, turning his big yellow car into the gate of Manor House.

Too bad, he reflected, waiting for someone to answer the bell, that he couldn't meet the late lamented herself. Jan had made her come so alive, he felt he'd recognize her if he met her in the street.

"If that's the press again," hissed Kay as the bell shrieked. "No, don't you go, you'll let them keep you talking all afternoon."

When she saw a big red-faced chap in deplorable suitings she tried to shut the door at once, but an immense foot in a bright brown brogue intervened.

"Name's Crook," said the apparition, in a voice that she thought admirably matched his clothes. "Representin' Miss Van Damm."

"Miss Van Damm is not here," insisted Kay. "And kindly remove your foot."

"I'd only have to ring again if I did, and of course she's not here. She's down in the nick, making a statement."

"In . . . ?"

"That's what I said," agreed Crook imperturbably.

"And if you are from the papers . . ."

"I told you. Representin' Miss Van Damm." He hauled out one of his cards.

She didn't even bother to read it. "I've nothing to say to you."

"Idea was for me to do the talking. Sugar's been talkin' her head off all morning, probably like a nice cup of a char and a lay-down when she gets back."

"Roy," called Roy's wife imperiously, and out he came, cool as the proverbial cucumber. He nodded amiably to Crook, who took the opportunity to introduce himself.

"Jan's lawyer? We are having a double ration, aren't we? First the burglary and Mrs. Brown, sheer melodrama, and now the *au pair* girl. What's she been up to?"

Crook looked around him. The hall was nice if you liked that sort of décor—rug chest, flowers in a copper bowl, oil painting of Uncle Tom Cobleigh and his lady wife just above, a chair with an oak-tree design on the back, nice Eastern mat, none of your British is Best here . . .

"Of course, we could talk in the hall if that's the way you want it," he said amiably. "Only, it's quite a story."

"Come in here," offered Roy.

The room looked a bit empty with all the glass cupboards unfurnished—have to buy some nice ornaments to fill in the gap, reflected Crook. They'd never see the originals again. He wondered if he'd be offered refreshments in a glass, but the thought didn't seem to have occurred to either. So laying aside his appalling brown bowler hat, worn in honor of the police, he unfolded his story.

No one could say Kay was backward in coming forward, as nurses used to put it to their charges, but even she seemed silenced as the tale wound to its end.

"Nice to know where she is!" Roy commented to give his wife a chance to get her breath back, surmised Mr. Crook. "The kids 'ull be glad."

"You mean they're back here?" exclaimed Mr. Crook. "Jan hoped their auntie would keep them under cover just for a brace of shakes. Nine days' wonder, you know," he added encouragingly.

"Their aunt brought them back this morning," said Roy. "Thought their right place was with their parents in times of crisis. It's been whine whine for Jan ever since their arrival."

Kay had found her voice at last. "I never heard anything so outrageous," she cried. "The girl's a monster. To find the dead body of a woman you've been working with for months bundled into a cupboard and walk out leaving her there! What made her come forward now? I suppose the police were on her trail."

"She came because of this young chap who owns the scooter—seems to think he's being detained on a murder charge, but even the most enterprisin' rozzer wouldn't try and make that stick. More likely the constable tried to lay violent hands on the scooter"—he spoke with feeling, realizing how he'd react if someone tried to play fast and loose with the Scourge—"and he retaliated by laying violent hands on the bobby. Still, it shows a nice feeling on Sugar's part, wouldn't you say?"

"Poor little devil!" said Roy softly. "What a ghastly situation. And no one to turn to. Did you give her our address?" he added to his wife.

"Well, really, we were entitled to five days' free of staff complications."

"You might think so, but it doesn't seem to have worked out that way. When you think that in ten years' time Dawn might find herself in a similar situation . . ."

"Dawn has parents and a proper background."

"Just my point," said Roy promptly. "Jan's got no one, you can't count that lunatic aunt—she's a waif, if you like. What would you do if you found yourself in her shoes?"

"I hope I should have the common decency to ring up the police," said Kay icily.

"He wouldn't be much of a substitute for a mother-figure, though, and we're supposed to treat these girls like our daughters."

"P. C. Trubshawe's about as alarming as a teddy bear, and you know it."

"Ah, but she doesn't know Ted, which is a good testimony in itself. Just consider, Kay. She'd found herself stood up by that young swine . . ."

"I've warned her again and again not to go about with every loose-minded young man she meets. And surely anyone would have had the decency to call the authorities. And what does she do? Just fastens the door and goes to bed."

"There wouldn't be much point leaving the door ajar," pointed out Roy sensibly. "Anyway, the history of crime is peppered with disappearing corpses. And where should she go if not to bed?"

"I don't know where she thinks she's going to stay," continued Kay remorselessly. "I can't have her here with the children?"

"Why not? Do you think she's a corrupting influence? You know very well she's no such thing. And the kids adore her."

"And every time they go out they'll be followed like cats trailing the Pussy's Butcher," cried Kay hotly. "Is that what you want?"

"Quite apart from sending the kids into some sort of trauma if you refuse to have her back, have you considered the interpretation people in general will put on it? They'll say you think she was mixed up in the plot. Yes, of course they will. Ask Mr. Crook here."

"I ain't the police," said Mr. Crook quickly. "I don't have to have theories. But your husband's right, you'll be attractin' the fuzz and their cohorts, and I don't see that's any improvement on the press. You can shut the door against them; the fuzz is different again."

"Wouldn't you know?" cried Kay viciously when Crook had departed to collect Jan. "Of all the *au pair* girls coming to this country, we have to pick the one involved in a murder."

"You might say that of all the *au pair* girls coming to this country, and many of them according to all accounts pretty helpless, we've had the luck to get the one who's achieved the devotion of our daughters. The wolf of Rome who suckled Romulus and Remus can't have taken more care of her charges than Jan. Why, she's their focal point at present, and well you know it."

"I'm sure it's not healthy," insisted Kay. "They have parents."

"Who to them probably appear as old as the hills. They're probably secretly amazed we haven't been dead for years."

"It's like living in a bastion," grumbled Kay. "You never know when a reporter won't fall out of the sky like a bird falling out of a tree. When Jan comes back I shall insist on her staying in her room till after the inquest—we can tell the children she's got a heavy cold."

"Won't that involve calling in a doctor? That'll set tongues wagging again."

"Not for a cold. Oh, Roy, can't you see how intolerable this is going to be for weeks to come? These press monsters will be following them around, trying to bribe Dawn with great vulgar boxes of chocolates to talk."

"If they do that, your daughter will tell them her mummy has told her never to take sweets from strange men. She's got all her marbles about her, has that girl."

"And then," continued Kay, undaunted, "there's the ques-

110

tion of delayed shock. It can hardly have penetrated yet, what has actually happened to Mrs. Brown. When it does . . ."

"I should koko," said Roy unsympathetically. "Your kids aren't fools, this is probably the most exciting thing that has ever happened to them, bar getting born, and they won't remember anything about that. Kids aren't hothouse plants, Kay, they're as tough as wild flowers. You can dig and dig and not uproot them. Oh, cheer up. It's not every household that can boast a murdered woman. It's not even as if the kids had liked her."

"If Jan had behaved like a normal humane person and called the police at once . . ."

"It wouldn't have helped Ma Brown, and the girl was in a bit of a state."

Kay remained unmoved—and who can blame her? "As for this Crook person—I wonder who he thinks is going to pay his fees."

"He seems able to look after himself," said Roy carelessly. "Hadn't you better have something hot, coffee or something, for when Jan comes in? If anyone's suffering from shock, I should think it would be her."

The inquest on Mrs. Brown was fixed for the following Monday, there being, as Roy observed, an epidemic of corpses in the neighborhood just then, thanks to a motorcar pile-up just outside Buzzard Major. Mr. Crook decided it wouldn't do any harm to attend the inquest, and it never hurt a possible suspect for it to be known that he/she was legally represented. A few words with Jan before she took her place in the witness box wouldn't come amiss. He drove down late Saturday evening and went up to the Manor House after breakfast the next day.

The children were feeling their isolation from Jan. Mostly they spent their time in the garden or did lessons supervised by

Kay. When they went out she went with them, which wasn't nearly so much fun, as she never let them speak to anyone.

Kay found them insufferable, always asking awkward questions.

"If Jan's ill, why doesn't she have a doctor?"

"You don't have a doctor for a cold."

"You can have a doctor for anything, now that you don't have to pay them," argued Dawn logically. "He might give her some medicine."

"She's having some medicine."

"Why isn't it making her well?"

"She's got to get over the shock—about Mrs. Brown."

"But she didn't like Mrs. Brown much," urged Coral reasonably.

"You can be sorry people are dead, even if they're not your best friend."

"Are you going to the funeral?" asked Dawn.

"Daddy thinks we should, as she had no one else."

"We've never been to a real funeral, have we, Coral?" insinuated her sister hopefully.

"Little girls don't go to funerals."

"We're having one this afternoon," announced Dawn, head in air.

"Whose is that?" murmured Kay.

"A blackbird. That cat must have got it. It's a shame. It wasn't doing the cat any harm."

"Mrs. Brown wasn't doing anyone any harm," Kay pointed out, feeling this might be an opportunity to point a moral.

"Perhaps she was like the woman on TV," suggested Dawn.

"A Wicked Woman," agreed Coral enthusiastically.

"What nonsense," declared their mother. "Of course she wasn't a wicked woman. It was wicked men who broke in and stole Mother's treasures."

"No one knew the woman on TV was wicked till she Poisoned Her Husband."

112

"Mrs. Brown's husband died long ago. [Had he, though?] And don't start saying perhaps she poisoned him, because she did nothing of the kind. [Well, of course not. Murderers aren't like other people. You can always tell.]"

"What's that?" breathed Dawn as an immense yellow Rolls drew up at the gate.

"Oh no," murmured Kay. "There can't be two like it in the country. Go into the garden and play quietly."

"Is it the doctor?" Coral wondered.

"Certainly not. It's a friend of Jan's."

"You said Jan couldn't see anyone."

"This is different."

"Mummy means it doesn't matter if *he* gets a cold," Coral pointed out sensibly.

"Isn't anyone going to take us to church?" wondered Dawn.

"Not today."

"We might have a service on the lawn, then. I'll be the vicar, Coral, and you can be the choir and we'll both be the congregation."

This arrangement seemed to both of them perfectly sensible, and they disappeared through the French windows as Mr. Crook clobbered the front door.

"Young Jan knows how to pick 'em, doesn't she?" approved Roy when Crook had taken his departure. "Staying over tomorrow just to give her moral support. Have you got all the right things to be chief mourner at a funeral?" he added.

"Do you really think it's necessary . . . ?"

"Of course. She can't be buried like a pauper. Six years is six years."

"I wonder you don't suggest Jan comes too."

"Of course she can't come. She'll have to look after the kids. Where are they, by the way?"

"Singing matins on their own account. And this afternoon

they've a very private funeral. Some bird they've found. All very morbid, but I suppose they enjoy the dressing-up. They've got a row of graves in the orchard already, from field mice to a squirrel they found on the common. One thing, it'll keep them quiet, and now we've had that bolt put on the inside of the door, no one can steal upon them unawares."

"Wish they'd invited me to the funeral," said Roy wistfully. "Years since I went to a funeral I could enjoy." He didn't expect to enjoy Mrs. Brown's much. "I could have dug the grave."

"They'll enjoy doing that."

"Or tolled the bell like— Who was it tolled the bell for Cock Robin?"

"I do wish you'd stop talking about funerals. I should hardly have expected," she swung off at a tangent, "that Crook creature would impress a jury."

"He doesn't have to impress a jury, no one's accused Jan of strangling Mrs. B."

"The police may not, but I bet everyone else in their secret hearts thinks she's responsible, she and that young layabout she was going round with. He seems to have gone pretty neatly to ground."

"I don't believe a word of it," declared Roy. "And let me remind you there's a law of slander. A chap like Crook would slap a suit on you quicker than light if you even dropped a hint against his client."

He walked across to the window and flung it wide. The strains of "All Things Bright and Beautiful" floated in.

"It's a pity we couldn't go to the real church," said Coral soberly. "The vicar might have preached about Mrs. Brown. She sang in the choir. It would have been nice to hear what he said. Dawn, I have an idea." She confided it to her sister.

Dawn nodded approval. "A very good idea. After the funeral, I think. They won't want to come to that."

"Isn't Jan's friend staying to lunch?" Dawn asked as they

114

came in, closing their illustrated prayer books and putting them on a shelf.

"He's staying at the Come and Get It till after the inquest," Kay pointed out. "He'll have his lunch there. He'll have to pay for it, anyway."

"What's an inquest?" asked Dawn.

"You wouldn't understand . . ."

"It's quite simple," her father assured her. "If you die suddenly, get run over by a bus, say, there has to be an inquest to agree how you died."

"I should think anyone could tell if you'd been run over by a bus."

"Unless you were pushed," Coral suggested.

"You've got the hang of it, my girl. There'll be an inquest on Mrs. Brown because she died unexpectedly."

"Can anyone have an inquest?"

"Not if you die respectably in your bed, with the doctor in attendance."

The children embarked on an interesting discussion as to whether they should have held an inquest on the blackbird, which carried them past the cream trifle stage. Then Coral went into the hall and commandeered a little sheep bell that stood on a shelf there, a memento of some trip abroad.

"Want any help with your funeral?" Roy asked hopefully. "A strong arm to dig the grave, say."

"Dawn was sexton and dug it yesterday," Coral explained.

"Ring the passing bell?"

"Coral's bell-ringer," said Dawn kindly, "and we aren't having any mourners. It's a private funeral, like it says in the newspapers sometimes."

"No flowers?"

"Coral's made a wreath of daisies, out of respect."

"How self-sufficient kids are," Roy sighed. He went to stand by the window to watch the little procession go soberly down the path.

The procession emerged from the potting shed, which had been utilized as a mortuary. The body of the departed lay in a cardboard box that had once held spectacles and was now covered by a cotton Union Jack. On top of this a prayer book was precariously balanced. Dawn came first, box in hands, chanting softly to the tune of "Who Killed Cock Robin?" Behind her Coral swung a stone on a string to represent a censer, and carried an unlighted candle with a piece of colored paper to represent the forbidden flame.

Gravely they moved to the orchard to halt beside the empty grave, the fifth of a small row. Dawn put the body carefully in the hole and began to intone, "Bird that is born of lady bird hath but a short time and is full of misery."

"He cometh up and is cut down like a flower," chanted Coral. "Is anyone watching?"

"He is at the window," sang Dawn. "In the midst of life we are in death."

"Because of the orchard cat. Go forth, Christian bird . . . Has *he* gone?"

"He has gone, but he will come back soon. They always do. Lord, have mercy upon us."

"Amen, hallelujah. Have you the clods?"

"I have them." Dawn took a small earthy handful from the pocket of her jeans. "Dust to dust, ashes to ashes . . . Now she is there."

"She is saying, 'They are having a lovely funeral.'" The children's tones never changed. Together they stooped to fill in the grave. Coral's trowel was an old iron kitchen spoon; Dawn had a toy spade. "Now for the tombstone."

Coral took the square of paper Dawn drew from her pocket and read in low impressive tones:

> "Here lies a bird
> In the orchard found.
> But now interred
> In the gentle ground."

This was placed on the grave with a stone at each corner; then they formed a cross out of two twigs tied together with a piece of wool.

"*Requiescat in pace*," Dawn said reverently.

"You were clever to get Jan to find out what that meant. It's all over the churchyard. She's gone now, she won't be back for ages."

Dawn nodded. "Grownups always do things by twos."

"Like having children, do you mean?"

"Some people have two at a time, like Mrs. Placket."

"I know. Dawn, one day you might be Poet Laureate."

"Yes," agreed Dawn placidly. "Have you got your money?"

Coral patted her pocket. "It won't be enough for anything nice, but Mr. Pringle won't mind."

"Come on, then, before they start coming back."

They tiptoed down to the garden door, on which a new bright steel bolt gleamed in the sun. "No one can get at them now," Kay had said.

It was a lovely afternoon, the light falling on the ripening fruit and adding a silver sheen to the impertinent daisies even Kay's resolution couldn't keep under. Behind them the parallel rows of the espaliered pear tree were white against the walls of the house.

"What are we going to say?" wondered Coral as carefully they eased the new bolt out of its socket until the blue-painted door swung wide.

"We shall tell him about the letter."

"Suppose he's like most grownups and won't listen?"

"Of course he'll listen. He's Jan's friend. He'll be very glad to see us. And she'll be glad too. After all, she can't be held in . . . in . . ."

"Coventry?" offered her sister helpfully.

"Incommunicado—forever. She must be very tired of that room."

As Kay was saying "They're safe for another half-hour at

117

least" they were crossing the common and trotting down to the village.

"We'd better go to Mr. Rayner first," said Coral in business-like tones. "Being Sunday, he may shut early."

"You think of everything," conceded Dawn gracefully.

So they went first to Mr. Rayner's. He kept the general shop in Buzzard Minor and was prepared to oblige on Sundays with practically any goods you could mention. Ted Trubshawe knew this but tactfully turned a blind eye. You have to act human to people, was his motto.

Eight

Mr. Crook sat in the private sitting room of the Come and Get It, making hieroglyphic notes on slips of paper. To him came the landlord saying demurely that two ladies had called and would be glad of a word.

"Mention about what?" murmured Mr. Crook.

"They said they had important news."

Mr. Crook glanced at his watch, a great turnip affair most men wouldn't have been seen dead with. "Must be urgent," he agreed. Any man bar a policeman would wait till opening time. Being Sunday, the bar didn't open till seven P.M. "Still," he suggested, "me stopping on the premises . . ." He caught the landlord's eye and desisted. "Tea?" he suggested, not very hopefully.

"The ladies might prefer milk shakes," returned his companion and went to fetch the visitors, who were waiting with exemplary patience in the entrance.

A moment later they were ushered into Crook's sitting room; he'd brought some work down with him, knowing that a village on an English Sunday isn't the gayest place to find yourself.

"The Misses Banks," the landlord said.

"You're Jan's friend," said Dawn, coming forward and offering her hand in a very grown-up way. "I'm Dawn and this is my sister, Coral."

"Pleasure's mine," said Mr. Crook respectfully, "and it's

true what you said about being Jan's friend." He placed chairs for them on either side of the desk.

"It's about Mrs. Brown," Coral explained. "She was Mummy's housekeeper."

"He knows that," said Dawn.

"And she's dead."

"Murdered dead."

"And," continued Coral indignantly, "Mummy thinks it's Jan's fault, just because she found her."

"Mummy should tell that to the police," suggested Crook. "They find more corpses than anyone."

"Remember that, Coral," warned Dawn impressively.

"What were you going to tell me about Mrs. Brown? Something Jan told you?"

"Jan doesn't tell us anything. We aren't allowed to see her."

"She's shut up in her room," amplified Coral. "Mummy says it's a feverish cold, but she hasn't had the doctor in."

"Does she go out at all?" wondered Crook.

"She doesn't come out of her room except to go to the bathroom."

"We aren't supposed to go out either," confided Dawn.

"What will your mother say when she finds out?"

"Oh, she won't think of looking for us for half an hour, and we shall be back by then."

"But we had to tell you about the letter," explained Coral.

"We didn't know if Jan had told you."

Mr. Crook shook his head. "She must have forgotten. Which letter was that?" He felt like a bird watcher, fearful of startling his objective.

The two children answered together, "The one she bought from the shop."

"Mrs. Brown? How enterprising! I thought H.M. Government had a monopoly of the mail."

"She bought it from the shop," insisted Dawn. "We saw her."

"We saw her," confirmed Coral. "We thought it was funny she was going to the lolly shop, because she always said lollies were bad for your teeth, so we hung about till she came out. And she hadn't got any lollies . . ."

"Unless she had them in her pocket."

"But she had a letter in her hand."

"Perhaps she'd just taken it out of her bag to post it," suggested the resourceful Mr. Crook.

They regarded him with joint scorn. "She went right past the letter box on the corner."

"Whereabouts is this shop?" asked Mr. Crook, diplomatically conceding this point.

They told him—up a road called Sleepy Hollow Lane, past a pillar box near the Unicorn Inn.

"I'll find it," promised Crook. "Unicorn, you said. A fabulous animal."

"Of course," Dawn pointed out seriously, "it isn't really an animal at all."

"It's a whale," supplemented Coral. "And it has a horn."

"That's what unicorn means."

"It lives in the sea," Coral added.

"But they die if you try and catch one."

"They never taught me anything as useful as that when I was at school," mourned Crook.

"Not school," chorused the children. "The TV."

"When I was your age we didn't have TV," explained Crook. "Of course," he added quickly, "that was a long time ago."

"What Daddy calls the age of the dinosaurs?"

"About then. Still, a few of us contrived to slip through the net."

Dawn brought them back to the point at issue. "Why did Mrs. Brown have to buy a letter?"

"Not buy. Collect. People can arrange to have their letters sent to another address if they like."

Coral frowned. "But Mummy wouldn't open *her* letters."

Dawn demurred. "Daddy says she has an electric eye and can read through the envelopes."

"When Uncle Jim sent me five shillings," contributed Coral, "Mummy took it and bought me a book about someone called Jean Dark. And what I wanted was a perfectly lovely one about a bear who lived in a basement and ate policemen."

"While we were in the shop," fluted Dawn, "a lady came in and asked if there was anything for Black. We thought that very funny."

"Black and Brown, you see," explained Coral.

"Only she didn't get one and she went away."

A sudden explosion attracted the attention of all three. The heavens opened, the rain came down in torrents; where there had been a clear sky only a few minutes before was nothing but blackness and threats. The window glass shook.

"And we didn't bring our snickers," mourned Coral.

"It would have been worse if it had rained during the funeral," said Dawn.

"Run you back," offered Crook. "Pleasure, I assure you. Anything I can do to help a partner . . ."

"Are we partners?"

"Brought me a piece of first-chop info, didn't you? Now wait for our next great installment." He rose and opened the door. "Wait here. I'll bring the Superb along."

"Is that your car?"

"Too true she is."

"Have you got an automatic back wheel brake?"

"She wouldn't know what to do with one if I gave it her. I'll bring her round to the door, and when I toot, come flying like the wind."

A minute later he tooted. "Don't forget you-know-what," said Dawn.

"I've got mine in my pocket," beamed Coral.

They dashed out into the waiting car. "Is she a dinosaur?" asked Dawn respectfully.

"She's been called worse," beamed a responsive Mr. Crook. "Make the most of it, girls. You will not look upon her like again."

Kathleen Banks came reluctantly through the drawing room and opened the French windows. Since the burglary she came in here as little as possible, not yet able to accept with equanimity the sight of the broken showcase and the patches on the walls.

"Dawn!" she called. "Coral! Time to come in."

No faintly expostulating voices answered her; there was no sound of soft feet on path or lawn. She called again, more sharply, then went out into the garden, looking left and right. They had these idiotic phases when for some reason or other they couldn't answer. Once they'd been deaf-mutes; last month they'd been giraffes.

"But, Mother, we couldn't answer," Dawn had protested. "Giraffes can't make a sound."

"Then why not be lions and roar?"

"Because lions can't eat the leaves off the trees." That seemed to them a perfectly logical reply.

Coming through the garden, crossing the lawn, she could discern neither hide nor hair of them, nor hear the suppressed squeals that sometimes betrayed their whereabouts. She called again in less dulcet tones. She frowned. The sky was darkening ominously. She knew these sudden storms. On the path by the orchard the spade and the iron spoon lay neatly side by side. Four stones weighted down the hand-printed epitaph; tomorrow or the next day they would raid the greenhouse for a scrap of broken glass to protect the memorial from the weather. Automatically she picked up the tools and returned them to the shed. A minute later she realized that the garden door stood slightly ajar, the bolt pulled back.

Kay was not an emotional type, but when she saw that, her heart moved uncomfortably in her breast. If the children had wanted to go to the Village Green they could have gone out by the front. So—had someone knocked on the door, called them by name, persuaded them to withdraw the bolt? But to what purpose? They had been told by Roy to pay no attention to any questions they might be asked, even if they believed they knew the answers. But Coral rushed at every situation like a bull at a gate. Of the two, Kay thought she had the stronger character. The only safe thing, she and Roy had decided, was to see that the pair were never off the premises unaccompanied, which sounded easier than it proved in fact. They were like quicksilver, and with Jan laid by, Kay felt her hands uncomfortably full. Hitherto invisible men—women also, for that matter—seemed to spring out of the ground or pop up from behind walls. All very well for Roy to say "It'll only be a nine days' wonder." Already the affair seemed to have stretched on for longer than that, and so far, she reflected resentfully, nothing to show. No arrests, no prospects, and they were like people living in a castle with the drawbridge pulled up.

Kay went through the blue door, but there was no sign of the children on the other side. On the further road a car went past, then two boy cyclists racing one another in what appeared to be a reckless manner; overhead a plane clamored through the clouds. Back through the orchard she came, running over the lawn. Roy, whom she met in the hall, refused to share her dismay.

"Take a hold of yourself, Kay," he said. "Probably slipped out to get a couple of choc lollies."

"They don't have to go out by the back for that," insisted Kay.

"They do, you know. You'd have stopped them like a bullet if they'd tried to make it through the front hall."

"Would they have any money?"

"I wouldn't put it past Coral to get 'em on credit. Not to worry, Kay. No one's going to kidnap our brats. And I'd be sorry for anyone who tried."

Their voices aroused Jan, who came hurrying down the stairs. "The children," she said in accusing tones. (Just as if she were the mistress of the house and I was the nursemaid, thought Kay resentfully.) "What has happened to the children?"

"They've gone for an itsy-bitsy walk on their own," Roy assured her. "The fact is, Jan, the sooner you get your temperature down, the better it will be for all of us."

The telephone shrilled suddenly and Kay jumped. "That may be someone ringing up about them."

"If there'd been any sort of accident, you'd have had Trubshawe here in person," her husband told her. "We still believe in the personal touch in this neck of the woods." He lifted the receiver.

"Who? What . . . ? Oh yes. Yes, I see. Right away? Many thanks." He hung up. "That was the landlord of the Come and Get It. Our pampered children are being brought back by car, by courtesy of one of the guests."

"You mean a stranger?" shrilled Kay.

"That is where Mr. Crook is staying," said Jan. "No harm will come to Dawn and Coral if they are with him."

A minute or so later the big yellow car drew up at the door and the little girls came dashing through the rain.

"Where have you been?" their mother demanded in what might be called ringing tones.

"Young ladies were caught in the rain," said Mr. Crook, who had followed them and stood in the doorway.

"We hadn't got our snickers," added Coral.

"You weren't supposed to be out of the garden," scolded Kay.

"We wanted to get something for Jan," explained Dawn. "Something better than medicine."

Kay's elder daughter plunged her hand into the pocket of her cardigan and brought out a small parcel packed in iridescent green paper.

"A Venus Bar," she announced. "One hundred per cent

cream, glucose and chocolate. You need feeding up, Jan. Nothing's so nice when you're not around."

"I bought four sugar mice," said Coral, producing a small paper bag in her turn. "Mr. Rayner was very kind when we said we wanted them for Jan. He let us put them on the bill."

"There's the making of a financier in you, my girl," approved Roy.

"I told you never to accept lifts from strangers." Kay's voice was stern.

"This wasn't a *stranger*," reproved Dawn. "This was *Jan's friend*."

"Happy to oblige," beamed Mr. Crook. "Drew a nice little dividend myself, I shouldn't wonder. What's the one about the mouths of babes and sucklings? If you were a bit older," he added appreciatively to the little girls, "I'd have you both on my payroll."

And before anyone could think of an answer to that one, he had gone.

The woman behind the counter in the shop near the Lonely Unicorn might have been cast in a tableau for Mrs. Noah of Noah's Ark fame, so stiff and unbending was she. Even her clothes seemed made of wood—a tightly buttoned blouse, a round hat with a six-inch brim, skirt straight as water. Her face was thin, sallow and as tight as a rat trap. In front of her was a pile of the weekly magazines, a rack of stationery and various packets of paper-covered sweets and chocolate bars. Behind her were a few shelves and drawers; a black cat, as remote as an aged witch, blinked from an open doorway on the right.

Crook came bounding in, as resilient as a sorbo ball. "Any mail for Brown?" he asked.

Mrs. Noah didn't bat an eyelid. "Which Brown would that be?"

"Get many of the same moniker?" asked Crook affably.

"You'd be surprised. Smith, now—that's mostly for the hotel trade. It's not often I get a Smith here. But Brown, Black, Grey—funny really, my maiden name was Green. But you were asking for Brown."

"Felicia," amplified Mr. Crook.

"There's one you won't have to be bothering about any more," Mrs. Gale told him staidly. (She had her name above the door.) "But perhaps you're a stranger here."

"If letters didn't come for the dear departed," Crook pointed out, "what 'ud be the sense of a Dead Letter Office?"

The woman shrugged and turned to sift through some envelopes in a tray behind her. "You didn't say who you were."

"Representin' the deceased." He laid his card on the counter.

"Nothing for Number Twenty-seven," said Mrs. Gale. "That's the number I gave her."

"Bit of a shock, dying the way she did," Crook offered.

"Them as plays with dynamite can't complain if they get blown up," retorted Mrs. Gale in oracular tones.

"Like that? I wondered. A good client, would you say?"

"I don't differentiate," the woman said. "It's cash on delivery."

"Regular?" hinted Crook.

Mrs. Gale stiffened. "You wouldn't be the police?"

"I told you—representing the late Mrs. Brown. If I was the police, I'd have to declare an interest, wouldn't I? Had them here yet, by the way?"

"No reason they should come here that I can see. No law about having your mail sent to an accommodation address."

"They might be interested in the correspondence."

"I couldn't help them. I only accept the letters, not read them."

"Same party always called for them, I suppose? Well, it's not likely there'd be two."

"I don't want the police round here. Everyone knows the

police are bad for trade. And I've done nothing against the law," she reiterated.

"Neither had Mrs. Brown so far as we know, and see where that landed her."

"Asking for trouble she was. Woman her age should have more sense."

"Some young chap?" offered Crook.

The little eyes opened, dark with suspicion. "I didn't say . . ."

"Well, she wasn't having letters sent here from her auntie. How do you know the right chap's calling for them?"

"They have numbers. Nobody knows the number but me and whoever's concerned. If someone comes in and asks for that number, I hand it over. Now, when you came, you said Mrs. Brown."

"And I should have said Number Twenty-seven?" guessed Crook.

"I might have asked the name as well, but without the number, nothing doing."

"Suppose two chaps came along?"

"Then the customer has given her number to two people. I've a right to suppose that. I'm not the police to ask questions."

"Get a lot of people trying to put one over?" hazarded Crook.

"Husbands and the like?" She nodded. "I have my rules and they don't change. Whoever asks for a letter with the right number, I'm not to know he's not the one the letter was written to."

"Have much trouble?"

"It's the client's trouble, not mine. But no, things go pretty smooth. Mind you, the clientele changes pretty often. Folk don't like being bothered. It may sound very romantic at the start, but someone's going to notice you coming up here every week, if it's only another client. Of course"—she shrugged—"they could change the address, though this is a nosy part of the world and the fewer folk are in your secret the better. Who told you about Number Twenty-seven?"

"Interested party saw the lady calling for a letter. Asked me to inquire. How about the other half, chap who collected the mail?"

"He'd be another number again."

"And you wouldn't remember what that one was."

"He'd be Twenty-eight, of course."

"Just Twenty-eight?"

"Just Twenty-eight. Robinson he called himself."

"Young chap?" asked Crook, remembering Elsie Farmer's confidences. "Sounds like the same one. Well, it's not likely he'd be running two young chaps."

"I can't say anything about that. I'm only the middleman. Folk that don't want a parade of their affairs bring letters here, someone else calls for them. Everyone's got a right to their privacy."

"Barring corpses," amended Crook. "They don't have any rights." He considered. "Come in a car, I suppose."

"You show me a young chap that doesn't travel in a car, and I'll show you the KohiNoor diamond," said Mrs. Gale unexpectedly.

"Long, wide and handsome?"

"I didn't notice."

"Which one was doing the paying?" asked Crook.

If he had hoped to startle the woman into an admission, he failed.

"I told you, I don't read the letters, just take them in."

"So you did." He brooded. "Wonder what he had on her," he speculated.

"Why should you think it was him? It was her got killed."

"And you don't kill the goose that lays the golden eggs."

"It makes sense."

"Unless the goose cackled too much. Always fatal to pay the first installment. One thing leads to another."

"People have a right to spend their money the way they please," insisted Mrs. Gale. "My sister was left five thousand pounds by her granny, and she bought herself a husband. My mother was all for her buying a little drapery business, done better that way if she'd known, but she said no, Norm was what she wanted."

Mr. Crook came back to the subject of the dead woman. "It's not natural," he argued. "Six years and no one knows anything about her. Coming here about a couple of months would you say?"

"I didn't."

"That's what my informant told me. Would you recognize him again, the young chap, I mean?"

"What do you think?"

"I think you know a lot more than you're telling."

"I just know what you've told me."

"Then it's true you don't know much. Well, ta a million."

He went back to the Superb. How much further had he got? The young man Number 28 might be the same as the one who used to meet Mrs. Brown in Firlmere. On the other hand, the murder might be a common or garden crime by a gang of thugs and nothing to do with Number 28 at all. Only—he kept coming back to the same point—what made Mrs. Brown open a door in the evening when she was alone in the house unless she knew who was on the other side of it?

Nine

The result of the inquest was much what Crook had anticipated. The police had no one in their eye against whom they could bring a concrete case, whatever supicions they might harbor, and the verdict was murder by some person or persons unknown. Jan, naturally, was the star witness, and gave the court a fine run for its money. The words monstrous, inhuman, incredible and makes-your-blood-run-cold echoed through the court.

Jan proved stubborn and consistent. "I could tell the police nothing about her, I was not there."

"You could have told them Mrs. Brown was dead," Kay had insisted.

"They would find that out for themselves, that is what the police are for. Country people are not fools."

The verdict, of course, left the affair wide open, the police could continue ferreting and questioning and suspecting till the cows came home.

"Which is just what they will do," prophesied Crook. He frowned. "I don't like these untidy cases."

"Untidy?" questioned his associate, Bill.

"Unsolved. In a sense, that girl was my client, and I don't like to think that two years hence chaps may be pointing her out as one of the lucky ones who got away with murder."

"Not like you to worry about a case after it's closed," said Bill. As a rule his partner treated his cases like letters that have been digested, answered and filed away while their recipient sits back to wait hopefully for the next post.

"If she'd been accused, there's a number of things I could have done," pursued Crook doggedly. "For one, I should have fitted the deceased with a back history. It's only in fairy tales that people fall out of the sky fully grown and with no past. What do we know about her? That she came from Harrogate six years ago . . ."

"Alleges she came from Harrogate," suggested Bill.

"Bringing a written reference from a Mrs. Arnold whom no one's ever seen and who is now said to be in California, possibly under another name. The fact is, Bill, we don't know nuffin' about the dear departed, including why she was blackmailed, but my guess 'ud be it has something to do with her Harrogate past. No, I know it didn't come up at the inquest, because there weren't witnesses, and without proof, there was no sense dredging it up. It's a funny thing, Bill, when chaps talk of blackmail they always associate it with one of the major crimes—murder, bigamy, drug trafficking—but some of the things that freeze a chap's blood—and that's truer still of a dame—turns out to be something quite small. Fraud on a big enough scale can become almost respectable, whereas pinching a lady's handbag or writing an unsigned letter is downright low-class. Have you seen anything of Snuffy Ayres lately?"

"Glimpsed him in Harton Street on Monday," offered Bill. "He's a busy little man."

"And we'll make him busier," said Crook briskly. "A nice trip to Harrogate to taste the waters might do him good."

Snuffy was a tidy little man with a big head; otherwise he was so much like everyone else, you could see him twenty times and not recognize him on the twenty-first. "He may not look much," agreed Crook, "but he brings home enough bacon to supply the Dunmow Flitch."

"You're going back some way expecting chaps to remember . . ."

"Not so far as Adam," interrupted Crook, "and everyone remembers him. Y'see, if the trouble started in Buzzard Minor, someone would have caught on. And why should a lady who's been working in Harrogate suddenly come south where she don't know a soul? Quite a classy place, Harrogate, I've always understood. And Mrs. B. was quite a classy dresser, so why suddenly uproot yourself and make for the Back of Beyond? Stand-offish maybe, but not invisible or wanting to be. She had her bingo and her choral society, and now suddenly she turns up with a boyfriend and all is wrapped in mystery. Yet in three years she must have formed some ties in the bleak north, and there should be as many openings in Harrogate as down south. And I wouldn't call Mrs. Banks the easiest woman I've ever met, but she takes on a living-in housekeeper on a bare written reference. I wonder if California ever heard of a Mrs. Arnold . . ."

"Of if Harrogate ever did," suggested Bill pleasantly.

"Well, she had to come from somewhere. It strikes me, Bill, that this young fellow may be tied up with the line of local burglaries that have never been solved. Usually it's an inside affair, a secretary or a chauffeur. I dare say X had his eye on Sugar at the outset. Foreigner, not likely to be scrupulous, you know the way their minds work—and then he recognizes Mrs. B."

"He also having hailed from Harrogate?"

"Could have worked on a paper there, say. It's six years ago. And he decides to put the screw on. Better for him than Jan, who's always got the kids in tow. Kids are about as safe as an open petrol can when lighted matches are flying. They see too much and what they see they tell. So—Mrs. Brown is a pure bonus allotment. Of course, to date we don't know what he remembered about her, but it was something she wanted covered up, and she was prepared to meet him at a strange pub and carry on a clandestine correspondence with him to keep matters dark."

"And how long would she have gone along with that?" Bill wondered.

Crook sent him a sharp glance. "A very good question," he said. "I may be able to answer it when I get Snuffy's report. Must have come as a shock to her after six years."

"You're tying this up with something that happened in Harrogate?"

"Don't it seem that way to you? If anything had happened here, we should have heard."

"If this Mrs. Arnold really went to California . . ."

"She ain't likely to be much help to us. No, I'm relying on its being something that got into the papers, something X could prove if Mrs. Brown refused to play ball."

"Like looking for a needle in a haystack," offered Bill bluntly. "She may not even have been calling herself Brown up there."

But Crook only said, "That's what we're paying Snuffy for. If she hadn't had some publicity, she wouldn't have come dashing half across the country. And the odds are it was something she couldn't afford to have made public. It strikes me Mrs. Brown was the original mystery woman. Most people let things slip without meaning to: That was the year we went to Majorca. Or when Mr. Brown died—or eloped—or cut his throat. But if she had any buddies, they aren't coming forward, and no one, so far as can be discovered, ever heard her talk of Harrogate. So let Snuffy see what he can worm out. In another profession he could have made his fortune. Water diviner in a desert, say—Snuffy would have had it blossoming like the rose."

Snuffy accepted the commission with the calmness with which he accepted all jobs, and traveled up to Harrogate forthwith. He had two possible sources of information—the local press and Mrs. Arnold, if she hadn't gone to California. There was no proof that she had done so, only Mrs. Brown's statement to a possible employer. Mrs. Banks might take everything at its face value, but Crook was a lot more suspicious. If you didn't want awkward questions asked, you saw to it that the source of answers was out of reach.

Mrs. Margaret Arnold was a well-to-do widow living in a Nash-design house in Trouville Row; she had lived there for some years before her husband's death twelve years earlier. A long time ago she had employed a housekeeper called Mrs. Brown, a reliable but somewhat secretive type. But that, Mrs. Arnold thought, was her privilege. You didn't want a gossipy staff. She had once been told by the charwoman who came in twice a week that Mrs. Brown was the original sphinx, but it didn't occur to her, in her busy, interesting life, to wonder at anyone who, living under your roof for years, never dropped a hint about herself. (It hadn't occurred to Kay Banks to wonder either. People kept themselves to themselves and no doubt had their own reasons. If they wanted to make confidences, there were people outside the house more suitable for this purpose.) Until the surprising debacle, after three years of unimpeachable service, Mrs. Arnold really hadn't thought much about her housekeeper. And it had never occurred to her to ask about the husband. Mrs. Brown had simply said she lost him some years ago, and you could make what you liked of that. Anyway, there had been no spectacular rising from the dead in her case. So that she had a considerable shock when, six years after Mrs. Brown's departure, her present *bonne à tout faire*, a Portuguese brunette as different from Mrs. Brown as is chalk from cheese, marched in one day carrying a card inscribed Mr. T. F. Ayres, with a London address and a scribbled note along the top.

"What is it, Olivia?" she said, scarcely looking at the card. "You know I never buy at the door."

"The gentleman wrote a message."

Mrs. Arnold sniffed. She was as suspicious as the comfortably rich have every right to be. She bent over the card. *Request a few words regarding the late Mrs. Brown*, she read. *No connection with press or police.*

Mrs. Brown? Mrs. Arnold considered. It took a minute or so to remember she had once had a housekeeper of that name. But surely, after all these years . . . Still, being healthily curious—and looking back, the woman had been a bit of an enigma—she agreed to see Mr. Ayres.

In he came, an unobtrusive little man just like someone out of a film.

"Sit down, Mr. Ayres," said Mrs. Arnold briskly, "and explain yourself. This Mrs. Brown, who is she?"

"She told her employers down south that she had worked for you as housekeeper for three years."

"That Mrs. Brown!" said Mrs. Arnold thoughtfully. "Why on earth should she crop up again after all this time." She looked at the card, frowning. "I see you call her the late."

"You—didn't see the papers?" said Snuffy respectfully.

"I'm just back from Paris, where I've been staying with my daughter. No, I haven't seen any English papers for some time, and I doubt whether Mrs. Brown was important enough to make the *Matin*."

She had that polished, self-sufficient look so often to be found in Parisians. She wasn't a great beauty, but she had a great air of sophistication. Snuffy knew exactly how to place her.

"Mrs. Felicia Georgina Brown—to give her her full title—was murdered over the August bank holiday." He spoke with such sedate gentleness that for a moment what he said didn't sink in. Snuffy went on, "We have reason to believe she was being blackmailed."

"I can't help you there," said Mrs. Arnold.

"We believe it may be on account of a certain matter that—er—terminated her engagement here."

"Oh!" said Mrs. Arnold thoughtfully. "So you've heard of that."

"She kept it very quiet for six years. Now we believe she was being blackmailed on that account."

Mrs. Arnold stretched vigorously. "What nonsense!" she said. "I've always believed Mrs. Brown had a sudden *crise de nerfs*. At her age it's not unusual. I mean, shoplifting is one thing, but to take something so conspicuous—as if in her position she could wear an Otto Lucas hat. On her it would attract attention anywhere. And what's more, I don't believe she ever intended to take it. I believe the story she told in court, and in a sense I believe it was Witchiter's fault."

"Witchiter being the name of the milliner," contributed Snuffy softly.

"They had this idea of having what they call a hat bar, with reasonably priced hats, and letting customers try them on, and then round the wall they have the models to tempt people to spend more than they can afford. Of course, it was madness of Mrs. Brown to put a model on, she knew she couldn't afford it and really couldn't wear it if she bought it, but she said she just wanted to know what it felt like. Do you know, Mr. Ayres, that's almost the first time I ever heard of her being human. Then this friend—well, acquaintance, I don't think she had any friends—came in and started talking and Mrs. Brown says she completely forgot she was wearing this hat, and she walked out of the shop and it wasn't till she saw herself in a glass . . ."

"She could have taken it back," said Snuffy softly.

"She said she was afraid they would try and charge her for it, as she had worn it out of doors, if it was only a couple of hundred yards. And she couldn't afford it. That's what she said. Of course, she put herself completely in the wrong by taking a handbag from Witchiter's Bag Department a day or two later. She was seen to do that and she hadn't made any attempt at payment. And then the story about the hat came out. They'd found her own hat, a dowdy little affair, in the department after she'd gone. I still don't understand about the bag. Even she couldn't pretend there was a mistake about that."

"It follows as the dawn the dark," Snuffy assured her lyrically. "You get these self-service stores cases. Woman buys a number of articles, puts them in a basket and pays for them, gets a few more things she puts in her own bag and doesn't pay for. She isn't caught, but she knows that was just her luck. Next week she pays for everything; then when she's unpacking the basket she thinks, Last week I had half these things without a penny, and it's not long from there to feeling herself cheated because she's paying for stuff she might have had for nothing. So next time she slips the odd job into her own bag. If she doesn't get caught, she's a bit more adventurous. Of course she got picked up eventually because she got careless; she kept going to the same store, instead of ringing the changes. Probably told the court she considered she had a right to what she could get. It was a game like noughts and crosses. The magistrate didn't believe her; in fact, her candor probably exacerbated her sentence. I daresay Mrs. Brown felt a sort of triumph when she took the handbag; it was probably the first thing she had actually stolen; you could call the hat an accident, silly but not deliberate."

"These amateurs!" said Mrs. Arnold. "They think they know it all. Why, even Oliver Twist wasn't allowed to 'swipe wipes and tickers' till he'd been taught the right way to do it."

"Ladies have a kind of natural belief in themselves," Snuffy pointed out. "Come to that, most criminals have. Look at that man who drowned six wives in their baths, or not six perhaps but several, anyway. He got away with the first one, so why bother to think up a different method each time. Vanity, you see. No one's so clever as I."

"Are you trying to tell me Mrs. Brown started on a second round of shoplifting after she left Harrogate?"

"Oh no. She'd learned that lesson. Three months she got, didn't she? She must have fallen foul of the police, they always make it tough. Only, after all this time it seems probable that someone's bobbed up who recognized her, and of course she couldn't afford to let Mrs. Banks know about the past. According to her—Mrs. Banks, I mean—Mrs. Brown had a written reference, signed by you."

"She came to see me when she'd completed her sentence and said she was going to leave the neighborhood and would I tell any future employer that she'd been perfectly honest in dealing with my affairs and had carried out her duties to my satisfaction. I agreed to do that, so long as I wasn't asked to speak to the woman or have her personally referred to me. That's when the difficult truths come out, when you meet face to face. I was pretty sure Mrs. Brown would never repeat her mistake, it was like an illness that you don't get twice. As it happened, I was planning to go abroad, my daughter was expecting her second child, so it all worked in very well. She never wrote to me— Did she stay in one situation for six years?"

"Oh yes," said Snuffy. "Much valued, I understand."

"Valued but not liked," suggested Mrs. Arnold. "Oh, she was competent enough, I'd have expected her to have too much sense to get herself murdered. It was probably the trial over again. She annoyed the police, so she got a prison sentence instead of a fine; she made things awkward for her blackmailer and— What happened?"

Snuffy told her.

"Does anyone know who the blackmailer was, that is, if you're sure she was being blackmailed?"

"She was meeting some young fellow on the quiet, and leaving letters at a convenience address."

"Couldn't she afford to disregard him after six years?"

"She'd made quite a position for herself, locally as well as in Mrs. Banks' house. She couldn't afford to let anyone know she was an ex-convict. That's how she'd have been regarded."

"Did she think she could go on paying blackmail forever?"

"Perhaps she was just marking time, buying silence until she could think of something else."

"Pity she didn't go the whole hog and kill him," said Mrs. Arnold bluntly. "Protecting her employers' property."

"It's easier said than done," offered Snuffy respectfully.

Charm he ever so wisely, he got nothing more out of Mrs. Arnold. Mrs. Brown had never spoken of husband or children; it seemed to be generally assumed that she was a widow.

"If your interest's neither police nor press, what are you doing here, anyway?" she demanded.

"So long as the case remains open, suspicion is bound to attach itself in one direction or another. I came up here to try and verify certain facts that might help to point to the truth. I'm employed by a lawyer watching the case for a third party."

When he had gone Mrs. Arnold rang for her housekeeper. "Olivia," she said, "I don't care what hour of the day it is, it's time for a glass of wine. Mrs. Brown used to make herself fairly conspicuous in life, she doesn't seem to have changed her habits in death."

"So—where do we go from here?" asked Bill thoughtfully, laying down the xeroxed copy of the local paper containing the report of proceedings in the magistrate's court. Even here Mrs. Brown hadn't rated much space. She had created a little interest mainly because of the position of her employer, and her hitherto excellent record. But she had never had the wit to gather to herself friends, either of the mammon of unrighteousness or the other kind, and it was only too obvious nobody had cared very much.

"And X didn't care either," opined Crook. "To him she was the key to the castle, well, the Manor House, and provided that turned in the lock, it had no further interest for him."

"But for you?" hinted Bill.

"There's something screwy here," said Crook. "Granted she'd go to practically any lengths to prevent the past bein' revealed, why didn't she play her cards clever? Good at bingo, they tell me, had a head on her shoulders, so why not cover herself all along the line? Y'know, Bill, there is a mystery here. She showed no more nous than a dame who goes out in a rainstorm without an umbrella. X has got the scene set very nice, might have been tailored for him—the boss and his ever-loving the other side of the Channel, kids with their auntie, Sugar out of the way. He can't have believed she'd come back when she found she'd been conned, not till Wednesday, anyway, not with Ma Brown sniffing at the door like the famous wolf. So why don't Mrs. B. lock the back door and leave the key under a stone by the step, the way they always did, and go off to her bingo same as always? When she comes back the house has been done, she raises the alarm, all the alibis an archangel 'ud need, no danger to herself, no danger to X either, seeing she wouldn't admit to knowing him. Of course, the lady from the Pumpkin and Pie might have opened her mouth a trifle wide, but I doubt it, Bill, I doubt it. Licensees don't like the fuzz on the doorstep any more than anyone else; I daresay Mrs. Noah has her own reasons for keeping her lip buttoned. No, you take it from me, Bill, it was good old human vanity that brought Mrs. B. low, as low as a coffin."

"You think she thought she was more than a match for him and meant to show him?" hazarded Bill.

"I can't think of any other reason. Point is—what? No sense trying to turn the tables and threaten him with blackmail, too much a case of the pot calling the kettle black, and bring her too much into the open. So—she meant to defend Master's valuables with her life? Trouble about that is you usually fall between two stools. You don't save the valuables and you don't save yourself. She must have been a suspicious lady, Bill."

"I daresay she wasn't much liked," Bill allowed, "but her reputation at the Manor House seems unspotted. Would her neighbors immediately think she was in cahoots with the thieves?"

"You know what they say—virtue like happiness has no

history. And there's no doubt about it, she was a bit of a dark horse. And if X was picked up, he'd have spilt the beans all right."

"So what's your idea? She faced him in the hall with a hot rod? They didn't find one on the premises."

"Probably wouldn't have known how to use one if she had it. Besides, she had to get hold of one first. They're among the few things you can't buy these days at Woolworth's. She might have taken the fuzz into her confidence and got them to come round, but we know she didn't. Anyway, she wanted, if possible, to keep out of the picture." He shook his big red head. "No, Bill, our one hope is that X runs true to type, gets curious, gets impatient, loses his nerve, tries to make things safe for himself. Or do as the police do. Wait for information received."

It might be some quite inessential detail that would reopen the case; he arranged to have the local paper posted to him. He had been heard to say that you could get more news out of the local rag than from half a dozen of the big national dailies. And having done that, he waited.

And a night or so later an unoccupied house was broken into not ten miles from Buzzard Minor.

"You'd think X would have the sense to lie low for a while," expostulated Crook. "Not likely there are two gangs operating in the same neighborhood. But that's how these chaps get themselves nicked. Vanity again."

Not a rich haul, the police allowed, but some quite nice things taken—radio, cassette recorder, a handful of rings, china, a diamond watch . . . small beer and to date no hint of a clue.

Ten

The police hadn't much hope of recovering the collection of Battersea enamels, easily the most valuable part of the haul from Manor House. The silver would have been melted down long ago, there never had been any hope of recovering that; which left the scrolls, the miniatures and a miscellany of ornaments. Kay badgered the authorities for news.

"You're wasting your breath," Roy assured her. "If anything turns up they'll let you know. But hardly anything ever does."

The authorities sent a list of the missing objects to all reputable dealers and visited a number of known fences, but they clung to their belief that the enamels had been taken out of the country before the crime was reported. Among the fences was a man called Josiah Lang, who called himself a working silversmith but who had excited the attention of the police on a number of occasions. Mr. Lang, naturally, knew nothing of the affair. "Turn my place over," he offered. "Anything you find here, I can account for."

The police didn't doubt it. They were pretty sure he'd slipped through their net before now, but he was too fly to get himself incriminated.

"Keep your nose clean, Josh," they advised him, but if he'd seen anything of the Banks silver, you could be sure it wouldn't be on the premises now.

Not long after this visit from the police Mr. Lang had

another caller. A slim-built young man in his late twenties turned out of the main street at Camden Town and descended a flight of steps into a basement, where he stopped at a drab painted door. He pressed an electric bell and an instant later heard feet coming along the passage. He knew he was being identified through a peephole which enabled the tenant to identify him, though he himself could see no one. After another moment the door was opened and a small man, vaguely reminiscent of one of Dickens' more malevolent characters, stared up at him.

"Mr. Lang," said the young man ingratiatingly.

Mr. Lang scowled. "I told you to keep away from here," he said in a grating voice. "I warned you, I don't have any truck with violence. I've got a reputation to keep up."

"I've got some good stuff for you, Mr. Lang," the young man said.

"Then you can take it elsewhere," said Josiah. "I told you, I'm not interested."

"You will be," the young man insisted. "It's just up your street." He gave his name as Terry Woods, but it didn't seem unlikely that he had different names at different periods of his career, and in different parts of the country.

Heavy feet passed on the pavement. A curious head peered over the railings. Lang caught his visitor's arm and pulled him roughly inside and down a dark passage to a largish room at the back of the house, where they wouldn't be seen.

"You want everyone should hear my business?" he demanded, pushing the door closed with his foot. The room was furnished with a desk, a table and a number of chairs and cupboards. "You don't know the English language?" he went on angrily. "You want I should put it in writing? I don't want to have no more dealings with you."

The young man was carrying a battered suitcase, and this he now opened and began to set some articles out on the table.

144

His companion's eyes widened, but his hands remained by his sides. "So who did you strangle to get these?" he demanded sarcastically.

"Never laid a finger on anyone," returned the young man in virtuous tones. "Tell you the truth, the house was left empty. Fair ask for it, some of these chaps. Left the kitchen window open, too."

"An obliging kitchen maid," offered Mr. Lang in the same voice. But his eyes were taking in the details of the goods the young man was offering him.

"What are they?" asked Mr. Woods. "No, I've had my eye on the place for some time, but the right opportunity didn't get offered. Don't even keep a dog," he added.

As though fascinated, Mr. Lang drew on a pair of gloves and gingerly handled the fruits of the robbery. "Silver," he said in accusing tones.

"Well, some," the young man acknowledged, "but you always say silver finds its own level, Mr. Lang."

"It has to be melted down, it is an expensive process. All those cups and salvers the last time, all inscribed. It deters from the value . . ."

"As if I didn't know, you old rogue!" muttered Woods under his breath. "But no inscriptions on any of these. And a good weight." He picked up a heavy silver sugar castor. "And some of the ornaments 'ud fetch their price."

"But distinctive," sighed Lang. "Very distinctive. Too hot to handle at present, and that's money out of my pocket."

Woods saw that he meant to have them, but at his own price. "I've expenses, too, Mr. Lang," he reminded the older man.

"Goods you must keep out of sight are dangerous as a bomb. And if the police should find out about you and that unfortunate woman, that housekeeper—what does that make me?"

145

"Whyever should they?" Woods argued. "The case is closed. Anyway, I never laid a finger on the woman. It was Bernie . . ."

Mr. Lang flung up his hand. "I don't want to know no names. Is he with you in this?"

"He's not even in the country. He'll lie low for quite a while, I shouldn't wonder. Anyway, till the smoke dies down."

"And when do you suppose that will be? Only this morning in my newspaper there is the record of a man arrested for a murder nine years old—nine years, and they don't forget."

"It was her own fault," said the young man, sounding sulky for the first time. "If she didn't want trouble, what was she doing leading me up the path . . . ?"

"So she led you, is it?"

" 'Come at the weekend,' she said. 'Everyone will be away, the house will be ours.' "

"So she knew why you were coming."

"Well, not because she was Helen of Troy," agreed Mr. Woods.

"Then—you had something on her?" Lang's voice was sharp.

"We all make mistakes," Woods said.

"But"—Lang sounded puzzled—"if she knew why you were coming . . ."

"Of course she knew. Only a fool would have put up a fight— Mind you, she wanted it to look as if she'd struggled, but she didn't have to lash out like a wildcat. Anyhow, the stuff was insured, wasn't it?"

"Perhaps," said Mr. Lang, "you did not mention that you were bringing a friend. Any more than you told me, when you came with the silver, that a woman had been killed. I read it in the papers. There is the name—Roy Banks—there are the inscriptions—and the poor woman, found in a boot cupboard. A boot cupboard."

"We couldn't leave her lying on the stairs," Woods protested. "Not with that chap wandering round the house and trying the doors. We weren't to know who he was or how long he was going to hang about."

"So that is why you left by the French windows?"

"The car was that side of the house. That was her idea. 'You know how they gossip in a village,' she said. 'Not like living in a town. Here your business is everybody's business, and knowing Mr. and Mrs. Banks are away and the house is empty, tongues might wag . . .'"

"So intelligent a woman should not have been so easily deceived by you," said Lang scornfully.

"We couldn't risk someone peeping through the letter box. And she'd said no one 'ud be back before Wednesday. How could we guess that stupid girl would lose her luggage and come home?"

"It was not she who gave the alarm," Lang reminded him. "It was the open window . . ."

"I told you, we couldn't take the chance of running into the chap."

"You might bang him on the head, also. But he was not an elderly woman taken by surprise . . ."

"I've had enough of this," cried Woods in disgust. "If you've got such a tender conscience, why haven't you gone to the police? I'll tell you. Because you want to play as safe as the rest of us, safer if you know how. We take the chance getting the stuff. How about that little lot? There's others, you know, might be more interested."

Lang looked with loathing at his young companion, but Woods wasn't for the moment seeing him. Instead memory conjured up *her* face, at first startled, then apprehensive, then terror-struck—that was when she saw Bernie with the stocking drawn over his head. Then she'd lost her own and started to scream. She'd have shut him out if she could, but she was caught unprepared, standing there wearing her ridiculous chain with her bag looped over her arm.

"Be quiet, you old cow," he'd said. "No need for anyone to get hurt. The stuff's insured, isn't it?"

"You've come to rob," she said, and the way she said it made him laugh and that got her in a fury. She started to shout.

"Shut her cackling mouth," said Bernie. "Where's this stuff?"

And at that she'd hurled herself on them, didn't give them a chance, really. Anyway, they'd meant to tie her up, leave her till someone came by, they said a dog could live four days comfortably without food, and in four or five days someone would be back. She'd need time to cool down or she'd go straight to the police, and she knew who he was—anyway, knew the name he'd told her. And there was that woman at the paper shop, suppose she edged into the picture. Not that he thought all that out at the time. He'd never thought it 'ud come to this.

"Take care!" he'd warned Bernie. "She could have a weak heart or something."

"Pity she hadn't got weak lungs," Bernie had muttered.

Still, he hadn't meant it to end this way either. You couldn't call it murder. She'd have scratched their eyes out, given half a chance. Lucky really that barmaid from the Pumpkin and Pie had said she wouldn't recognize him again. One thing, he hadn't given her a chance. It might be good sense to leave the neighborhood soon, but not in too much of a rush. No one was looking in his direction, so far as he knew. He didn't count Josiah. He'd cut his own throat before he'd go to the police. His real moment of danger had been when he nearly collided with that silly girl on the scooter. He couldn't have anticipated her, but the rain and the darkness were on his side. No jury would take any notice of evidence so slight as that. Pity really, he thought casually, she hadn't broken her neck, too. With Bernie out of the way, there wouldn't be anyone . . . He hadn't counted on the old man reading the papers, but he wasn't really any danger. It was his own skin he cared about, no one else's.

He came round from his brown study to find Lang's eyes on

his face. He waited a moment to see which way the cat was going to jump. Was Lang going to cling to his assertion that he wanted no more truck with a chap whose record might get him clapped into gaol for murder? His impulse was to gather up the stuff and scarper.

"Sorry you're not interested, Mr. Lang," he'd say. "You're cutting off your nose to spite your face, but if that's the way you like it . . ." And off on a jaunty step. Only, he couldn't afford to play it that way. In a sense, the fellow was his security. Let him take the stuff this time and he was making himself accessory after the fact. He might lie himself black in the face to the fuzz, swear he'd never connected the stolen trophies with a dead woman, but the fact would remain that he'd been prepared, for his own profit, to do a deal with a murderer—that's the way he'd put it. Instead Woods put on a hard face and asked, "Are you going to make me an offer, Mr. Lang? If not, I can take it elsewhere."

Mr. Lang considered. He saw the situation quite as clearly as Woods did. It was improbable there'd been violence on this occasion, but he could make a hard price for the goods. Already he had a market in mind for some of them. He never kept stuff long. Play safe, was his motto. The police might come calling, but they'd never pinned anything on him yet.

The customary haggling began. From his first derisory offer Lang rose slowly; Woods couldn't afford to be too choosey. Eventually they fixed on a price, not much to the young man's satisfaction. But each felt he had something on the other.

Woods came cautiously up the back steps, casting glances left and right, like a good child waiting to cross the road. Not many people were about tonight, and those that were, were busy with their own affairs. The interview with Mr. Lang had gone off no worse than he had anticipated. He had, he felt, shut the fellow's mouth, since how could he go to the police and acknowledge that he was a buyer of stolen goods, or pretend he hadn't noticed the similarity of the names and monograms? He still considered he had had a rough deal over the Manor House affair. Needless to say, the thought of murder had not been in his mind when he called that evening—as he had assured Lang—by Mrs. Brown's invitation. It must have been a shock to her to see the stockinged head behind his own, but a reasonable woman knows when she's playing a losing hand. Tie the old girl up, safer for her really, they'd agreed. All she has to say is that she opened the door and two hooded men pushed her back into the hall. The most unreasonable employer must know a middle-aged woman can't stand up to two intruders, and she wouldn't open her mouth about Harrogate. She hadn't got much, poor old mare, but she had a respectable position. Besides, see how easily she'd come to heel.

It had been a rare piece of luck seeing and recognizing her one day in Buzzard Major. He'd covered the trial for a fading daily and he remembered her in the dock. Meeting her eased away a lot of difficulties. Mind you, he'd played it slow, the careful casual telephone call, the "chance" encounter. He wondered how far she'd fathomed his plans. Blackmail on a mild scale, probably she thought it 'ud stop there, and his demands had never been heavy. He couldn't get her to talk much about her employers, but finally he wrung from her that invitation to come and see for himself on the Thursday evening, everyone 'ud be away, she had the place to herself till Tuesday night, anyway. They'd find her before then, of course, village people were as nosy as they come, someone would realize the papers weren't being collected or the milk taken in, which was, of course, exactly what had happened.

He found he was shivering suddenly—at the thought that that girl, the *au pair,* might have come back earlier. He hadn't really thought the woman had collapsed, a faint perhaps, shock . . . He had left the house far behind and was walking through the dark streets. A bit of luck for him that that barmaid at the Pumpkin had said she wouldn't know him again. There was only the old girl at the paper shop, and if she'd confided anything to the police, the press would have got hold of it before now. Suppose she, too, was lying low? Perhaps there'd been a note from Mrs. Brown confirming their meeting on the Thursday, perhaps the sealed envelope still lay in the drawer at the back of the shop.

"What happens to letters that aren't called for?" he'd asked once, and Mrs. Gale said she kept them for a month and then destroyed them unread. She'd probably said precisely the same to Crook, but neither of them could be sure it was the truth. She'd not gone to the police at the time of the murder, but that might simply mean she was playing a waiting game.

Too much luck to hope she'd fall under a bus or choke on a mouthful of lobster thermidor, thought Woods.

At about the same moment Lang was thinking precisely the same about him.

The clock on the wall of the little paper shop near Sleepy Hollow Lane said 5:25. The proprietor walked restlessly to the door and looked out on the darkening evening. It was always the same, right through the week, even if the mornings contained promise of a bit of sun later, a scrap of blue sky, a drop in the force of the wind, once the tea hour was past and the light died, the sullen gloom came down. She thought—an unusual thought for her—of sun-drenched countries, fields of flowers, warmth. She'd have looked a queer bird in such surroundings, in her drab gear, her wooden rosy-cheeked face—even her hands seemed less than human, moved by some mechanism perhaps.

The shop closed at five-thirty, not likely anyone would come after that. If they wanted cigarettes, the Lamb and Fleece opened at five-thirty, and the sort of women—they were mostly women—who came for surreptitious letters were at home being dutiful wives and mothers, their madness and hope and fear hidden behind their concealing features. Mrs. Gale had no curiosity about these correspondents. Few of the women were really young, some sent for advertisements they wouldn't like to have sent home, some were doubtless seeking a bit of a change before it was too late from the endless round of cooking, cleaning, washing that was their life. Mousy creatures on the whole, the bad lots were much more brazen, the permissive age they called it and they took advantage of the fact. That Mrs. Brown now—no one ever seemed quite sure about her, a woman of mystery, six years in the place and for all anyone knew, there'd never even been a Mr. Brown. Still, that was for the police, not for a woman who's got her own bread to earn. Not a sign of him since Mrs. B. was found, never came to ask, didn't go to the police either, but maybe that wouldn't be difficult to understand.

The clock struck the half-hour and instantly she collected the hanging files of magazines from either side of the door and threw a cover over the trays of chocolates and sweetmeats. She emptied the till, leaving the drawer pulled out so that any intending sneak thief could see how little return he'd get for his pains. She opened the letter drawer, four envelopes as yet unclaimed, but the month of grace was up for none of them. She pushed the drawer closed and turned the key. Their contents were nothing to her, just a go-between, that's how she thought of herself. Why, she wouldn't know half of them if they came in unannounced.

Remembering her visitors, she found she was thinking about that queer chap who looked as if he might have come out of a kiddies' playbook—the Nightmare of the Nursery, say— barging in with his questions about Mrs. Brown, deceased. He'd given her quite a turn. Mind you, she was within her rights, no law could touch her, she gave a service, and it's still called a free country. She wondered what his interest in Mrs. Brown had been. Mr. Brown? she wondered. But no. Someone would have ferreted that fact out. The young fellow hadn't turned up again either. Counting on the fingers of one hand, she was surprised to realize what a short time ago it all was. Still, memories were short, it wasn't likely the police would ever get any of the stuff back. There'd been another break-in, she'd heard, only a night or two ago, but no violence there.

Mrs. Brown was different—blackmail, most like. It generally was when the woman was so much older than the man. She'd read about the rendezvous at the Pumpkin and Pie, likely the same chap. The old girl wouldn't have had two of them on a string. Hard as a gin trap, she'd been, but the forces of evil got her in the end. If there was any justice, they'd get him, too. Only, these young fellows were like rats, went back to their holes.

She gave a final glance round—why was she wasting her time on Mrs. Brown, she'd gone for good—pulled on her old coat and locked up. Her car, a battle-gray affair that looked as if it had been made of a couple of biscuit tins, was parked on a little patch by the shop. It was a ramshackle affair, time really she took it for an overhaul, but it got her from place to place and that's all she asked of it.

She was remembering past clients—there'd been a clergyman once, but he hadn't lasted long, they'd taken his body out of the river and a merciful coroner brought in a verdict of death by misadventure. There'd been a letter come for him the next day but she'd burned that pronto. You never knew where you were with the police, and she didn't want to get mixed up in other people's scandals. All the same, there was more to that Mrs. Brown's death than a break-in by thugs, though she didn't suppose anyone would ever know what it was. That foxy chap who'd called himself a lawyer—Crook, his card said, an ominous name—well, death had put one over even on him.

Why have I got that crowd on my mind tonight? she wondered. She hadn't let herself get turned on even by the clergyman, and he wasn't the sort of client she anticipated. She worked on a small scale, mostly local. The M.I.5 agents and the porn boys used quite different pipe lines. People were fairly desperate when they started using accommodation addresses— if you excepted the fading forties who wrote surreptitiously for hormone creams and mixtures guaranteed to pep up your sex appeal—but she'd never had to face any limelight. It never came out about the clergyman calling and the great gingery fellow hadn't wanted any floodlight either.

Getting into the car, she took one last glance up and down the road. It was quiet enough at any time, and now, with the light darkening and the promise of rain in the air, no one was abroad, no hurrying figure who might be a client hastening to catch her before she closed for the night.

She had got off punctually tonight because she had shopping to do, a rare enough occasion for her, who looked as though her clothes were painted on to her body. What she mainly wanted was a new pair of shoes, and she always went to Oliver's at Waterlow Cross, where they had a good choice and an assistant who knew how to fit a customer. She didn't believe in buying cheap shoes, it was never an economy in the end.

She slowed down by the Lamb and Fleece, where she put her car into the Customers Only park. She always stopped here at the end of the day's work for a Guinness. As she approached the door of the saloon bar it was flung violently open and a young man emerged.

He's starting his drinking early, she thought as he cannoned against her, nearly knocking her down. He put out an instinctive hand to steady her. A light fell on his face, and she thought incredulously, It can't be. Not with me thinking of him not ten minutes ago." And aloud she said, "Why, it's Mr. Robinson. That's funny. I was just remembering you."

The hand fell away from her arm. If she hadn't been erect, she could have fallen.

Then the young man spoke. "You've got it wrong, auntie. My name's not Robinson."

"I'm not your auntie any more than your name's Robinson. But then, I never supposed it was. It's nothing to me what you choose to call yourself. I was wondering if I should try and get in touch, but then I didn't know how to contact you, did I?"

"Why should you want to get in touch with someone you've never met?"

"Oh, it wasn't that there was another letter for you. I wouldn't have kept that, anyway. And then I never do intervene in my clients' private affairs. I'm only there as a sort of post office, and post offices are impersonal enough. But this fellow asking questions."

"What kind of questions?" It was as if he couldn't prevent himself asking.

"Well, about Mrs. Brown, of course. You remember her, Number Twenty-seven. I did wonder if he'd come to find out about you, this man, I mean, though he did say he wasn't from the police, just that he was making inquiries. I didn't tell him anything, of course. I couldn't deny Mrs. Brown, naturally, she'd been seen leaving the shop."

He said flatly, "I don't know who you're talking about."

"This Mrs. Brown, the one who was found murdered at Manor House. You must have heard, it was all over the papers. Are you sure you haven't time to come in for a drink? I can't stop talking outside here. I've got some shopping to do, late night at Waterlow Cross."

"Accident on the main road," he warned her. "Car overturned. Wait till tomorrow."

"Then the shop wouldn't be open. No, I'll have to go by the shortcut."

"Can't have much respect for your car. That her there?"

"Never judge a book by its cover—don't they say that? It 'ud surprise you what she can do. Well, mustn't wait. You know where I am if you should change your mind. Next move 'ull be up to you."

"You're daft," he said scornfully and moved away.

She saw him go swinging up the street as she pulled open the saloon door. She found she was trembling, not with fear but with a kind of exhilaration. People might suppose hers was a mysterious, even an interesting, life; it wasn't, it was as dull as ditchwater. When she heard about Mrs. Brown's death, she thought straight off, I hope they don't connect me with this, though she hadn't had any real fears—her clients couldn't afford not to be discreet—until this chap came calling, and he hadn't come back. Not that there was much mystery about Mrs. Brown. She'd opened the door herself, expecting a friend—odd, though, that the friend had never come forward. Still, it wasn't likely the young fellow would come back. She couldn't do him any harm, he only had to say she'd got it wrong, just his word against hers, and it's a man's world, after all.

Still, no doubt about it, he'd been a bit shaken when she said his name. She hadn't any doubts, but there was no need for him to take on. She didn't want trouble. Even if she wanted to harm him, she hadn't the means. Still—she flattered herself she had been able to see the thoughts going through his mind like goldfish swimming in a bowl—he was afraid of her, well, apprehensive, anyway. I wonder what there was between the two of them? she thought, fetching her Guinness and carrying it to her usual small table. There were very few drinkers sitting at tables alone, herself and one or two who were clearly waiting for friends.

"Find it a bit lonely, don't you?" said the barmaid once. Solitaries often sat up at the bar, where they might get into conversation, though this one could hardly be any man's choice.

But Mrs. Gale said she saw people all day, it was nice to have a bit of quiet without feeling you were drinking on your own. She didn't approve of that, that was how you got overfond of the bottle, and she liked the sensation of people all around. And, of course, though this she didn't say, if you kept your ears pinned back, you might pick up something. Ears open and eyes down, that was the ticket.

There'd been a poster all over the country during the war—*Walls Have Ears*—sometimes with a picture of old Hitler crouched under a café table, sometimes just a big ear on the wall. Perhaps it had made people cautious during the war, but

156

they'd forgotten soon enough. And if you came to the same place every day, you got to recognize some of the regulars and their companions, and you never knew when it might come in useful. Let patience have her perfect work. And even if nothing came of it, it gave you a sort of feeling of power knowing something the subject didn't realize you knew, and you had to get your fun as you could. There wasn't much lying about these days, not for middle-aged women who looked as though they'd come out of the Ark. She was so pleased at this sense of power, even though it might prove quite valueless, that she broke her rule by having a second Guinness.

"You're going it," encouraged the barmaid. "Birthday?"

Expecting me to buy her one? reflected Mrs. Gale. Not that she would. The woman had free drinks enough, a favorite with the men, easy to see. But presumably an unpopular barmaid wouldn't hold down her job two weeks. Something in being independent, thought Mrs. Gale.

She was startled to find how time had gone on. Talking to that young chap and the second drink had whittled the evening away. She didn't mean to be hurried over her purchases. Buying shoes wasn't like buying stockings or underwear, where you simply had to ask for the right size. If you were hustled at the shoe shop, you could emerge with something that might half cripple you. And with shoes the price they were . . .

She remembered the accident in the town and decided to take her chance on the shortcut. It was a stony road with too many potholes, but it cut off quite a slice and a roundabout and now she hadn't any time to lose. There was a steepish hill down past the chalk pit, but after that the road ran straight and true into Waterlow Cross. Not likely there'd be much traffic about this time of night, with the weather ready to break any minute. Plenty of fellows used the local bus or relied on shanks' mare. She had a rugged journey to work, and the little car was her only luxury.

Putting the thought of Robinson and Mrs. Brown out of her

mind, she began to think of the shoes she was going to buy. She always bought plain black, not for her the absurd shoes the girls bought, with their two-inch soles and six-inch heels, but suddenly she remembered an advertisement put out by Oliver's featuring colored suede shoes with sensible rubber soles. Nothing gaudy, of course, leave the reds and the bright blues to them as fancied them, but there'd been a very pleasing dark green shade, lace-ups, colored laces if preferred. Oliver's would think she'd taken leave of her senses, but tonight—could it be that chance encounter?—she was feeling adventurous.

Might even get myself a new hat, she thought. It's about time. Green instead of black. Wonder what Katie could have put in that second Guinness. This isn't like you, Priscilla Gale. I do believe you're excited.

She couldn't make a great pace, the road turned and twisted too often, making passing dangerous. Anyway, she was never one for speed. Start in time and you'll never be late, was her motto.

She had reached the top of the slope and the lights of Waterlow Cross gleamed against the horizon. But there were nearer lights, something was climbing the hill, something much too big to be on a side road. There were complaints locally, here as everywhere else, about the big lorries using the narrow lanes. "P'raps they'd like us to fly," suggested the drivers. "We've as much right on the roads as anyone else. Not our fault if they can't take the strain." Of course, this driver wouldn't expect to meet much traffic on such a night, and perhaps he also had been warned of the accident. She braked prudently. The lorry driver must have seen her, would realize it was going to be a tight squeeze. Still, she was a good driver and so, presumably, was he.

Something was going wrong. She had braked, but the car seemed to be accelerating. The steering wheel bounced in her hand; they seemed to be all over the road. She wrenched the car round, but it was like something with a separate will of its own.

The faint rain that starred the windscreen was deceptive. Lights seemed to be rushing at her, voices were screaming. Or was it birds in the gaunt trees by the roadside?

The lorry seemed to be moving steadily upon her—why didn't the driver pull over? She made a further assault on the brakes, and the bottom of the hill rose to meet her. Now panic came into its own; the car was out of control. There was a sharp bend beyond the chalk pit. Someone—providence? the wind? a child?—had left a great branch sprawling across the road. If it hadn't been for the lorry, she might just have avoided it. As it was, she hadn't a chance. The lights ran together, there was darkness behind them.

I'll never get those shoes, she thought.

Eleven

"She must have been a nutter," declared a shaken lorry driver to the police when they arrived after what seemed an endless delay. "Came rocketing over the ridge like a bat out of hell. Didn't seem to have any control over the car at all. Of course, it's not much of a road . . . You can see for yourself if I'd drawn any further off the road, I'd have been in the chalk pit."

"These roads weren't meant for that kind of vehicle," the constable warned him grimly. "What was wrong with the main road?"

"What's wrong with the main road is that it isn't a by-pass. Besides, it's market day or something hereabouts. Place choc-a-bloc—I didn't reckon to spend another night on the road, and my guv'nor's fussy about timekeeping. Of course, once she touched the lorry—must have gone over a pothole or something—she was done for. The car bounced off like a ball, turned over. She'd got her seat belt fastened, though it didn't do her much good. Brakes must have failed," he added.

"That's something we'll not be able to prove," the constable said. "The car's a write-off."

And the same could be said of the driver. The steering wheel had buckled, with pretty ghastly results. Even the lorry driver, who'd seen accidents enough in his time, felt green.

"When was this?"

"About—oh, say, forty minutes ago. Well, mate, you know how it is. When you want someone to come along, the road's as empty as a bar at closing time, and I couldn't leave the lorry. In the ordinary way I'd have had my mate with me, but he fell off a pavement—just a bit higher than ordinary pavement—and cracked a bone in his leg. He's tucked up in hospital, and like I say, I couldn't leave the lorry. There were two hijacked only last week, and I have my side of it. I've got a wife and four kids. A chap came by at last on a motor scooter and he said he'd call you, get an ambulance. It's not as though it made any difference," he added desperately. "She was a goner from the minute the car overturned. Do you know who she is?"

"Local number," said the policeman laconically. "She'll likely have her papers in her bag. Where's that flicking ambulance? Or are they stopping to make one? It won't be able to get past you," he added in the same severe voice. "You'd better get up to the top and wait. There's a lay-by . . ." He made a note of the number and inspected the driver's papers.

"You going to be long?" asked the driver.

"No longer than we can help. And if you're afraid of being back late, you'll still be home before she is."

The driver got into his cab and pulled slowly up the hill. The ambulance came; between them they eased what had been Mrs. P. Gale only an hour ago out of the wreck.

"Did the lorry ruddy run over it?" ejaculated one of the ambulance men. "What's a lorry doing on this road, anyway?"

"No law against it," said the policeman, who clearly wasn't going to take sides.

"The locals have been asking for one long enough," returned the second ambulance man. "Now I suppose you'll do something about it."

They found Mrs. Gale's driving license and other papers, all correct, all up-to-date, a clean license. They ran Katie to earth, as being presumably the last person who had spoken to the deceased.

"She came in as usual," Katie said. "Every night she came after she shut up the shop. Never met anyone here, always took her glass and sat by herself at that little table by the wall if she could get it. No use asking me about her, because I didn't know her. Has—had the little shop in Sleepy Hollow Lane—papers, sweets, you know. Don't know how she made a living, it was so out of the world, but the schoolkids played in the field at the back, probably bought their Mars bars there and teachers might pick up a paper. And of course there were the letters."

"Letters?"

"It was one of those places where you can have letters addressed to yourself, letters you don't want other people pawing over."

"Many people use the service?" the policeman wondered.

"If there'd been a service like that near me when I was a girl, I'd have used it," declared Katie. "My mother opened all my letters right up to the time I was nineteen. And people like to have some sort of privacy in their lives."

"She didn't seem any different this evening? Didn't say anything?"

"She never said anything. Oh yes, she had two Guinesses instead of one. It's the first time I've ever known her do that."

"Waiting for someone?"

"If she was, she didn't wait long. I did ask if it was her birthday, but it wasn't that. Besides, you don't reckon to buy your own drinks on your birthday. Oh, she could have walked the tape line, if that's what you were thinking of."

"The road she was on wasn't on her way home, not the quickest way anyhow."

"Then p'raps she wasn't going home."

When it came to domestic details, she could supply none. If she had friends, she didn't meet them at the Lamb and Fleece.

The garage said that the car was in good working order a fortnight ago, when Mrs. Gale had been supplied with two new tires. It was an old model, and pretty soon she wouldn't be able to get spares for it, but she kept it well, and there was no reason why it should suddenly fold up on her. In her place he wouldn't have taken it down the shortcut, it wasn't a good road, drivers had been agitating to have it resurfaced for some time. No joy there.

Mrs. Gale had lived alone for several years in one half of a twin pair of cottages, two up, two down. Of recent years bathrooms had been built on to the ground floor. The tenant of the other cottage said she'd lived there for four years, but she couldn't supply any information about the dead woman.

"Kept herself to herself," she said and nodded. "Only time we had words really—and you couldn't call that a conversation —was when my pussy went over the hedge into her garden. 'I'll thank you to keep your cat the right side of the fence,' she'd say to me. 'He's damaging my garden.' Well, you can see for yourself it 'ud need the atom bomb to do that. No more than a dust yard, that musty old privet and a few dandelions."

She didn't have visitors, she never went away. The neighbor didn't even know if she was a widow or a deserted wife.

The news appeared in the local press; a few people wrote to protest about these side roads being used by heavy traffic. The police put up a notice forbidding transit of any lorry over a certain weight. They made the usual inquiries, but no relations surfaced. They put a notice on the shop door to say *Closed* and anyone anticipating letters could call at the station, but no one came.

"It's like that woman at Manor House over again," people said.

No one had seen her chatting to a strange man outside the Lamb and Fleece within an hour of her death, or if anyone had, he wasn't talking. She was like a bubble on a pond. The waters ripple, the bubble breaks, the pond looks the same as before.

Mr. Crook read the account in the local paper and readily identified his Mrs. Noah.

Now, what danger was she to anyone? he reflected. Mind,

164

there's no evidence it was anything but pure accident, but here's Mrs. Brown meeting a young man—nameless—and she's blotted out. Then another nameless young man, since I doubt if his birth certificate is registered under Robinson, hangs around an insignificant news vendor and she vanishes.

"What's worrying you?" asked Bill.

"Well, this case ain't closed, and I still feel responsible for my client. Too much mystery here, Bill. They'll bring in a verdict of death by misadventure, of course. Don't they say things go by threes? I'll just nip down to Buzzard Minor, I think, breath of country air won't come amiss, and see if I can pick up any unconsidered trifles the police have overlooked."

"Going to give them any warning?" asked Bill.

But Crook said he thought he'd let himself come as a nice surprise. "I don't want Sugar's to be the third funeral," he added. "And I'd just as soon know what she was up to. Wouldn't surprise me one little bit to know she had some little notion of her own up her sleeve along of her arm."

Kay hadn't been able to replace Mrs. Brown, and her suggestion that Jan should lend a hand with the housework had met with a cool response.

"Well, what did you expect?" said Roy. "I should think she has her hands full with the kids, taking them to and from school, doing their room and her own, washing their smalls and entertaining them in her spare time. I don't know what the *au pair* society would think of what she does now, without making her a general dogsbody."

The children agreed with him.

"She has to wash our hair," clamored Dawn.

"And make fudge now we can get into the kitchen," added Coral.

"Just what you'd expect of a daughter in an emergency," said Kay crossly.

"You have very idealistic notions about daughters," her husband murmured. "I'm afraid your own may disappoint you if you will maintain such high standards."

The upshot was that Kay found herself doing a disagreeable amount of housework and the food all came out of the freezer.

"Advertise in the local press," advised Roy. "They'll come in their droves."

But it didn't work out that way. Kay was shaken by the demands of the daily woman, who had promptly raised her fees by twenty percent on the ground of increased duties and the fact that it wasn't everyone who wanted to work in a house where a murder had taken place.

"I don't want a freak hoping for another crime," Kay said. "I shall have to give Mrs. Best her raise or she'll go, and heaven knows what stories she'll spread in the village. There's something to be said for having deaf-mutes in the household."

"Well, they don't get a murder every day of the week," said tolerant Roy.

Jan unexpectedly came to the rescue, offering to undertake the cooking, provided she was in charge of the kitchen.

"We can help," said the children eagerly. "Much more int'resting than homework."

"I don't know whether we'll get anything fit to eat," wondered Kay dubiously.

But they were in for a pleasant surprise.

"That girl's got a fortune in her fingertips," said Roy frankly. "No wonder Ma Brown would never have her near the kitchen. And how lucky for us that she prefers kids to kudos. Oh, come, Kay, you can't expect her to turn to and sweep floors when she can feed us like this."

Kay, as the phrase goes, could scarcely boil an egg. Mrs. Brown had been conscientious but uninspired; a joint was a joint and foreign dishes were so much flummery. Jan admittedly was more slapdash and certainly more extravagant, but every meal was a surprise and usually a tantalizing one.

●　　●　　●

"Do be quiet, children," implored Kay. "I've got a splitting headache. Dawn, go up to my room and fetch the aspirin. It's on the table by my bed."

"Mrs. Brown didn't approve of you taking aspirins," said Dawn self-righteously. "She said they're a drug, like tranquilizers and sleeping pills."

"Then Mrs. Brown was a smug old hypocrite," retorted Kay. "I daresay she didn't take aspirin, but I know at one time she took sleeping pills, because she offered me one when I had a bad migraine. I must admit it was some time ago," she conceded grudgingly.

"What's a migraine, Mummy?"

"A particularly atrocious form of headache that practically incapacitates you."

"Then you can't have migraine, can you, Mummy, because you're not incapacitated."

"Don't argue so," pleaded her mother. "Just get the little bottle. Good heavens, who can that be?" For the front-door bell pealed through the house.

"Let me open the door," begged Coral. "It might be the Queen."

"What on earth would the Queen be doing down here?"

"Her car might have broken down," called the resourceful Dawn over the banisters.

"In any case, why hasn't Jan opened the door?"

"Oh, Mummy, you know she went out on a bicycle to do the shopping. Isn't food more interesting now Jan does the cooking?"

"In any case, I won't have you children opening doors," scolded Kay. "The press are still hanging around, waiting for some new development."

"Like vultures," suggested Dawn, now running down the stairs, a little bottle in her hand.

"I could stand just behind you with a jug of water and

if it was the press I could pour it over them," offered Coral eagerly.

"It's probably Jehovah's Witnesses. I know they've been at Firlmere."

"What would they want?"

"To convert you to their way of thinking."

"I should point to my ears, which means I'm deaf, so I can't hear. Mummy, that's the third time the bell's rung. Whoever it is might go away."

"Anyone who rings three times will ring four," said Kay gloomily, crossing the hall. The next instant the children heard her exclaim, "You again! You don't mean something fresh has turned up?"

"Don't read the papers?" wondered Crook. "How about this Mrs. Gale?"

Kay stared. "Where on earth does she come in?"

"Got herself killed on the roads. It was in the local."

"I mean, how does that affect us?"

"Your Mrs. Brown used to call there for letters."

Kay looked disbelieving. "Who told you so?"

"Mrs. G. admitted it. Besides, I have a witness who saw her leaving the shop."

"What was she doing having letters sent to an accommodation address?"

"You'd have to ask her, wouldn't you?"

"But she's dead."

"They're both dead. That what's troubling me. Here's Mrs. Brown known to be meeting a young man on the sly—and she's gone. Here's Mrs. Gale visited by a young man who called for Mrs. B.'s letters—she told me that much herself, though she'd have denied it if she could, her clients' secrets were sacred, and now Mrs. G.'s gone. I want to make sure Sugar ain't the next on the list."

"Why on earth should you think she was in danger?"

"She was on the road that night when a car came from the

direction of Manor House. She can't identify the driver, but he can't be dead sure of that, and anyway, she could make a good guess. Everyone else who knew him is out of the way."

"You can't be serious about this," protested Kay.

"I didn't come all the way down here just to give the Superb an airing," Crook assured her. "Just see to it she don't go walks on her owney-oh, or go listening to the nightingales in the wood—I'm sure you have them."

"I've better things to do with my evenings than listen to nightingales, and so has Jan. How long is this going on?"

"Till the police get their man," said Crook simply. Over Kay's shoulder he caught sight of Dawn peeping through a crack of the living-room door. She was still clutching the bottle of aspirins. "Hullo, it's Lady Molly," he said. "What have you got there?"

"It's Mummy's aspirins. She's got a headache. Mrs. Brown never had headaches."

"That's what she told you. But to let you into a secret, I found out she had a headache that last night, that's why she came back early from the bingo. And—hold on to your hat—she took a little box out of her bag and took an aspirin."

"She kept it on her dressing table," objected Dawn. "She said they were breath sweeteners. I asked her once if she'd give me one to see what they were like, but she said children who needed breath sweeteners had senna pods."

"I thought they went out with the old Queen," said Crook. "Still, I'm only an old bach."

"Perhaps they were sleeping tablets," put in Coral, coming up to join in the conversation. "She had some, she told Mummy."

"She wouldn't be taking sleeping tablets in the middle of a party."

"She came back from the party."

"Ah, but she didn't go home straight away. She dropped into the Pumpkin and Pie for a pick-me-up, and then she walked home and went up to her room and parked her coat and came back to the hall. She couldn't have done all that if she'd taken a sleeping tablet, she'd have been dead on her feet."

Kay gave a shocked gasp, but the children didn't seem to notice. "Perhaps it was a breath sweetener and she didn't want them to know," offered Dawn.

"You take a sweetener after a drink, not before it," objected Crook. "Ah well, I'll try and sort it out. You know, I wouldn't change you for the cleverest pair of monkeys in the business."

"Did we help?" asked Dawn interestedly.

"You told me something I didn't know. Where's Sugar?"

"Doing the shopping."

"How come you ain't with her?"

Two eager voices assured him she'd gone on her bicycle.

"Don't you have bicycles?"

"Mummy won't let us, not till Coral's eight."

"Then what's wrong with shanks' mare?"

"Why don't you go to the gate and see if you can see Jan?" suggested Kay. "I wish you wouldn't put ideas into the children's heads, Mr. Crook," she added as they departed, "like suggesting Jan may be in danger."

"I explained to you, it's the young-man syndrome. We've dealt with Mrs. Brown and Mrs. Gale" (he didn't refer to her as Mrs. Noah in this house, he didn't think his reference would be taken up) "that only leaves Sugar. She was meeting a young man on the strict q.t. Well, no one seems to have noticed them, he hasn't surfaced since he stood her up, having maneuvered her out of the house for the August weekend, never called, never telephoned—and no one else seems to know anything about him. The young go around in tribes these days, but not this couple. He didn't come on the demos, didn't join the gang wherever it was meeting, it was just Sugar he was interested in, and it wasn't little Dan Cupid, because look at the way he ditched her when it suited his book."

"Why did he ditch her?"

"Because she'd served his purpose. Leastways, he found someone who'd serve it better. Leastways, that's how I read the situation. Say he wanted to know if this house was worth burgling. He wasn't a big operator, didn't carry a gun—no evidence of rough stuff in the other cases, and the fuzz are inclined to link him up with them—something nice and easy, and of course, it's always better if you can get a bit of inside info. I daresay Sugar chatted as much as the next lass, but what he wants is to find out how he can get in, what burglar alarms there are, who's on the premises. And—suddenly he switches his interest, he's seen drinking with Mrs. Brown, the house-keeper. From all accounts, she ain't the sort to attract a young man, so where's the catch?"

There was a clamor of voices at the gate and Roy came romping in. "Saw your trademark," he told Crook. "The kids say you've come to save Jan from a fate worse than death."

"From my point of view," said Crook, "there's nothing worse than death. But if you mean am I worried about Sugar, yes, I am."

"Did you know Mrs. Brown was using an accommodation address for her letters?" Kay asked her husband.

"I didn't know she ever had any. Perhaps that's why."

"Letters that were called for by a young man."

"I don't believe it. Unless"—his face darkened—"you mean he had some hold over her?"

"Seems like that."

"What on earth could he know?"

"She'd been in some trouble with the fuzz in the North. Shoplifting. Oh yes, I've got it all in black and white. That's why she lost her job, not because the lady went to California. Three months she got."

"You mean she'd been in prison?" Kay sounded appalled.

"And this chap must have known it. A bit of a bonanza for him to come face to face with her after—what?—six years. Must have been in Harrogate at the time and recognized her. I'd say she's not the sort that changes much. Shock for her, too. She's kept it dark all this time. Now he reckons he'd got her on toast. Get Sugar off the premises at a time when the family's going to be away and Bob's your uncle."

"You don't mind chancing your arm, do you?" suggested Roy.

"We know she was expecting a visitor, we know the visitor's fancy drink was whiskey. She never touched the stuff herself."

"I don't see it," said Roy bluntly. "If she'd met him in the hall and cracked him over the head with a bottle, that I could credit. But to knuckle under to a young thug and let him blackmail her into letting him into the house . . . Anyway, if they were such buddies, why does he have to strangle her?"

"I doubt if that was any part of the original plot," Crook said.

"It still doesn't make sense, taking a chance like that—and for what? A bit of shoplifting. That's the one crime that's practically respectable nowadays. Natural protest of the under-valued in an aggressive world. Get the right doctor and you're a victim of society. What did she take, anyway?"

Crook told him.

"And that's the lot?"

"It's quite enough," said Kay. "She went to prison, after all."

"Had the wrong lawyer," said Roy. "Why, you're always reading in the papers about ladies of title having a blackout and helping themselves. What harm could this young chap have done her?"

"He could have told me."

"That's what she should have done. After all, she'd been here six years. Don't tell me you'd have given her the push, not with us living in the middle of nowhere and you liking house-work about as much as a rabbit likes a snake. It's not like forging a check or ill-treating a child. You ask Crook."

"She'd do a lot to prevent it reaching the bingo crowd," Kay insisted.

"So why didn't she do something? She just knuckled under, and got herself killed in doing it. That can't have been part of her plan."

"Well, of course it wasn't," agreed Crook. "She only had to go to the police; only, I daresay she'd seen enough of them for one lifetime. She might have stopped to wonder who was going to listen to a young shaver like that, but from all accounts she was the independent kind. She wouldn't hand over the family treasures meek as a lamb. I've been wondering about that all along, and your little girl put the ace right into my hand."

"Dawn did?" Kay sounded incredulous.

"She said Mrs. Brown once had sleeping tablets."

"That was a long time ago."

"They don't go off, though. Tell me something. What happened to the dear departed's bits and pieces?"

"She didn't have many. What there are, are cluttering up my room waiting for them to be claimed, I suppose. It doesn't seem to have occurred to anyone I might want the room for someone else. I thought they advertised if no next-of-kin came forward."

"And they haven't been touched?"

"The police went through them, that's all. They didn't learn much."

"Maybe they didn't learn as much as they might. Maybe the solution to the mystery lies there."

Kay looked horrified. "You mean you want to turn over my late housekeeper's possessions?"

"With you for witness," urged Crook. "Of course, we can call in the fuzz if you insist, but they won't be too pleased."

"I don't know what you're driving at," Kay said.

Roy chimed in, "I must say, Crook, you don't mind chancing your arm. What else have you got up your sleeve?"

"I'm just wondering why it is that a lady who don't approve

of aspirin should take one in full view, with comments, on the night of her death."

"Because she had a headache."

"So why not retire to the Ladies and have it nice and private? But no, she has to tell everyone. And if she had a headache, why go to the bingo at all? She could just say she didn't like to leave the house. And if she had such a purler, what was she doing buying whiskey?"

"Which she didn't open."

"Not her fault, I daresay. Visitor came too soon, perhaps. It 'ud astonish you how many crimes depend on split-second timing. A minute or two less at the Pumpkin and she might have brought it off."

Coral came hurrying in to say Jan had just turned the corner, and Crook knew an odd stab of relief. His hunches were sometimes pretty extravagant ones, but he didn't want his protégée to miss the bus, as Mrs. Brown clearly had.

"It's a relief, isn't it?" said Coral in a grown-up voice. "It would be dreadful if anything happened to Jan."

A new thought struck Kay. "How did you know about Mrs. Brown's pillbox?"

Coral looked surprised. "We saw it on her dressing table."

"What were you doing in her room?"

"She used to let us polish her silver brush and comb that her mother gave her. You never let us do yours, Mummy. Is it because Daddy gave it you? Why didn't Mr. Brown give her hers?"

"Did you ask her?" asked Crook.

"She never talked about Mr. Brown. She never even had a photograph of him."

Dawn came in, followed by Jan. "The shops were so full. Mr. Crook, you came to see me?"

"Just to make sure you were O.K. And don't do any more shopping excursions on your own. Take the little girls with you. They're better than a brigade of Guards."

"I was on my bicycle," said Jan, not very graciously.

"People fall off their bicycles, as you should know."

"We'll keep an eye on her," promised Dawn.

"How about keeping an eye on the lunch?" suggested Kay.

The three flashed off in the direction of the kitchen and the other three went upstairs, Kay still obviously uneasy.

"I don't know if we should be doing this," she said.

"Assisting the police in their inquiries," Crook encouraged her. "It's not like it was proof, it's only a hunch. If anything comes of it, then we can think again."

The dead housekeeper's room was as cold as a tombstone and almost as barren. Mrs. Brown's few possessions—her toiletries, her bag, the yellowed photograph—had been stored in a dresser drawer. The top of the dresser was bare.

Crook snapped open the bag and tipped it up. A small octagonal pillbox in green and gold came sliding into his hand.

"Still in the bag," he pointed out. "Unless you . . ." He glanced at Kay.

"It's precisely as she left it—or rather, as the police left it."

Crook pressed the catch and the lid flew up. The box was filled with small white tablets.

"Aspirin," commented Kay scornfully. "Just as she said."

"Oh, I don't doubt the pill she took at the bingo was aspirin," Crook concurred. "It's the others. Look." He shook some of the tablets out. "They look the same to the casual eye, but some are a bit thicker. I don't think they're all aspirin, but we shall soon know."

"You mean . . . ?"

"I mean I thought of gettin' a professional opinion. Oh, come, where's the harm in that? None of them was used to commit a crime. But if it turns out they're all innocuous, we can forget about them. If they ain't, the sooner we know the facts the better. Remember, so long as the case remains open you're liable to have the fuzz knockin' on your door day or night.

Solutions are what the police are after and they'll stop at nothing to get them."

"I'm still not sure you should take the pills," said Kay uncertainly.

"What do you want to do, my love?" Roy asked. "We shall look a proper lot of Charleys if they all turn out to be harmless."

"In any case, whatever the lady's intentions, they had nothing to do with any crime," Crook reminded her.

"How can you be so sure?"

"The whiskey bottle wasn't opened. I'd say she was en route for the kitchen when she was stopped by the bell. Not that that had to make any difference to her plans. 'Come along in. This way. My sitting room's down beyond the kitchen. Now make yourself at home, and I'll get something for us to drink.' He don't sound the kind that expects to make himself useful. So—crumble the tablets, pour out the whiskey, good and strong—he always took a double, remember . . .'"

"There's one thing you seem to have overlooked," observed Kay. "How was she going to explain his presence in her sitting room? I've always heard it wasn't so difficult to commit murder, it's disposing of the corpse. Or do you suggest she was going to put him in the boot cupboard?"

"He wasn't going to be found on the premises," said Crook patiently. "But a chap who's taken a powerful dose of barbiturates—that's where your daughter came in, telling me Mrs. B. had once had sleeping tablets—ain't going to be too lively at the wheel of a car, driving on a wet road with plenty of turns in it. Run up a lamppost or off a cliff as easy as winking. He wasn't going to die of poison—but if she had her way, he was goin' to die."

"You're very glib with your theories, Mr. Crook, but they're not proof."

"That's why we ain't taking them to the police. It's beside the point really what these tablets are, seeing they were never

176

used. But it fills in a gap in the Mrs. Brown story. I wouldn't like to think she gave in as easy as that."

"What if he'd got home safely, after all? Had you thought?"

"No harm done. He couldn't go round broadcasting where he'd been or bring any accusations against her. Mightn't even suspect what she'd been up to, and anyway, there was no proof, she'd see to that. She couldn't try the same trick twice, and if anyone had come looking for the little box at the weekend, aspirins is all it would have held."

"Might even have made him a present of the rest of the whiskey bottle, so there'd be no proof it was ever on her premises," capped Roy.

"If he had been found, he either wouldn't or couldn't talk," continued Crook. "Proves one thing, though. She didn't expect him to have a mate. Must have realized then she was for the high jump, he couldn't be certain she wouldn't spill the beans. Shoplifting's a little thing compared with losing your treasures —the snuffboxes were quite something, I understand."

"They were unique," snapped Kay. "And the police haven't a notion where they are."

"Probably have quite a lot of notions, but they can't move. My guess is that collection went out of England on a night flight. Much too hot to hold here, and you can't melt snuffboxes down. Put it whichever way you like, she died defending your property."

"Would you say that?" asked Roy dubiously. "It looks to me more as if she was fighting for her own reputation."

"And a lot of good that did her," commented Crook. He patted the pocket where he'd put the little pillbox. "Say good-bye to your daughters for me, and remember what I said about Sugar. Keep an eye out for her and if anything unusual turns up, however small, get in touch. I feel we aren't at the end of this story yet."

·   ·   ·

"Very interesting, Mr. Crook," said the chemist to whom he took the box of pills. "It's like you said. There's two different sorts here. One lot's plain aspirin, lots of ladies carry them around, especially in towns where they'd naturally need them more. The other's a barbiturate, pretty strong, she'd only get that on a doctor's certificate, and most doctors wouldn't just give it to a casual patient. A few of those 'ud send a chap off pretty quick, though they wouldn't do him lasting harm, provided he wasn't walking along the Queen's Highway or some place where the traffic could get at him."

"Or climbing a roof. It's all right, Mr. Porter. I don't think any of these were used. I just wanted to know."

Mr. Porter was looking puzzled. "You say the lady carried these in her bag?"

"Well, not most of the time. Most of the time she kept them on the dressing table."

"It's to be hoped out of the way of children. They could do a child a lot of harm, and they don't think, children don't. Curious as cows that'll come right across a field to take a snuff at you."

"They were in the box in her bag at the time they were found," amended Crook.

"Curious," said Mr. Porter, "very curious."

Crook looked at him inquiringly.

"Even if she was going away for a night, she wouldn't need above one or two. And if she was going for a week, she'd not be carrying them in her bag."

"You never can tell with dames," said Mr. Crook. "Well, thanks a million, and stop looking as though you were judging the world on the Last Day. I promise you none of them was used for an improper purpose. The lady was carrying them to be on the safe side. And as it happened, she found she didn't need them, after all."

Wouldn't like his job, Mr. Porter reflected as the Superb drove away. Nothing what it appears to be. Might as well be a human corkscrew.

178

He returned lovingly to his counter, where he knew the value and the power of everything. Don't know how he ever sleeps of a night, he thought.

Mr. Porter turned to greet a new customer who wanted brushless shaving cream and toothpaste, the sort of sensible straightforward things we all want. He hoped that whatever Mr. Crook was up to, he'd leave his, Mr. Porter's, name out of it.

Twelve

Mrs. Gale's death excited no speculation, even locally. After all, it happens every day of the week. There are crashes on the M.1., the M.4., all the motorways. Tragic headlines are common reading.

CARS COLLIDE—FIVE DEAD
TRAFFIC PILE-UP, 4 Dead, 12 Injured
PETROL LORRY OVERTURNS IN MAIN STREET
DRIVER KILLED

It's a shame, a pity, someone must be to blame, but it's someone else's responsibility to pass judgment. So an elderly nondescript driving a tinpot car and crashing a dirty great lorry with fatal results isn't going to attract a lot of attention.

The coroner's jury brought in a verdict of death by misadventure, with a rider as to the inadvisability of outsized lorries using side roads, and that, so to speak, was the end of Priscilla Gale. Like the late Mrs. Brown, she appeared to have neither kith nor kin; odder still, she had no local connections, most people couldn't have told you the address of the place where she slept or even what the initial P stood for. Her table at the Fleece and Lamb would be empty, but someone else would come along, they'd soon forget her. After the funeral a board appeared outside the shop offering these commodious premises on lease, but it was some time before anyone took up the challenge. The premises might have suited Mrs. Gale, but they weren't everybody's cup of tea. The room behind the shop was cramped and dark—Mrs. Gale had used it mainly for keeping stock in—there was indoor sanitation but no bath . . .

"These are not being offered as residential premises," the agent pointed out acidly. "And they would amply repay some initial outlay."

The first people to consider the place seriously was a married couple called Henson. They agreed together that it had possibilities, though it needed money spent on it for their purpose. They never considered carrying on where Mrs. Gale had left off, but having regard to the rather solitary aspect of the place and the fact that there was a fair number of dwelling houses in the neighborhood, they thought they might open a fish-and-chips shop. They weren't without experience, and they wouldn't come into competition with the Fleece and Lamb, who only did sandwiches and no evening meals at all. This being the country and not a great seething town, their plans were speedily approved and a license granted. The contents of the house were offered with the lease, but the furniture was minimal—an aged couch, a chair, a table, some shelves, an old electric fire. The only thing worth considering, said busy, managing Mrs. Henson, was a nice little chest of drawers. There were a few things in it—writing paper, a bottle of ink, some accounts—nothing of any note, but when she was fitting fresh paper to the shelves Mrs. Henson found a sealed letter under the original lining, addressed in printed characters to Mrs. F. Brown at the Swallows Nest address.

"I suppose she kept the letters here that were waiting to be called for," Mrs. Henson told her husband. A few letters, about four, had been found by the police and taken to the local station, where presumably they'd wait till the Day of Judgment.

"Must have slipped under the paper," agreed Mr. Henson cheerfully.

"It was more as though it had been put there," said Mrs. Henson.

"Well, no one's come for it," her husband reminded her. "Put it in the bucket, unless you'd prefer to take it to the police."

"When people use accommodation addresses, it's usually because their business is private," said Mrs. Henson slowly. "This Mrs. Brown's business is her own affair."

In any case, you don't want to start a new business with the police hanging around; people do jump to some very odd conclusions, and the police are right enough in their own place, which isn't your house. They had great hopes for this new enterprise. In the spring and summer there'd be a steady trade from cars and motorbikes. The shop wouldn't be too far from the houses for mothers to send their kids along or kids to spend their own pocket money on chips—a lot of your profit depended on chips, you couldn't afford to let them grow soggy. Hot, brown and succulent, that's what people expected, and they'd depend on the locals, which included anyone within an easy bike ride, for the winter trade. Anyway, a new enterprise always succeeds at first, and it's up to the proprietors to keep up the standard. They'd roused quite a lot of interest already. The locals said it must be costing them a pretty penny, what with paint and new counters and the big frying machines. They were all prepared to give the place a go. But they wouldn't like it so much if they found the police loitering on the doorstep.

"Best thing would be to return it to whoever sent it," discovered Mrs. Henson. She couldn't steam the envelope open because it had been sealed with cellophane tape. She could tell from the feel of it there was nothing but a sheet of paper inside. No notes, f'rinstance. She'd heard some of the gossip about the dead woman's private postal service, but she wasn't curious, she'd her own affairs to stick to, thanks, and other people could stick to theirs.

The name Mrs. F. Brown didn't mean a thing to her. She came from a different county, and it wasn't as if it had been a sensational affair, and the papers played it down in a way that would have been unthinkable a generation ago. It wasn't even as if it was the sort of name that would stick in your memory. No one had been arrested, there hadn't even been a picture in the national press.

"It's funny," she brooded to her helpmeet. "Look at the postmark. She'd kept it quite a while. Funny it wasn't called for."

"Perhaps she got herself killed before she had a chance of passing it on."

Beattie Henson considered. "It could be important to Mrs. Brown."

"If it was important, she'd have made inquiries for it."

"Do you think I should return it to sender?"

"Oh, do what you like," said Sidney Henson, who'd had enough of the subject. "In a lot of countries you put your name and address on the back of the envelope. That would have saved us a lot of trouble."

"Whoever wrote it may be worrying because he or she hasn't had a reply."

"I'm going along to see those chaps about the kitchen fitments," said Mr. Henson. "One of us has to get things done."

When he had departed Mrs. Henson got a knife and slit the envelope. As she had suspected, there was only a single sheet of paper inside. But if her intention had been to return it to the writer, she was foiled by the fact that the paper contained no signature. In printed letters the message ran: THIS TIME THE PRICE IS FORTY POUNDS.

"I told you to chuck it away," said Sidney. "Now look where you've landed us. One thing, whoever wrote that must have got tired of waiting for his forty quid."

"I wonder who Mrs. Brown was," reflected Beattie.

"Such an unusual name," gibed her husband.

"Do you suppose we ought to tell the police?"

"God give me patience!" groaned Sidney. "If Mrs. Brown wanted her affairs made public, she'd have gone to the police herself. Chuck it away and forget about it."

184

A Nice Little Killing

But Beattie Henson wasn't like that.

While Sidney had been busy chasing around after the workmen and seeing suppliers, Beattie shopped for curtains and linoleum, and she had got into the habit of dropping into the Fleece and Lamb for a snack midday. The little shop was pandemonium, and anyway, it was a good thing to get your face known when you were going to depend on local trade for your living. She and Katie got on a treat; people relied on Katie to know about newcomers, and no one could accuse Beattie of reticence.

She brought patterns to show the barmaid. "Got that at Minson's," she'd say. "I'm the chauffeur in my family. Drive Sidney in, then have a go round the shops, back here for a snack, pick him up of an evening. It's surprising how much there is to do when you're closing down one business and starting another. Mind you, we were doing well, but it was too crowded at the end. You want to be able to breathe, and Sidney got his price easy as easy. It's nice to make a change before you're too old, and I've always liked the country myself."

The day after she opened the letter, she said to Katie, "Who's Mrs. Brown?"

Katie put on a face of mock seriousness. "I seem to have heard that name before."

"Mrs. F. Brown. We found a letter addressed to her in a drawer among Mrs. Gale's things, must have got slipped under the lining sheet. You don't know where we could find her."

Katie's face had altered; all the mock humor had departed. "I could make a good guess," she said. "You really don't know?"

"You said yourself it wasn't an unusual name."

"It's the F. Come to think of it, Mrs. Brown was just the sort to use an accommodation address. A woman of mystery they called her. I remember about the time she was killed . . ."

"Killed?"

"That's right. Some thugs broke in—well, got in, anyway; the talk was she was expecting a friend and they came instead.

Only—the friend never turned up when the police started asking questions. There was quite a talk about it at the time. Mark you, if I worked at Manor House with that snoopy Mrs. Banks, I wouldn't want my letters picked over." She cocked a speculative eye at Beattie. "No idea what was in it, of course."

"You can't go opening other people's letters," said Beattie righteously. "I did wonder about sending it back to the writer if we could find out who that was, but seeing she's dead . . ."

"It's a proper turn-up for the book, isn't it?" said Katie. "And it's no use asking Mrs. Gale, because she's dead, too."

"Nothing to say she'd know what was in it," Beattie suggested. "Envelope was sealed with cellophane."

"She wasn't taking any chances, was she? Coming," she called to some new arrivals who were fidgeting at the further end of the bar.

A new, very young, very eager voice spoke in Beattie's ear. Its owner was a young cub reporter still wet behind the ears, just started on the local *Argus*.

"That's quite a story you've got there," he encouraged. "There was a lot of talk about Mrs. Brown, no one seemed to know anything about her. And now this Mrs. Gale, another woman of impenetrable secrets—the Last of the Lonelyhearts," he improvised.

"Seeing they're both dead, there's no sense stirring up dust," said Beattie sensibly. Whoever had been trying to raise forty pounds from the late Mrs. F. Brown clearly hadn't been lucky." Sidney's right, reflected Sid's wife. Let sleeping dogs lie.

"What did I tell you?" exploded Sidney when she told him that evening. "I said to put the damn thing in the basket. You can't help her, and you surely don't want to help a blackmailer."

"I wonder what she did—to get involved, I mean," reflected Beattie. "Still, it's like you say, Sid, there's no sense carrying it any further, seeing they're both dead, and the blackmailer isn't likely to come forward. Only, I don't see how he can be anything to do with the one that killed her. You don't kill the goose that lays the golden eggs."

"I promise you one thing," said Sidney, who seemed to have the proverbial little black dog on his shoulder that night. "By this time next week half the clientele of the Fleece and Lamb will know Mrs. Brown isn't the only one who got herself murdered. Who is this young chap?"

"Just someone drinking at the bar." Beattie sounded suitably vague.

"So what did you really tell him?"

"It's more what he told me. I didn't know anything. How could I tell him?"

"Who were the chaps who were expected to make bricks without straw? They should have gone to work in Fleet Street, where half the time they don't know what straw looks like."

"This isn't Fleet Street," Beattie reassured him comfortably. "Anyway, we don't even know if it's the same Mrs. Brown. If I used an accommodation address, I wouldn't use my own name. I daresay it's some son got into a bit of trouble and they're keeping it from his dad."

"Funny message to send your mother," Sid grunted.

"Camouflage," said his wife primly. "What did Warren have to say about the fittings? How soon do you think we can open? We ought to be thinking about getting some leaflets done and distributed."

Wifelike, she decoyed him from one problem to another. By the evening's end he'd almost forgotten there was such a person as Mrs. Brown.

All the same, she'd come back into the news. If she didn't make the front page, she headlined in the middle of the local *Argus*.

Crook didn't seem pleased. "Never any sense stirring up the

mud," he said. "This'll put X on his guard. Why don't these chaps have the sense to let sleeping dogs lie?"

The letter had been posted from Buzzard Major three days before Mrs. Brown came by her untimely death and had never been collected. Crook wondered why Mrs. Gale had hung onto it, it was about as harmless as a stick of dynamite. Once the news had broken, you'd have expected her to burn it or shred it up fine; but she could have had her reasons. Letters were sent to her in order to be collected; this one hadn't been. Ergo, the writer knew she had passed the point of no return. Point was, did he know it hadn't been collected. He couldn't very well turn up and put the question point-blank to Mrs. Gale. With Mrs. Brown's name being bandied from lip to lip, he'd want to lie as low as he could. And now the story was oozing out, like water from a cracked pipe. And still, if he had the sense he was born with, he'd continue to lie low. Only, there's a lot in the one about murderers returning to the scene of the crime. It's as though they need that extra assurance that's all going well, they didn't forget anything. And, of course, they want to hear what people are saying. Crook wasn't concerned with the murderer's feelings; he never had time to spare for anyone but his client.

"If Sugar gets any of these mysterious communications, let me know pronto," he said to Roy. "I've told her—naturally—but you know what dames are. All your good sense can be water flowing under the bridge, and I like to think there's someone keeping an eagle eye on her besides your dauntless young."

"That man Crook is a menace," declared Kay. "Since he appointed Dawn and Coral ladies-in-waiting on the *au pair*, they can't talk of anything else."

"I wonder they don't insist on staying away from school to look after her" was Roy's heartless comment. "I daresay they'd learn just as much from her."

Jan took them into the local village school each morning.

Kay had wanted them to chum up with two or three other "daughters of gentlefolk" who lived in the neighborhood and shared a visiting governess, but Roy would have none of it.

"These are the ones they're going to compete with and work with and eventually marry into," he assured his wife, "and unless you want them to be old maids, you'll go with the running tide. Trying to stand in the path of the contemporary educational trend is about as sensible as old King Knute trying to stem the tides. They belong to their generation, and you've no right to try to haul them out of it."

"My mother would turn in her grave to think of her granddaughters at a comprehensive," said Kay, and he thought what a ridiculous expression for a time when practically everyone is cremated. "She and my father made a lot of sacrifices to send me to St. Clements."

"And where did that get you?" demanded Roy. "Right in the heart of the working classes. Well, of course we are. What do you think I do all day if it's not work?" He went off whistling.

P. C. Trubshawe came to call at Swallows Nest in the course of his duty. Beattie thanked heaven Sid was in town.

"I can't tell you anything," she assured him firmly. "I wasn't here at the time. I only know we found this letter, and I wish I'd taken my husband's advice and thrown it away at once, but I did think we might be able to return it to the sender." She was planning what to tell Sid when he came back. Already she'd been long enough in the country to realize she couldn't hope to keep this official visit a secret. Some helpful neighbor was bound to spill the beans.

"Have you the letter now?" Ted Trubshawe asked, but she told him no, she'd destroyed it. From Mrs. Brown's point of view it was out of date.

"It wouldn't have done any good to keep it, even if it does refer to the right Mrs. Brown. It wasn't signed and it had no address, just a plain sheet of paper with printing, and it said the price now was forty pounds."

"Or else?" hinted Ted.

"Nothing about or else. Though I did think it might be blackmail, but it could be something else."

"Didn't tell anyone else?"

"Well, my husband, of course. And he said it was nothing to do with us and to throw it away. But I had this idea we might be able to return it to the writer."

He didn't comment on that. "Anyone else?"

"I told Katie, the barmaid at the Fleece and Lamb, and she told me about this Mrs. Brown at Manor House. But of course, it doesn't have to be the same one. There are lots of women's names beginning with F. besides Felicia. There's Freda and Florence and Fenella and Frances and Fay."

"But they don't live in this manor. It's a pity, really, you threw the letter away if you were going this far. The writing might have helped us."

"Oh no," she said sharply, "the words weren't written, just printed in black ink on a plain bit of paper that could have come from anywhere. And the postmark was Buzzard Major."

"You didn't think to bring it to us before destroying it?"

"If Mrs. Brown had wanted you to know, she'd have come to you herself. I really can't think why she didn't. After all, the police aren't allowed to reveal names, are they? Not when it's blackmail."

"We don't know yet for certain that it was blackmail."

"So why not use her own address?"

"She might have been buying something on the installment plan and have got behind with her payments."

"Wouldn't she have got a headed letter for that?"

"It 'ud depend what she was buying?"

Beattie's eyes widened. "You mean—porn?"

"Or perhaps a share in a race horse not honestly come by.

The possibilities are endless. Blackmail's like a main line station," he added, surprising them both. "The lines go in all directions. It can start when you're still in the nursery. 'Drink up your milk, Harry, or else . . .' "

"But the blackmailer wouldn't come to you, so why does anyone pay?"

"You don't have to be threatened with the police—your husband, perhaps, a child, your employer, anyone concerned. The writer won't be best pleased to know someone else has opened his letter," he added dispassionately.

"But I don't know who it was," protested Beattie. "I couldn't do anyone any harm. Come to that, Mrs. Gale mightn't have liked it known what sort of correspondence passed through her hands. Oh!" She drew a deep breath. "In a minute you're going to tell me her death wasn't an accident, either."

"Crowner's Court brought in a verdict of Death by Misadventure," said Ted stubbornly. "Can't go against that. Anyway, according to the driver, who survived, there was no one else on the road."

Another thought struck her. "You don't think my husband and I are in any danger?"

"Not if you don't know anything and the letter's destroyed. Of course, he may not know that."

"He may be a maniac writing anonymous letters all over the place," cried Beattie. "This may only be one of a crowd."

"Perhaps," agreed Trubshawe, but he didn't sound reassuring. In his opinion villains never knew where to stop.

Anonymous letters were certainly in the news. The next one was addressed to Jan and sent to the Manor House. Crook, returning from a romp around town, found his telephone ringing, and Roy Banks's voice at the other end.

"Your hunch paid off," he said. "Letter came this morning,

same as all the others, I daresay. Nice neat print on a cheap envelope, nice succinct message—keep your nose clean, though he doesn't put it so neatly on the enclosure."

"Who got it?" asked Crook. As if he didn't know.

"Came for Jan."

"And she brought it to you?"

"I took it to her. 'Your secret adversary's on the warpath,' I told her. 'How about calling in Mr. Crook?' Funny thing, she doesn't take it very seriously. Look, I'm not so far from your office at this moment—I commute, you know—say the word and I could be round in a brace of shakes."

"Be my guest," offered Crook.

A few minutes later he heard feet on the stairs. He himself came up like the proverbial policeman, thump, thump, but this chap came flying up two steps at a time.

The letter was like dozens of others Crook had seen. It wasn't the work of an illiterate person, but it showed no particular originality. Paper, pen, envelope were all what you might expect. The wording ran: KEEP AWAY FROM THE POLICE. THEY COULD BE DANGEROUS.

"Is this the first Jan's had?" Crook wondered.

"Unless she's sent one to you."

"She hasn't."

"Mind you, she doesn't seem to take it very seriously. 'Why should I go to the police?' she says. 'What good could they do me?' "

"Camouflage," said Mr. Crook modestly. "For police, read Arthur Crook. It may not occur to anyone you'd act as a go-between, so we might still have a little time."

"You really do think she's in danger," said Roy.

"Same like St. Paul, we stand in jeopardy every hour, only some of us more than others."

Crook didn't very often find himself thinking along official lines, but he would have agreed with P.C. Trubshawe that villains seldom know when to call it a day.

"According to her, she doesn't know anything that could make her a danger to anyone. Does she, Crook?"

"Depends how much the lady's confided in me. You have to remember she did see a car driving fast away from the Manor House the night Mrs. Brown bought hers. Oh, she says she wouldn't recognize it or the driver, and so far as the driver's concerned, I daresay that's true, but a car's different. It was a long car, she said, dark—she might believe she saw it and passed on the information. Mind you, she could be wrong forty-nine times out of fifty, but your villain banks on the fiftieth chance. And considering their records, these chaps have very sensitive consciences, always wondering if they're going to be found out and trying to take security measures. And so they put themselves right back in the limelight, which is what X is doing right now. 'Tain't as though she's the only source of danger either. My old mum, who had a code of conduct that 'ud have satisfied the Archangel Gabriel, used to quote 'Oh, what a tangled web we weave, When first we practise to deceive.' "

"I'm not with you," acknowledged Roy frankly. "Who or what is the other source of danger?"

"The chap who knows he was concerned in Mrs. Brown's demise; his hands may be tied, but it's never possible to be certain which way the cat will jump. And there's a thing called Queen's Evidence."

"You mean his partner in crime? I thought you took it for granted he was out of the country."

"If he's got any sense he'll put himself somewhere where he can't be extradited till the tumult and the shouting have died down, but that's not the one I had in mind. There's a third party to all these crimes, the chap who disposes of your ill-gotten gains."

"In a word, the fence."

"You know all the fancy names," Crook congratulated him. "Yes, the fence. Now, I wouldn't say as a class they set a high moral standard, but most of them do draw the line at murder.

Just think what this particular fence must have felt when he read about Mrs. B.'s hurried departure from the scene, and he realized he'd been melting down and otherwise disposing of all those silver cups and pots which carried your identity."

Roy considered. "The news didn't break till about Sunday, did it? Too late for him to try and get out. Still, aren't his hands tied?"

"If he's going to be implicated in a murder, he's going to do all he can to help the fuzz. And they'll believe him. No one wants stuff from a house where someone's been knocked off. I don't say they'll pick him up on this case, but they could get him later on and ends might tie up. X has got to mind his p's and q's so far as that chap's concerned. The sensible thing will be to stay away from him in future transactions, but then he's got to find a new fence, and it's wonderful how the whispers go round. Oh, I don't say X will try to touch him, but the fewer people have even an inkling of your secret, the safer for you, and if X hadn't got ants in his pants about Sugar just possibly bein' able to put a name to him if they should come face to face . . ."

"Is it likely?" interrupted Roy.

"It wasn't specially likely that X should run up against Mrs. Brown, but we're pretty sure that's what must have happened. After six years she must have thought she was safe. Like I was saying, if he hadn't got the wind up he wouldn't have sent Sugar this card. So far as she's concerned, Mrs. Brown belongs to the past, let her stay there. All the same, Sugar ain't showing much nous if she proposed to shrug this sort of thing off. Playing with wolves is always a mug's game, however nice and tame you're persuaded the wolf is. Even if you chain him up he can sometimes break out. It's like playing with mosquitoes," he added, cheerfully changing his metaphor. They may not look much, but they can give you malarial fever—or could when I was a boy," he added cautiously.

"You're not suggesting your fence could be the next on the list?" Roy sounded a bit derisive.

Crook forgave him; he (Crook) had forgotten more about crime than this pleasant chap was ever likely to know. "My fence, as you call him, can break his neck four times a day between now and Christmas, and I should koko," he said. "But like you pointed out, he's got something to bargain with. What's Sugar going to do about this card?

"That's a compliment to you, really," put in Roy unexpectedly. "She thinks of you as the parfit gentil knight [Crook looked as if he were about to vomit] who, representing right, always wins in the end. Anyway, what can she do? She's told you as much as she knows; she's not likely to have a sudden divine revelation, naming the criminal."

"She's there, that's her mistake. Or rather, was her mistake. She was there on the night Mrs. Brown copped, and someone had arranged she shouldn't be there, leaving him a clear field. And now—where is she now?"

"You mean as of this minute? At a guess, I'd say toiling in the kitchen, being hampered by my delightful children. But if you're really feeling anxious, I can always ring through."

"Did she know you were going to see me today?"

"Well, I didn't know myself," Roy pointed out reasonably. "And even though you've got the card, it's hard to see what you can do about it. However, if it'll ease your mind— Use your phone?"

"Why not?"

Kay's voice came through as clearly as though she were speaking from the next room. "Good heavens, Roy. What is it now? This telephone's never quiet for a minute. If it isn't me, it's Jan."

"You mean she's just had a call? Where is she?"

A faintly derisive note crept into Kay's voice. "What an old fussbudget you are. She's always having calls, you should know. If we didn't need a phone for ourselves, we should have to install it for her benefit."

"Where is she now?"

"She's gone out. Roy, the girl's of age, I can't keep her chained to the leg of the kitchen table."

"Did the children go with her?"

"She must have a little time to herself. Anyway, I don't know what you're fussing about. She's gone to meet your precious Mr. Crook. From your point of view, she's safer than if she had the whole C.I.D. behind her."

"Is that what she told you?"

"That she was meeting Crook? Certainly. There's been a development and he's driving down—some man rang up from London. Roy! Roy, why don't you say something? What's the matter?"

"Simply that I'm phoning you from Crook's office and Crook is sitting on the other side of the desk, and no one—but no one—has rung Jan on his behalf to say he's coming down."

For once she was silenced.

Crook reached over and took the instrument out of Roy's hand. "Mrs. Banks, how long ago did Jan go out?"

"About ten minutes, I should think."

"Did she say where she was going?"

"To meet you."

"Did she say where?"

"I didn't ask. I supposed it would be at that hotel where you stayed before."

"If I was going to be so close, I wouldn't need to get a chap to put a trunk call through from London, and she wouldn't have needed to fly off like a bat out of hell." He thought an instant. "Is Lady Molly there?"

"Lady . . . ? Oh, you mean Dawn. Why should she know more than anyone else?"

"If Jan told anyone—and I bet her informant played it very sleuthlike—it's most likely to be one of your kids. But I daresay he was cunning enough to tell her to keep the whole thing under her own hat."

196

"In any case, the children went off to the village when they found Jan was going out. They've got a new hobby, they sit up a tree half the day and identify birds. They wanted a pad and some crayons so that Coral can sketch them while Dawn dictates a description. Dawn explained to me a tree's like a watchtower, you can see for miles. Mr. Crook, you don't think . . ."

"Be seeing you," said Crook, and put the receiver down.

He shouted for Bill to put him in the picture. "Get on to that perambulating policeman," he said. "Tell 'em all to keep their eyes skinned. He'll be worth ten of any of the townees from Buzzard Major. Girl's on a bicycle, so it won't be close at hand or she'd have taken the kids with her—this must be half-term or holiday time or something," he added vaguely, "seeing their mother said they'd probably be up a tree. So she's going too far for the kids to walk, and they haven't got bikes. Any special rendezvous in the neighborhood where a couple mightn't be interrupted?" he added to Roy.

"Derelict huts in the woods—that sort of thing? I daresay. But only a local would know about them."

"We've thought all along it was a local," Crook pointed out. "If this ties up with Mrs. Brown—and if it don't, what's it in aid of?—it has to be someone who knew the ways of the household. Why didn't your wife find out where they were going to meet?"

"Probably didn't think it was her business. She regards you rather like the Wizard of Oz, someone outside the normal run of humanity."

"Coming?" asked Crook, making no comment on that.

"Going to Buzzard Minor?"

"What do you think? Mind you, we've lost a lot of time, but X won't know we're on the trail. Maybe told the girl to keep her lip buttoned. 'We don't want any publicity, do we?' "

His voice screeched to a hideous falsetto, and then he was bolting down the stairs, with Roy in his wake. He still clung to the hope that Jan would have told one of the children where she was going, and pretty soon he'd stop the car and try to get through on a pay phone. It was the one contingency he hadn't anticipated, and from his point of view, so much wasted effort—if the girl had known anything, she'd have come into the open before now, nothing of the shrinking violet about her.

Thirteen

In Buzzard Minor, Dawn and Coral surveyed one another dolefully.

"Mr. Crook did say we weren't to let her out of our sight," Dawn observed.

"But she's going to meet Mr. Crook, she said so," her sister reminded her hopefully.

"They may try and stop her before she gets there."

"Did she say where she was going?"

"She said she couldn't say, because she was told not to."

"Why should Mr. Crook not want us to know?"

"Perhaps he wanted it to be a secret."

"We can keep secrets."

"Perhaps he thought Mother would ask a lot of questions, and you can't tell your mother you don't know."

Dawn had a flash of inspiration. "Suppose it wasn't Mr. Crook at all?"

"Oh, it wasn't. Don't you remember? Whoever it was said Mr. Crook was on his way, something had developed—Daddy was talking to her this morning. They had a letter."

Dawn's eyes widened. "A threatening letter?"

"She didn't show it to us."

"Perhaps she rang up Mr. Crook."

"And he said he'd come down, but she wasn't to tell anyone."

"I don't see why she couldn't tell us. He said we were as good as the Horse Guards or something."

"Did you see which way she went?"

Dawn pointed. "She went thataways. If Mother would let us have bicycles, we could have followed."

"She wasn't going into Buzzard Major, then, because that road doesn't go that way."

"It goes to Waterlow Cross, at least that's where the bus stops."

"But she didn't go by bus."

"We could go by bus," discovered Dawn. "The bus goes faster than a bicycle. Then if we saw her we could keep her in sight and find out where she was going. Yes, I know the bus goes faster, but it stops and waits for people. I remember Jan saying if you were in a hurry it was ackshully quicker to take your bike, what with shortcuts that a bus can't take." She stopped abruptly.

Coral took her point. "If Jan was going to Waterlow Cross, she'd take the shortcut through the woods."

"But she'd have to come out on the road again," argued Dawn. "And Mr. Crook did say . . ."

("I wish you paid half as much attention to me as you do to your precious Mr. Crook," Kay had been heard to mutter. "Sometimes I think you need hearing aids when I'm talking to you.")

"What do you suppose has happened? He usually just comes straight down, doesn't he?"

"Perhaps," said Dawn, "he's coming by train."

"But Mr. Crook always comes by car."

"P'raps he's afraid of being followed."

"Or perhaps the car has broken down and he had to get someone else to ring up in case he missed his train."

"I don't think Mr. Crook's car would dare break down."

"Then perhaps someone's slashed the tires. Or perhaps he

thinks a platform is safer than a secret rendezvous. Dawn, how much money have you?"

"I was going to buy a new sketch pad for our bird-watching and you were going to buy colored crayons so we could get an impression down right away . . ."

"So we'd have enough for the bus. What time does it go?"

"I'm not sure," confessed Dawn, "but it doesn't really matter, because Daddy says it never keeps to its timetable. Come on. We can tell Mummy we're going to the village. So we are—Waterlow Cross village."

Kay met them on the stairs. "Where are you off to now?"

"We're going to the village. As we haven't got to look after Jan for once . . . Mummy, do you think Daddy would let us borrow that bird book of his for bird-watching?"

"If you mean the one that cost four guineas, I should say no," returned Kay heartlessly. "Bird droppings all over the cover . . ."

"We could put on a paper cover. Perhaps Daddy would give me a pair of field glasses next birthday."

"Have you any idea what field glasses cost?"

"Not if they're Japanese."

"That's something else you'll be able to ask him. Don't be gone too long. With Jan off to meet Mr. Crook, I could do with a hand at setting the table for lunch."

"If Jan isn't here, who's going to cook the lunch?"

"A very good question," said their mother. "I wonder if Jan's thought of it."

"Perhaps she'll bring us back some fish and chips . . ."

"I don't know what we have to have all the mystery about," grumbled Kay. "He could have told her to meet him for lunch and she could have left things ready before she went."

"Perhaps," said Dawn solemnly, "it's a matter of life and death."

"What nonsense has she been talking to you?" demanded Kay. "There's more to life than just cops and robbers."

"Like doing your lessons and putting your books away. Yes, and, Mummy, we must go now, in case the shop shuts or anything."

Kay opened her mouth to dispose of that one, when the telephone began to ring.

"Come on," said Dawn, clutching her sister's arm, and they ran out the back way through the garden and over the bit of common to the place where it joined up with what Buzzard Minor liked to think of as its main road.

At about the same moment Kay was saying, "Not Mr. Crook! Then who on earth . . . ? Is this somebody's idea of a vile practical joke?"

"Not much of a joke to Jan," Roy told her. "Mr. Crook's getting word through to Trubshawe, anyone who sees her will pass him the word, he'll be in touch— You best stay in in case there's any news, and when the kids get back, keep them in, too."

Kay would have asked more questions, but he cut her off. Crook was snatching up his teddy bear outfit and preparing to depart, and Roy meant to go with him. Kay reluctantly put down the telephone, thinking, This is what comes of having a foreigner about the place. We never had any trouble before she came, and now—Mrs. Brown murdered and anonymous letters (though she didn't know about this morning's yet) and death. And now, Jan gets a mysterious telephone call from an anonymous correspondent and is decoyed away heaven knew where. She even began to wonder if the children were safe in the village. She'd ring up Tempest's in a few minutes—the children bought all their stationery there—and leave a message that they were to come right back. It was terrible feeling so solitary, and it was clear Roy was going to cling to his precious Mr. Crook. Nobody was giving her a thought. She tried to think of anyone she could ring up, just for company, but there wasn't anyone— not anyone at all.

And when at last she did ring Tempest's, they hadn't been seen there that morning.

The children had been walking for some time when they heard the roar of the bus turning the corner, and they stopped and waved lustily.

"Where's the young lady?" asked the conductor as they bounced aboard.

"She's had to go on to meet a friend," explained Dawn, "and we're trying to catch her up. She's forgotten something."

And she waved the workbag she had thought to bring with her. The children settled down by a window and stared through the glass as though they would conjure up through sheer will power the figure of Jan on her bicycle.

They hadn't overtaken her when the first shotcut ran off the main road.

"She does go so fast," Coral complained.

Dawn turned to one of the passengers. "Do you know what time the train from London gets in?"

"At Waterlow Cross?"

"Yes."

"You want to watch out," said the conductor humorously. "There's going to be a rare crowd there today. Why they had to pick market day to open the new library . . . "VIP and all."

"All this fuss about books," sniffed an enormous country-woman laden with baskets. "Much better open a new crèche for the kiddies. I ask you, where does it get you, all this book reading? If you want diversion, there's the telly. Books just put ideas into people's minds."

"My father has a whole wall covered with bookshelves," announced Dawn. "He thinks they're better than the telly."

The fat woman sniffed; the rest of the company smiled. They all knew who the children were, and those in the know had been intrigued by the vision of the incomparable Mr. Crook and his British-Museum-type car. He (meaning Roy) was all right, give the time of day to a worm if he happened to meet one, but she was a stranger and always would be. She'd picked up a little bit of kudos when Mrs. Brown got herself murdered—well, you don't get a capital crime in your neighborhood every day of the week, but, come to recall, they'd been two of a kind, both thinking themselves better than common clay.

"Due in at twelve-four," said the conductor, reverting to the original question. Like so many of his kind, he was a walking encyclopedia of local information.

"Likely be late," sniffed the fat woman.

"Mr. Crook won't like that," said Coral.

A kindlier woman leaned forward to say, "That the friend you're expecting?"

"We weren't expecting him, but he sent a message and Jan went off in such a hurry. He calls us his partners," she added.

That set up a good-natured laugh; as was usual in the neighborhood, the whole busload joined in the conversation.

"Take care you don't miss him in the crush," said the conductor, and someone laughed heartily and said, "You have to be joking."

"Red carpet and all," said someone else. "Lunch at the Swan, no expense spared. Better if they had a stand-up buffet and gave the rest to Help the Aged."

It was obvious that they had got away from Mr. Crook and were back on the VIP from London.

Coral whispered to her sister, "Suppose she didn't go to the station, after all."

"She'll be all right with Mr. Crook," said Dawn reassuringly.

"I thought we would have seen her by now."

"This bus is slow," agreed Dawn. "It stops so often."

"It stopped for us," Coral reminded her.

A minute or so later they turned a corner and there—*mira-bile dictu!*—in the distance they saw a cycling figure. They had no doubt whose it was. This was one of those stretches of thoroughfare where the rolling English drunkard had been more sober than usual, and the road ran clear ahead for a considerable distance. The children relaxed.

"We said she'd be coming to the station."

The conductor appeared suddenly at their side. "Does the young lady know you're following her?"

Dawn swung the bag again. "She'll be glad when she sees us."

One of the passengers, one of those managing women who know all the answers before the questions are put, leaned across the aisle to say, "Does your mother know you're out without her? You're too young to be on your own in the sort of crowd there'll be at Waterlow Cross today, with this pop singer person coming down."

"We shall be quite all right," Dawn assured her, exchanging a glance with her sister. They'd no notion who the pop singer was. The speaker couldn't mean Mr. Crook, no one could confuse him with a pop singer.

The bus stopped again and an old lady was helped on. She was erect and spare but she carried a rubber-tipped stick. All the bus knew her, old Miss Peachum, one-time schoolmarm. The conductor's dad had been in her form once. A real tartar, he said.

"Station, miss?"

She nodded. "I have a fancy to see Cyril Ponsonby after all these years. Apparently he has made quite a name for himself after all these years."

"Ponsonby?" The bus looked politely puzzled.

"I believe he calls himself some fancy name now, but he was born Cyril Ponsonby—a great disappointment to his father when he took up with this pop music. A nice snug little corn chandler's business Harry Ponsonby had, all ready for his son to step into, but no, young Cyril had to get away to London and join what's called a pop group."

One of the women leaned forward companionably. "Hasn't been back for a long time, has he? Laying down the red carpet now he has come, I hear. Half the councilors turning out and lunch laid on at the Swan and all. It's to be hoped now he'll remember where he was born and do something for the town."

"Rafe Roister, that's what he calls himself now. Be mobbed, I shouldn't wonder. These teenagers go mad about him."

"Went away fourteen years ago," reflected Miss Peachum. "Well, once I set my eyes on him, I'll know how big he really is. The only pop I understand," she confided, "is 'Pop Goes the Weasel.' My Uncle Jim used to sing it—most comical he was."

You wouldn't have thought any of them was in a hurry to reach his or her destination, the way they leaned over and chatted and checked their parcels. Then they stopped again to set someone else down; she was hung with packages like a Christmas tree. No, she wasn't going to get trodden underfoot for any pop star, even if he was in the top ten. There was a bit more badinage and then on the bus went. If he really felt so strongly about his birthright, why hadn't he come back before? And now he was here, why wasn't he laying on a bunfight?

They smiled at one another after she'd gone. Fancy expecting the rich to do that sort of thing. Wouldn't stay rich long if they did.

The lights changed at a crossroads and the next thing they knew they were behind one of these long vehicles crawling like some mammoth caterpillar and taking practically all the road, and by the time they were free of that, there was no sign of Jan.

"Not to worry, girls," said Ron, the spirited conductor—life and soul of any party, Ron. "She'll have taken the shortcut down the gully. They all do it."

And so they did, though the next generation said it was

206

young to be tired of life, wasn't it? The road plunged downward, thickly grown with coarse grass, so if there was a stone or a coil of roots in your way, you'd never see it, but it got the ardent cyclist and motorcyclist off the road. Jan went down on Hugh Wheeler's scooter, on some other chap's motorbike or, as today, shot down under her own steam. She'd guide her machine among bushes skirting a malodorous pond, and so on to the path that led you back to the main road quite near the station.

Dawn looked anxiously at the watch on her wrist. "It's twelve o'clock—well, nearly," she whispered.

"I expect the train will be late," Coral consoled her. "Daddy says they always are."

And then they really were there, and a mountain of large well-fed females with shopping baskets as plump as themselves got up to storm the door. They hadn't appeared to be in a hurry till now, but now they couldn't get out fast enough.

"Just a minute, ladies," said the gallant Ron. "Miss Peachum's just alighting."

Nobody complained, nobody even looked put out. Poor old So-and-So, ex-schoolmarm, can't have had much fun in her time and now looking as if a breeze would blow her over.

"All right?" asked Ron, handing the old lady down.

Miss Peachum struck mistrustfully at the ground with her rubber-tipped cane, as if she suspected it might dissolve under her tread. Then she looked at the station, which stood at the end of a short slope. "It seems to have grown steeper," she said accusingly.

A large notice outside the station announced CAR PARK FULL; in the road immediately below was the car waiting to take Rafe Roister to the Swan, flanked by a few others for his entourage. There seemed to be a lot of commotion, with people still pushing up from the road in the hope of seeing their idol alight.

"The young ladies are going to the station," Ron suggested,

"they'll give you a hand, won't you, girls? Not to worry about your friend, she's bound to be here, unless she stopped by the lake for a swim." He laughed at his own ready wit.

The little girls were looking about anxiously, though it wasn't going to be easy to find anyone in that crush. Even from where they stood, it was obvious the platform would be packed. And still they came on. Not the housewives from the bus, who had better things to do—one or two had oiled unostentatiously into the Plough and Dragon not a hundred yards away. You didn't stop for elevenses on a market day but you didn't go without your refreshment.

Miss Peachum set her hand on Dawn's shoulder. "Not too fast," she adjured her. "Your mother would be glad to know you weren't allowed in such a mob. And what school do you go to?"

They told her. "State education!" approved the old lady. "Mind you, I doubt whether you get the thorough grounding that was thought necessary when I was a gel. No O's and A's in those days, but none the worse for that." She looked about her appreciatively. "I wonder when he went away if Cyril appreciated the triumphal nature of his homecoming. Dear me, all those flags—Welcome Home—he can't think this much of a home to him. He'd be—let me see—about thirty-two . . ."

"Quite old!" said Coral politely.

"He won't think so." Her large handbag of artificial leather swung out and caught the child on the shoulder.

"Can I carry it for you?" asked Coral.

Miss Peachum screwed up the strap as if she'd bind it into her flesh. "That's the one thing I always carry myself," she said.

"Like the burden in *Pilgrim's Progress*," contributed Dawn.

"But someone could carry it for you," Coral insisted. "Bearing one another's burdens we His gracious law fullfil. Look, Dawn, did you see who that was?"

"Walk in a straight line, little girl," commanded Miss Peachum severely. "You might have had me off my feet."

"It was Hugh Wheeler," insisted Coral. "You know, he said

if Jan would go on his next demo, we could go with her in a cart, representing Help the Aged or something."

"Not a cart," corrected Dawn. "A float. I'd like that, wouldn't you, Coral? But perhaps Mr. Crook wouldn't let her."

"They wouldn't want him on a float. Mr. Crook's a friend of Jan's," she added politely. "That's really why we're here. He sent a message."

Someone barged into the old lady from behind.

"No manners nowadays," remarked the old lady. "Good heavens, who are those?"

She lifted her stick and pointed to a gathering of very young teenagers ("They're called teenyboppers," said helpful Coral), who, armed with rattles and colored balloons, were wedged in a solid mass just outside the station. The British Rail official in charge wasn't going to have them on the platform, though they clamored like a regiment of owls. They wore their darling's picture on lockets round their necks or screwed into imitation gold hearts dangling from their wrists. Some of them wore jerseys with R.R. in huge letters on the front. They stamped and pushed and chattered—Miss Peachum didn't think of owls, magpies was a better simile, a nasty thieving type of birds, very flashy, all that vivid black and white.

"Where are their mothers?" Miss Peachum wondered aloud.

"Roll on, Judgment Day," said a voice near at hand. It came from the driver of one of the cars. "They should give us danger money for this. Wild cats aren't in it."

There was only one main station entry and exit. Passengers arriving on the further platform climbed stairs to cross the line. The car park was this side, too, and every available inch was occupied. At last they were there; there weren't many people behind them now, they'd all pushed past.

"Best stand here out of everyone's way," an official suggested as they pressed through. "And don't let the little girls go off on their own."

Dawn opened her mouth to say they'd no official connection

with the ex-schoolteacher, but Miss Peachum said authoritatively, "Naturally, they will stay with me. Dear me, what a large number of police."

The exigencies of the local force had, indeed, been stretched to its limit and beyond. This sort of occasion provided a paradise for the pickpocket, since obviously the fuzz can't be in two places at once and their first job was to see that the guest of honor wasn't crushed under foot.

"Killed by kindness, in fact," suggested one officer to another.

"You'd be just as dead whichever way it was" came the swift retort. "You'd think chaps would have the sense to leave their valuables at home on a day like this, but— Just look at that woman's bag, not even shut and probably all the housekeeping in it for a family of eight."

The children's eyes flew like butterflies round the crowded platform. Another female group had assembled on the platform itself. These were the members of the Anti-Porn Pop Crusade, and they were there to protest again the hero's latest song, "Go Down on Your Knees to Love." Blasphemy, they called it, and one or two of the lines could be twisted into secondary meanings that couldn't possibly pass the bar of Puritans, Inc.

"Oh, please," besought Coral, "is there a band?"

"Mr. Roister's his own band, and by all accounts he's very good at the loud pedal. Perhaps he'll bring it with him on the train. Goodness knows," the officer went on to no one in particular, "why he had to come by train when he's got a car that's more showy than Queen Elizabeth the First."

"Perhaps he was afraid he wouldn't be able to park it," Coral said. "Dawn, do you remember when we had that comb and fife band last Christmas to represent the angels singing in the sky and Miss Temple said it was irreverent?"

"We'll never find Jan here," said Dawn. "Talk about sardines."

210

"They all have to come out of the same gate, so we're bound to see her sooner or later."

"Mr. Crook said, 'Don't take your eye off her.' " She moved away a step or two, and at once Miss Peachum's large bony hand caught her shoulder.

"You are to stay here," she said. "Until some other older person comes along I feel responsible for you. I can't imagine what your mother was doing allowing you to come unattended."

"But Jan's here . . ." Someone pushed her aside, saying to his companion, "He'll be in the middle section of the train. Never travel right in front or right behind. Then if there's a collision or a derailment, you stand the best chance."

The whole platform seemed to bristle with cameras. Most of the teenyboppers had one, and the press was quite respectably represented.

"Did you come just to see Rafe Roister?" Dawn asked Miss Peachum.

"Naturally I like to keep in touch with my old pupils as opportunity offers. Even after many years I can remember them."

"Perhaps he'll remember you," encouraged Coral. "Mr. Crook's going to be on the train too."

"Better not tell the police," said a humorist standing near by.

"Oh, the police all know Mr. Crook. He told us."

There was a gale of laughter that passed over their heads. "Rum some of the names chaps get saddled with," said the man. "You'd think they'd change them."

"Remember that grocer at Framley Cross? Trash his name was. Mind you, he did his best. Had T. R. Ash in big letters over the door, hoped newcomers would call him Mr. Ash."

"Hullo, train's signaled," someone said. "Stand by for broken ribs. Let the mob get off first and we can get on in comfort. If I'd realized they were having this kind of a do today, I'd have made the appointment for tomorrow."

"Stay exactly where you are when the train comes in," Miss Peachum said. "You shouldn't really be here at all without an adult . . ."

"We've got Jan. When the crowd thins we shall find her, and by then she'll have found Mr. Crook. We shall be quite all right, thank you."

A fervent voice close by said earnestly, "He's got ever such a lovely voice. Fill the whole station, I shouldn't wonder."

"Or empty it, according to your taste."

And then at last the train could be seen traveling smoothly towards them.

"What a pity it isn't steam!" the children said. "Then it could have puffed and puffed."

And now those who'd been waiting for their idol's appearance seemed to bunch yet more closely together, solid wedges of humanity. The teenyboppers held their rattles in readiness. A wind blew out a red and gold banner—WELCOME TO WATERLOW CROSS. The police stiffened, the pickpockets prepared to make a haul.

"There she is," cried Dawn. "Look, up there, away from the crowd. I wonder if we could reach her."

"You wouldn't get through," Coral said. "I expect he told her not to get lost in the crowd."

Jan was standing near the platform edge, making no effort to be the first to spot the hero of the day. She had his records, of course—well, some of them, anyway, what young person hadn't?—but she didn't suppose she'd see much of him. He was reputed to be rather short, so the crowd would swallow him up. She was surprised at the number of older women who were waiting, but it was said he enchanted all ages. Even Hugh Wheeler had come, though normally he'd be working for Mr. Pringle at this hour.

"Won't Daddy be surprised when he hears we were here when Rafe Roister arrived? Oh, the train's stopping. Look out for Mr. Crook, Dawn, unless he sees us first."

"He won't be looking for us. It's Jan he's coming to meet."

"He told us to keep an eye on her and that's just what we're doing."

Her sister nodded. "That's right. Everybody else is keeping an eye out for Rafe Roister."

Well, perhaps not quite everyone. Round the outskirts of the crowd, moving smoothly as a snake, lounged a young man, threading his way through the groups and making for the upper end of the platform where Jan waited. The autograph hunters had paper and pencil at the ready, cameras were poised, the teenyboppers prepared to applaud, the Anti-Porn crusaders to protest. One of the maestro's entourage opened the door of his carriage and stood holding it gently against the magical moment when the hero of the hour would reveal himself to his slaves.

And then it happened.

A scream as harsh as rending calico rang through the station. "Jan!" yelled a voice. "Look out!"

And like an echo came a second voice. "Jan, he's going to . . ."

Heads that should have been focused on Mr. Roister started to turn; cameras wavered in their holders' hands, voices started to clamor. Then flashlights half blinded the eyes of two little girls fighting to escape from authority in the persons of Miss Peachum and a uniformed porter.

"But it's Jan" came in passionate protest.

"And he was going to push her under the train."

Here was melodrama with a vengeance. It was a bit prodigal of life to spread the butter so thick when the rest of the week might be no more than dry bread. Miss Peachum's voice cried furiously, "What do you think you're doing? Has no one ever taught you how to behave in public?"

"He was going to push her under the train."

The incredible words echoed all round the station.

$\bullet$ $\bullet$ $\bullet$

In the carriage of the returning local hero everything was in readiness for the great moment. The erstwhile Cyril Ponsonby was on his feet, a short, compact figure wearing a suit that couldn't have cost much less than a hundred pounds, and the trendiest shoes Waterlow Cross had ever seen. He wore a shirt that beggared description and flashed a striking ring. Apart from that, there was nothing special about his appearance. As soon as the train stopped, the carriage door would be flung open and he would stand for a moment poised above the crowd to give the photographers their opportunity. Then he would thread his careful way through the adoring (and probably semi-hysterical) crowd to where the special car awaited him. The councilors waited too, those who had been deputed to be on tap. And then—this had to happen, attention that should be focused on him was being misdirected because of some half-crazy girl.

He hadn't seen the children or Jan. He had only a flash in which to make up his mind, but show biz is an affair of split-second timing. The train had barely drawn to a standstill when he leaped out onto the platform, his arms raised in a familiar gesture, and began to sing "Go Down on Your Knees to Love."

They had been right about one thing. It was a glorious voice, no one could blame its owner for rejecting the offer of a future partnership in one of the snuggest little corn chandler's businesses in the county. The teenyboppers' mouths fell open and for a moment their rattles were still; the Anti-Porn Crusade forgot to boo. The only people who remained impervious were the two shouting children and the odd couple standing near the spot where the engine had just rolled smoothly past.

Jan, who had been watching the approaching train from a convenient vantage point, as she had been instructed by telephone, had been startled almost out of her wits by that demented childish shriek. There wasn't even time to wonder what they were doing there, when they'd been left safely at the Manor House, and it had been instinct, not good sense, that

214

made her take a couple of inward paces that drew her away from the platform edge. The arm raised to give her the treacherous thrust under the wheels struck her shoulder, so that she staggered, but away from the train. She had been so engrossed in waiting for Crook that the rich preparations for the return of yet another Local Boy Makes Good had made no great impression on her. But a moment later the tumult began, rattles were shaken, detractors booed, cries of approval filled the air. The mob surged forward to touch its idol's sleeve, carriage doors clashed, Waterlow Cross was simply another station on the journey. Everything had happened so fast the conductor wasn't aware he had almost been a witness to a murder.

The sound of almost universal acclamation hummed round Jan's head like a hive of bees. Until her arrival at the station she had not appreciated that this was the day of Rafe Roister's triumph. She didn't belong to his army of fans, and in any case all her thought had centered on Mr. Crook, who was making this unheralded journey by a means almost unknown to him. Then, recalling the children, she swung round. "Dawn! Coral!"

"We're coming as fast as we can," said the staunch young voices, "but there's such a lot of people."

Then another voice spoke, not sympathetic, not even much moved. "You don't mind taking chances, do you?" it said. "If you've got a fear of heights, why stand on the very edge of the platform?"

She found her voice. "Someone pushed me. I was waiting for Mr. Crook. He said . . ."

"You mean Crook's here?"

"He was coming down on the train, this train."

"Then where is he?"

She looked round as if she expected him to materialize out of the clotted air.

"Did he tell you himself . . . ?" The voice sounded more impatient than ever.

"It was a message. I was to meet him . . ."

"And you fell for that? If Crook had wanted you here, he'd have told you himself. And stop shaking like an aspen. It's contagious."

She seemed to see him for the first time. "Hugh! Hugh Wheeler! But what are you doing here?"

"If you must know, I've come to collect some props for our next demo. I suppose they've been tossed out on the platform, if anyone could take their minds off this Roister chap. You didn't come for him?"

"I told you, I came for Mr. Crook."

"So you did. And he didn't turn up. Good heavens!"

For the impatient children had at last broken free of their captors and were forging through the throng like a miniature battering ram. (Miss Peachum had finally given nature best; the tumult and the shouting were too much for her, and she had allowed herself to be assisted to a seat just outside the station, provided by a Council kindly disposed towards the elderly. A good-hearted female sat beside her and patted her hand.)

"We'll look after the little girls," a policeman had promised. "Gone to their head, all this excitement."

All the same, there had been that mention of Mr. Crook. He remembered his coming down when Mrs. Brown got her comeuppance. He devoutly hoped he was another figment of the children's imagination, as well as that ridiculous charge of attempted murder. One thing, he was difficult to miss—and there was no sign of him.

The pop star, seeing which way the wind was blowing and knowing that children and animals always hog the stage, gracefully gave them best, got himself out of the station and into the waiting car and drove off, followed by the still hysterical plaudits of the teenyboppers. The Anti-Porn chorus dried up at once. There were plenty of other causes of which to disapprove, and they needed their breath.

The children panted up to Jan and caught her hands. "We

216

thought you weren't going to hear," they said. "Jan, he meant to push you off the edge."

"You want to be careful what you're saying," said the policeman. "Why should anyone wish to harm the young lady?"

Mind you, it happened. There'd been a recent yarn in the press about some foreigner who persuaded his newly married wife to insure her life for some fantastic sum, to be doubled if she died of an accident, and then took her out and pushed her over the cliff for the insurance money. But he didn't think this was a similar case. Most likely an accident, though admittedly this wasn't the crowded end of the platform.

"You'd have to ask him."

"And you think he'd tell?"

"He'd say he didn't know anything about it, at least I should think so."

An enterprising journalist or so had pressed up to collect any dirt that might be going. Hugh they recognized at once, he was always on the go.

"It's Mr. Wheeler. Got a statement for us, Mr. Wheeler?"

"He wasn't the one who tried to push Jan over," cried the children, and Dawn added, "He's Jan's friend. He's going to have us on a float at the next demo. It's for old people. 'In my end is my beginning.' "

"And we're the beginning," chimed in Coral. "That old lady might do for the end. What happened to her?"

"I expect she saw Rafe Roister. That's why she came. Not for us."

"Tell us what you saw while you were waiting for Mr. Roister," coaxed the journalist.

"Not Mr. Roister. Mr. Crook. Why isn't he here, Jan?"

"You don't have to be in a place because someone rings up and says you're going to be," pointed out Hugh. "Didn't phone himself, mark you."

"You mean it was a *trick?*" cried Dawn.

The policeman thought things were getting out of hand. "You want to be careful what you say. It's a very serious charge, you'd need proof."

"We saw—didn't we, Coral?"

"We didn't see who he was. Jan was standing by herself, and of course there were all these people. We thought we'd looked everywhere, and then suddenly somebody moved and we saw her . . ."

"And there was this man—he was going to push her over, really he was."

"Someone pushed me," recalled Jan. "I thought. Such a crowd—and then the children. I never noticed who it was. And the next thing Mr. Wheeler was saying you should not stand near the edge if you hadn't a head for heights. But I am not afraid of heights, and that was where Mr. Crook had told me to stand. And after all, he is not here."

"You were the young lady who found Mrs. Brown, weren't you?" asked the journalist, instantly prepared to find a tie-up between the two events.

"I did not know who put her there. Dawn, Coral, does your mother know you are here?" A fresh thought struck her. "Why should you think I would be at the station?"

"You set out thataways and you took your bicycle—and we took the bus. Mr. Crook had told us . . ."

"Better ring up and make sure they aren't dragging the ponds for you," suggested Hugh.

"We told her we were going to the village, we didn't say which village."

"She will be worried . . ."

"Mother never worries. And anyway, Mr. Crook said we were to keep you under our eye."

"And it's a good thing we did. If Coral hadn't seen him . . ."

The policeman was beginning to sound exasperated. "You can't print this story," he said to the pressman. "A little girl sees someone slip and thinks she may have been pushed."

218

"She was pushed," insisted Coral. "I saw him."

"You don't see him anywhere around now?" insinuated the reporter shamelessly.

"You should know better than to ask that," exclaimed the policeman, shocked. "The young lady was a long way off . . ."

"Coral sees everything," said Dawn. "She's the one who found the flycatchers' nest. Even Daddy hadn't seen it."

Coral stood deep in thought.

"Don't strain yourself," said Hugh. "He probably looked just like everyone else."

A porter came up. "Mr. Wheeler? There's a parcel for you."

"I'll come and collect it. And I shall have to be getting back to Mr. Pringle. That man was born with a watch instead of a heart, except where his plants are concerned. So long, Jan. Look after yourself. And don't let the kids commit themselves," he added in lower tones.

"We will ring your mother," said Jan decidedly. "There is nothing more we can say."

But Coral didn't stir. "I'm thinking," she said. "That man."

"You don't want to start making things up," said the constable quickly.

"Black," said Coral.

Dawn's eyes flew open. "Oh no, I don't think . . ."

"Black hair and black . . ." She caressed her own small cheekbones. "Whiskers?"

"Sideburns," said Dawn knowledgeably.

"Can't be more than a few thousand chaps answering that description, particularly in a crowd like this," said the reporter, preparing to depart. The rozzer was right. No sense wasting any more time. You wouldn't hang a dog on the word of a six-year-old.

D. C. Kite was frowning. It was a queer story and you never could be sure with kids. You had to take their evidence with a tinful of salt. Given imagination, they would fervently believe their own stories in the face of all reason. But if it was improbable, it wasn't impossible. What really bugged him was the mention of Mr. Crook. No point in the girl inventing that, and if Crook had been on the train, the whole station would have discovered it long ago. And in such a crowd, would any girl not a complete zany (though to be sure, with foreigners you could never be certain) take up her stand on the edge of the platform, where the arrival of the great locomotive and its retinue of carriages might make anyone giddy? There'd been the mention of Mrs. Brown, too, though that might be pure chance. But it would be a perfect opportunity for a villain who wanted someone out of the way—the crowded platform, the increased tension as the train drew in, the breathless gaping of the crowd, all eyes (including hers, of course) fixed on that part of the train where the great man might be expected to be traveling. What a chance then for a casual fellow to slip up and with one adroit movement knock the girl off her feet. History recorded plenty of similar occurrences, many, no doubt, recorded as accidents. The closeness of the engine would make her a little dizzy; was it luck or instinct or the echo of a child's cry that had made her step back as instinctively as an animal and save herself? He found to his surprise he was attaching serious consideration to a small girl's story.

"Whoever he was he's not here now," he said. "You'd better ring the young lady's mother. You won't get back from here in a hurry, not with the crowds on the roads."

"We could go back in a police car," suggested Dawn. "We've been in Mr. Crook's Rolls Royce . . ."

"I expect your mother will come for you herself," said Jan.

"A police car would be more interesting."

"This person who told you Mr. Crook would be on the train—you've no idea who it was?" D. C. Kite said to Jan.

"I thought it must be Mr. Parsons, that is his partner. He said it was urgent, and I was to tell no one where I was going. I thought perhaps he was coming by train because he was afraid of an ambush if he came by car. I thought he had discovered

220

something. But you should not be here," she added to the children.

"We used our loaves," explained Dawn. "The way Daddy always says we should."

"You came on the bus?"

"We did think we might get a hitchhike but the bus came first. Of course, we couldn't be sure, but we didn't think he'd ask you to meet him at the Folly in the woods— We often go there," she added for the benefit of D. C. Kite, "because the car wouldn't go up the lane."

For the second time that day they were interrupted by a shriek from Coral. "Look, look, there he goes through the gate. Now I've lost him again, there's such a lot of people."

Now that the great man's car had driven away, the crowd was pouring off the platform, few of them realizing the (to them) minor drama being enacted in another part of the platform. They were surging into the car park, queuing up at the bus stop, jostling one another down the lane.

"Not much likelihood of picking him up now," muttered the constable. "Only chance will be if he gets jammed in the car park. A chap like that isn't likely to have come on foot."

His uniform helped him less to thread through the crowd than he had expected, and it was no use proceeding without the children, since only Coral had seen him, and he doubted whether his superiors would accept her unsupported word. Only, this might prove to be a case of attempted murder and there'd been enough mysterious deaths of late. And chaps don't push girls off platforms for fun, not unless they're out of a bin, and if she'd stumbled and he'd put out a hand to help her, why had he vamoosed so quickly? Modesty's O.K., but it can be overdone, and though Jan wasn't a raving beauty, she was the sort of a girl who merited at least a second glance. They struggled through to the car park, which was full of impatient drivers waiting for a chance to get out, but for once the pedestrians had the drop on them.

Coral, perfectly composed, walked round the cars, inspecting each driver in turn. "Not here," she said. "Perhaps he's waiting for a bus."

But, of course, he wasn't.

"You'd best ring the young ladies' mother," the policeman repeated. He knew who they were, of course, everyone knew the Banks children. "They can stay with me."

There was a telephone box by the station entrance and fortunately it was unoccupied. Dawn's contention that her mother would not be worried was far short of the mark. Not normally given to overanxiety where her children were concerned, Kay was by now half frantic. She had telephoned everyone who might have seen them and received negative answers on all sides. This convinced her that Jan, that treacherous creature, had confided the whereabouts of her rendezvous with the pestilential Mr. Crook, and the children had gone beetling off on their own account.

Putting ideas like that into children's heads, thought Kay desperately. Jan should be looking after them, not they after Jan.

If they weren't back by the time of Roy's return, he'd lift the roof. In her mind's eye she had visions of them, in their logical if harum-scarum fashion, hailing strange cars, and even to so phlegmatic a mother the prospect was terrifying. When the telephone rang she dashed at it, and was so much relieved to hear Jan's reassuring voice that her feeling showed itself in a voice as sharp as cracked glass.

"Where are you ringing from? What are you doing there?"

"I came to meet Mr. Crook, but he was not there."

"Of course he wasn't there, he's on his way down from London. But the children . . ."

"They said they used their loaves. The police can explain," she added desperately.

"Where do the police come in?"

"They were on the platform, there was an incident . . ."

222

"I don't see what that has to do with Dawn and Coral."

"You will," promised Jan. "I must go back. The police are looking after them. There's such a crowd, this pop star . . ."

"I can't see why you had to go there on such a day." Light broke. "Is that why you're all there? To see the pop star?"

"I came to meet Mr. Crook. They followed me—on the bus. An old lady brought them up to the station." Dawn had vouchsafed that detail.

"You'd better stay with them till I get up there. You can come back on your bicycle."

Hanging up the receiver, she resolved that once Jan's period of service was over, she'd never have another *au pair* in the house.

Fourteen

The young man responsible for Mrs. Brown's death squeezed through the station gate and was swallowed up in the crowd that now streamed in the direction of Waterlow Cross, pursuing their idol to his hotel, where they would camp outside his window, waving their flags and sounding their rattles, in the hope of bringing him onto the balcony. Terry Woods went with the rest. He had come in a car, of course, but the entrance to the car park was blocked solid. It was improbable that any sane person would listen to a demented kid, and even less likely that he could be recognized, but there was no harm putting a sizable gap between him and the police for the next hour or so. Then he could snake back and collect his car.

He was almost rigid with rage at the collapse of what had appeared to be a virtually foolproof plan. He belonged to what Crook called the Security Brigade; he couldn't chance his arm, commit his crime and then get out and wait. He had to come nosing back to see if, after all, he had tied up all the ends, blotted out all the clues. Or he stood about in locals listening to other drinkers, waiting for any reference to his particular affair. All the amateurs do it, Crook said; not the pros, that's why they are pros.

He'd assured himself (and Bernie, his partner) that he'd left nothing to chance. He didn't go for the big jobs, leave those to the big fellows. No, he picked the small houses that might yield a quick and reasonable profit, and then did his homework. When

225

his choice fell on the Manor House he looked about for an inside accomplice. He didn't much fancy breaking in unless he could be sure the place was empty, and there was Jan, obviously hand-tailored for the job—young, an alien, no family, no obvious support, a here-today-and-gone-tomorrow girl. And easy. He never had any trouble with girls, though, they just fell off the branches into his hands. He dated her, took her around a bit and talked; and let her talk in return. You couldn't say the cat had her tongue, she was as forthcoming as anyone could wish; he soon knew about Kay's Battersea enamels and Roy's trophies. He learned the domestic setup too. Mr. and Mrs. Banks, two kids, housekeeper. The kids were a bore, but less than a dog would have been; kids sleep tight and he wasn't planning a daylight raid.

He teased her about her situation. "What's it like being a slave in a foreign land?" he asked.

Jan's temperament was naturally serious and her brief experience hadn't been conducive to humor. "I am not a slave," she retorted. "I am an *au pair* girl."

"Isn't that the same thing? Or do you get some free time?"

"Whenever Mr. and Mrs. Banks are at home at night, I am free. Only if they go out I must stay with the children. Mrs. Brown says they are no concern of hers."

"Doesn't she ever go out?"

"She goes to bingo on Thursday and she has a singing session on Wednesdays. Sometimes she has friends in, there is a sitting room . . ."

Better and better, he thought. "How about me coming in to cheer your solitude one evening when they're all out?" he suggested.

Jan stiffened at once. "Mrs. Banks would not like . . ."

"Oh, come on. What does she think I want to do? Pinch the silver?" He laughed. He thought it an excellent joke.

But Jan didn't join in the laughter. "She thinks if I am talking I may not hear if one of the children calls out."

"She sounds a real old weirdie to me. Still, you wouldn't have to tell her."

When she remained adamant, he became annoyed though he didn't show it. It had seemed such an open-and-shut case. And now this stupid girl was wrecking his plans. He half wondered whether he should abandon the siege, when he had a rare stroke of luck. Shopping by chance in Buzzard Major, he heard a customer at the next counter say, "And send it to Mrs. Brown, Manor House, Buzzard Minor."

It was the address, not the speaker's name, that caught his attention, but when he turned and saw her almost full face, he nearly gaped in astonishment. He knew her at once, even after six years. She hadn't changed so much as just grown older. It was easy to rub up against her in the street and say, "Hullo, remember me?" She looked at him in blank non-comprehension. Well, that wasn't surprising, he'd been a cub reporter on the local *Argus,* she wouldn't be aware of his existence.

"Harrogate!" he insinuated. "Six years ago. Local County Court."

She changed then; her always pale face turned a kind of saffron-yellow. "What do you want?" she said.

So that's when they began, the rendezvous at the Pumpkin and Pie. She thought blackmail was all he had in mind, small sums, she wasn't likely to have saved a lot in six years, but he loved his sense of power over her. There was no particular hurry; Bernie wasn't immediately available, they didn't always work in pairs. She'd held her present job for six years, she wouldn't want to jeopardize it. Besides, once the truth was known, she'd have to leave the neighborhood that had become her home. He'd wait his opportunity and get an invite some evening, and if she'd been surprised to see him again, she was going to be a lot more surprised when he came with a friend to spend the evening. The opportunity arrived at that August weekend. Mr. and Mrs. Banks going away, children going to their auntie. Casually he picked up Jan again. What, he wondered, was she doing for the August holiday?

Jan wasn't sure; she might join Hugh in his demo, they always had a bit of a party afterwards. The children being away, she'd have some free time and Mrs. Brown would look after the house.

"Don't they trust you?" he ribbed her, and she said, "Mrs. Brown trusts no one."

"No boyfriends?" he asked. "I know you've no family. Well, why not come to Greece with me. If you can afford to pay your own fare, that is. My parents live in Greece, they'd like to meet you, heard quite a lot about you. So—how about it?"

"You make a joke?" asked Jan.

"No joke, I assure you," he promised.

She still hesitated. "Mrs. Banks . . ."

"You don't have to tell her where you're going. Say you're visiting another *au pair* girl, why shouldn't she believe you?"

Together they cooked up the story of the friend in Eastbourne; they even had a phony address for her, but Kay didn't ask for it.

"I'm glad you've got somewhere to go," she said, and took no further interest.

Terry took Jan's savings with no more hesitation than he had mulcted Mrs. Brown of hers. He had no conscience where either was concerned. He had no conscience—period.

So there it was—beautifully set up, and the old hag actually played into his hands by inviting him to come to the house on the Thursday evening.

"They will all be out," she said. "Mr. and Mrs. Banks are going to Amsterdam, and the little girls are going to their auntie. I shall go to the bingo as usual, but I shall come back early."

"I held the gate open and she walked right through," Terry had boasted. "Didn't even have to invite myself."

(It would never have occurred to him that she might be up to his weight, might be laying her own plans for his ruin as assiduously as he was plotting hers. In fact, she was prepared to go further than he. Her death hadn't been part of the schedule, and if she'd behaved like a reasonable female—the things were all insured, for Pete's sake—she'd still be darkening the face of the earth.)

But it hadn't gone at all as he planned. When she opened the door, tall, sharp as a darning needle, wearing her fantastic beads, her bag slung over her arm, and found the two hideous images on the doorstep, stockings drawn over anonymous faces, instead of giving them best, she'd fought like a wildcat. He'd had to grow the sideburns if only to conceal the ugly red scratch she'd inflicted on his cheekbone. That had made him see red, and he chopped her sharply under the chin. Down she went like a bag of sawdust, crumpled up against the banisters.

"Look out," Bernie had said. "You don't want to croak the old witch."

"Oh, rot!" he'd retorted. "She's only shamming. Where's the rope and the plaster? I'm not taking any chances with this one."

Only, as it happened, they weren't needed.

It didn't occur to either of them to call it a day; they'd come to get the goods and get the goods they would. They left her sprawled on the stairs while Bernie stripped the drawing room, and he collected Roy Banks's silver winnings. Then, as they were preparing to depart, it came, the sound they couldn't have anticipated. Someone swung open the gate, steps came up the path. They froze where they stood. Terry hadn't any doubt who it was. He hadn't believed Jan, realizing she had been conned, would have so little spirit that she would come back to the Manor House the same night. Just what she would do he hadn't bothered to consider. Find a room perhaps, sleep rough, get a job washing up in caffs—there were plenty of alternatives. She might even pick up a fellow, though she was a bit of an iceberg for that. But here she was, ringing for admission. Thank God, she had no key. After a minute the steps moved round the house and the back-door bell rang.

"She won't go away," said Terry, "she's nowhere to go. The place looks dark enough from outside, she'll hang about waiting for the old hag to turn up."

"We've got to get out," said Bernie.

"She'd be bound to see us, back or front," Terry objected.

"There's the French windows. It's dark and it's raining. You can't see them from the back door."

Before they went they hustled their victim into a boot cupboard; a cellar would have been better, but the house didn't seem provided with a cellar. They had parked their cars at the side, lest they attract attention from the invisible witness against whom no man can be armed. Then they collected their swag and stole out by the French windows. They discovered these couldn't be fastened from the outside, but the long heavy curtains would disguise that fact, and anyway, no one was likely to try them before morning. As they came slipping onto the lawn the front-door bell pealed again. By the time they had stowed their bags into the boots of their cars—they were traveling separately, Bernie had a night-flight ticket to Amsterdam, where he had a possible client for the enamels; Terry would see Josh Lang first thing in the morning, make the best bargain he could and then get off to Brighton for the weekend—before their cars had purred away across the common, Hugh Wheeler gave up his siege of the darkened house and drove his motor scooter to the Huntsman. Terry waited awhile to give Bernie a good lead, but no one came back to the house.

Terry had another shock on his way home, when some crazy rider on a motor scooter, coming hell-for-leather round a dangerous corner, nearly ran him down. He didn't stop to offer his assistance; he could see the rider had become unseated, but whoever it was couldn't be badly hurt, since she (it looked like a girl, though you could never be certain) was already on her feet. He whirled round the corner before anyone could take his number or give him a hail.

He had no other encounters on his way back. He saw no one

on the stairs as he carried the case to his room. Here, with the door locked, he examined his haul. It was rather better than he'd anticipated, good solid-silver pieces, none of the gimcrack stuff you sometimes found on women's dressing tables.

Josh would diddle him, of course, but even so— A nice little killing, he thought.

Thus is many a true word spoken in jest.

Brighton calmed his troubled nerves. He had no difficulty in picking up a smashing girl, and if there was anything in the press about an old drab being found dead in a cupboard, why should anyone associate it with him? There'd been nothing in the Friday papers, so she hadn't been found by midnight; nothing in Saturday either. If Bernie had any wits he'd stay away till the dust blew over. He didn't like the situation. Burglary and larceny were one thing, but to date he'd never even been guilty of grievous bodily harm, let alone murder. Not that it was fair to call it murder, of course, and even the courts would reduce the charge to manslaughter. They hadn't even taken a weapon with them. Suicide would be a truer verdict. They were bound to find her soon. Someone would notice the milk bottles accumulating, the papers not being collected. In the meantime the sun was shining in Brighton, and when he got back, there'd been half a hundred households waiting to be robbed, in spite of all the police warnings. Sometimes he even thought, It's a shame to take the money.

He read about Mrs. Brown in the Sunday press. Foul play was suspected. How stupid could you get? How could the old girl have put herself in the cupboard? He had a momentary horrid vision of her popping her head out of the door, calling coyly to the next entrant, but she couldn't, of course. He'd fastened the cupboard before he left. For the next few days he tried to adopt an attitude of nonchalant calm. But he couldn't clear out for good and simply wait. He had to know if there were any developments, sneaked back to the neighborhood, where he wouldn't be distinguishable from a score of other young chaps.

Just to be on the safe side. He heard that Mrs. Farmer of the Pumpkin and Pie had been to the police with her story of the dead woman meeting a young chap surreptitiously—well, fairly surreptitiously—in her bar, but nothing had come of it. Of Mrs. Gale he never thought at all. He'd represented himself there as a young man called Robinson, and he and Mrs. Brown had never been seen together. Besides, women in her shoes never recognized clients, a matter of policy as well as, probably, a matter of fact. Just to play safe, he'd grown sideburns and let his hair curl over his collar. That should be sufficient disguise for an emergency that probably would never arise.

He didn't bother about Jan either. He'd been careful not to take her to places where her own crowd went, and anyway, it hadn't been so frightfully often. These girls lost their heads and came tumbling down as easily as learners on an ice rink. In any case, she wouldn't want to publish the story of her connection with him—no girl likes to look a fool.

So, he thought, he was probably in the clear. The case would remain open on the police books, but the odds were they'd never get the chaps responsible. What made him so sure? Ask Crook. He'd tell you it's vanity that brings most criminals down. So his chance meeting with Mrs. Gale had been a hideous shock; the sideburns hadn't helped at all, she'd recognized him at once, hailed him as Mr. Robinson, and he'd been so much taken aback that his denial had been a shade too late to be convincing. She'd been laughing, he remembered, as she pushed her way into the bar. Well, she wouldn't do much more of that. Once these rattrapped women opened their mouths, you could anticipate trouble. When she'd disappeared, grinning all over her stupid face, he'd stood thoughtfully in the road for a moment. Bar trade wasn't very heavy as yet, there were hardly any cars in the car park, the casual drinkers came up on their own flat feet. A young man having a bit of trouble with his car wouldn't attract any attention at all. And what an old rattletrap hers was! It couldn't surprise anyone if that ran off the rails into eternity.

His luck held; no one came past in the short time it took him to tinker with the brakes, and he was off and away long before Mrs. Gale had finished gossiping with the amiable Katie. There was nothing in next day's paper about the "accident" but the local weekly carried the story, and no one even suggested foul play. The car was in too bad a state to be used as evidence. He'd done his job efficiently as well as quickly. If he'd opted for an honest life, he could have done quite well as a motor mechanic. He sighed with relief. One more obstacle out of his way.

He wasn't afraid of Josh Lang selling him up the river, he couldn't afford to take the chance. That left only Jan. And he wouldn't have let a slip of a girl bother him if it hadn't been for the sudden eruption of Arthur Crook into the picture. And when he had come and gone, and a fellow could breathe again, suddenly he reappeared. Bernie had come back and they'd done one more job since then, a genuinely empty house this time, in and out like a pair of eels. And it was after that that Lang had showed his fangs and told him he could get out and stay out, he wasn't having any truck with murder. He wouldn't go to the police, of course, he had his own name to think of, but it was a shock just the same.

All the time he was remembering this sequence of events he was walking steadily down the road, moving with the slow steps of the crowd that still surged behind him. Now a laden bus went by and the cars were beginning to extricate themselves from the pedestrians. Soon it would be safe to return to the car park, where nothing would remain but the cars of commuters. By that time the police and the crowds would alike have dispersed, and no one had actually seen him except that nosy kid with her pointing finger and her yelling face. If he could have pushed her onto the line after Jan, he wouldn't have hesitated. It had been such a splendid opportunity and he didn't see how it could fail.

He was now some distance from the station and on a corner he saw a café restaurant offering hot lunches. He went in and sat at a table at the back. While he waited for his steak to be cooked he went on contemplating the morning's disastrous enterprise. It had seemed to him foolproof. The platform would be packed with oafs of both sexes; an anonymous message to Jan to be waiting on the platform near the engine would put her precisely where he wanted her. As the train came streaming in, all eyes would be fastened expectantly on one of the central carriages in which you could be sure the hero of the day would travel. She also would be expectant of the improbable spectacle of Mr. Crook traveling by British Rail. It shouldn't be difficult with the crowd clenching itself together, so to speak, in a paroxysm of excitement as the train began to slow down, to execute a single dexterous gesture that would topple her off her feet. Before anyone was aware of what was happening, he would himself be lost in the crowd, as shocked as everyone else.

And then—it was like a nightmare—that wild infantile scream. Jan had responded like a streak of lightning, turning in its direction, so that his lifted arm caught her on the shoulder, causing her to stumble, but *away* from the platform edge, saved from a fall by the density of the crowd. The demented child continued to shriek, attracting attention even from the worshiping mob. In the ensuing scramble it was easy to escape individual notice. He saw a policeman trying to force his way through the throng, the children pressing closely against him, while Jan had turned and was trying to force her way to meet them.

He had strictly, in his character as Crook's emissary, told her to say nothing about the rendezvous, but she had told the children, so much was clear. Never trust women, he thought, they can't keep their traps shut. All the same, he was surprised that she had involved the children, only, of course (on second thoughts), she had taken it all at face value. She'd swallowed his

234

second treachery as unhesitatingly as she had swallowed the first.

And now, he supposed, the malevolent Crook would come surging in again, additionally incensed at having his name taken in vain, and heaven only knew what absurd theory he'd propound. What with this setback and Lang's repudiation of him, it might be a good idea to take a bit of a holiday, overseas, say. The dust storm would soon die down—storms always did . . .

He pushed back his plate and thoughtfully stirred his coffee. The crowds had gone now, he'd oil up the hill and collect his car. The platform would be empty. Rafe Roister, to give him his fancy name, wouldn't be coming back here; he was doing what you might call a whistle-stop tour all round the county. Tomorrow there'd be another crowd on another station. He wondered if the fellow was even aware of the minor drama that had been enacted as he stepped from the train.

He paid his bill and went out. The road was pretty empty now, no police hovering, no hooded figure lurking. He walked easily up the hill, attracting no more attention than a buzzing fly.

He didn't notice the police car at first, drawn up in an unobtrusive corner of the park. Only as he unlocked his own car door he heard another door clash and there was a bobby walking steadfastly towards him. Automatically he glanced over his shoulder, because the chap surely couldn't be coming for him, but there was no one else in the park.

The officer came nearer. "This your car, sir?"

"Looks like it, doesn't it?"

"May I see your license?"

He stared. "What the devil for?"

"If you please, sir."

With a pretty poor grace he hauled it out and handed it to the constable, who glanced at it, as if noting the name and address, before he handed it back.

"Play over?" suggested the young man.

Another car door closed and he saw a girl crossing towards them. He stiffened. The officer waited until she had joined them, and then said, "Do you recognize this man, miss?"

She said in a low, incredulous tone, "Nikki! But it couldn't be you. How could I do you any harm?"

"There's some mistake," said the alleged Nikki levelly. "I don't know this girl."

Jan's head came up; the brilliant color that had begun to flood her face paled again. When she spoke her voice was as taut as steel. "You took my money," she said, "to pay for a ticket to Greece."

"My dear girl," he told her, "I've never been to Greece."

"But you took my money to buy the ticket. We were going for the August holiday."

"I spent that weekend at Brighton, if it's of any interest to anyone. And I daresay I could prove it if I were pushed."

Her voice was unchanged. "But you took my money to get a ticket for Greece."

"And I suppose you could provide half a dozen witnesses."

"I told Mr. Crook."

"You could have told the man in the moon, but it wouldn't give you a case." He turned to the constable. "As you can see from my papers, my name isn't Nikki."

"I never supposed it was, sir," returned the policeman woodenly.

"Then what's all this in aid of?"

"We'd like you to accompany us to the station."

"Are you charging me?" His eyes flashed. "What with?"

"The young lady's identified you . . ."

He turned on Jan. "What are you talking about? You'll never get away with this."

"Why did you want me out of the way that night?" demanded Jan, as furious as he.

"We'll ask the questions, if you please," D. C. Kite interposed.

Before he could answer that, a voice heard only once before and never, he had hoped, to be heard again, called clearly, "He's the one."

He lifted his eyes, incredulous with rage. A second policeman was approaching, holding the hands of two small girls. It was the younger of these, a midget kid really, who repeated in the same clear voice, "That's the one. I saw him. He was trying to push Jan under the train."

"Is this Children's Hour?" Nikki demanded. "Do I tell the next fairy tale."

"And I saw him going out of the station," the inexorable voice continued.

Nikki turned to the police. "I happen to be a free-lance journalist. I'm covering Rafe Roister's tour. I couldn't get near the car park when I came out, so I went along and had some lunch while I waited. The people there will remember me, I daresay."

"We saw him," repeated Coral. Her great blue eyes outfaced him.

"Did no one ever tell you it's rude to stare?" he shouted.

"Good heavens!" exclaimed the second policeman. "What's this?"

A large yellow Rolls of ancient lineage was bowling up the hill.

"It's Mr. Crook," cried Dawn, and she and her sister dived in its direction.

Jan was after them in a flash. "Wait till it stops," she cried. "Mr. Crook wouldn't run us over."

As the car came to a standstill Kay poured herself out. "What are you doing here?" she cried aggressively. "You told me you were going to the village."

"We didn't say which village."

"Did Jan tell you . . . ?"

"Jan didn't tell us anything. We used our loaves, like Mr. Crook said."

"More than my client seems to have done," remarked Mr. Crook. "What gave you the idea I'd be coming down on a disc jockey's train?"

The children flew to the defense of their darling. "We thought you might suspect an ambush, and on a train you would be safe." Mr. Crook wrinkled his nose. "You couldn't ambush a whole train."

"You'd be surprised," said Mr. Crook. "And seeing I wasn't coming by car, where was the sense in asking you to meet me at the station. You couldn't give me a lift on the back of your little bike." He seemed to notice Nikki at last. "Friend of yours?"

"He's the one who tried to push her under the train," cried Dawn, shocked. "Coral saw him."

"Don't think we were introduced," murmured Crook.

"This is Nikki," said Jan in a flat voice.

Mr. Crook's eyebrows shot up. "Number Twenty-eight?"

Nikki gave a violent start. "I don't know what you're talking about," he shouted.

"Mrs. Gale might have been able to help, but alas, she's no longer with us. If you don't want my client any longer . . ." He turned politely to the police.

"Miss Van Damm's coming to the station with us."

"It's all a load of cods-wallop," said Nikki.

"He took my money," asserted Jan.

"Get a receipt?" murmured Mr. Crook. "Always a wise thing to do."

"We're going too, aren't we?" urged Coral. "We can make statements."

"The charge involves obtaining money by false pretenses," D. C. Kite pointed out. "Not attempted murder."

"We saw him."

"What about my car?" Nikki demanded.

"We'll look after that. Give the officer the keys . . ."

He tried to protest, but it was a waste of time. Crook could have told him it would be. In cases like this the police always win.

"I'll drive you all back," Crook offered the Banks family obligingly. "Then I'll come along to the station and collect my client. And watch your step," he added to Jan. "A dove among serpents won't be in it."

Fifteen

Jan stood forlornly, watching the big yellow car disappear smoothly round the bend. Now she felt alone; even Hugh had deserted her. Looking across to where Nikki stood, she wondered at her earlier feeling of infatuation. He looked the same, well, practically the same, his voice and mannerisms were unchanged—but what madness to suppose there was any security there. And I believed him, she thought. I believed he meant to take me to Greece, to introduce me to his parents, and all the time he was leading me up the garden. She didn't expect to see her money again, but she didn't doubt the truth of what the children had said, that he had plotted against her, though as yet she didn't follow that to its logical conclusion. "Why?" she had asked him. "What harm could I do you?"

Nikki spoke. "I'm entitled to speak to my lawyer," he said.

"You'll have every facility for ringing him up from the station, sir."

"Not that I shall bother," said Nikki. "The situation's too absurd. You haven't got as much proof as would cover a prewar threepenny-bit."

"Why should I tell Mr. Crook you had taken my money if you had not?" demanded Jan.

"If you'd get into the car, miss, we can settle all this at the station. We just want a statement." That was the policeman

241

again. His voice was wooden enough, though his manner was persuasive, but he knew there was a lot more at stake. But this wasn't the moment for speech.

In point of fact, the police weren't at all happy about the situation. If Mr. Crook hadn't been involved, matters might even have been allowed to lapse. A rookie could tell you that the girl couldn't adduce proof of her story, though it was improbable enough to be true. But—she'd said she'd told Crook the facts on the day in question and Crook hadn't denied it. And there had been that odd remark of the girl's, "Why did you want me out of the way that night?" All in all, the best thing seemed to be to get the pair of them down to the station and see what higher authority had to say. Crook had said he'd be joining them there, at all events.

At the station the station sergeant regarded them dubiously. "Taking a chance, weren't you?" he said.

"The girl insisted on bringing a charge."

"She can't believe she can make that stick."

"There's Mr. Crook, Sarge."

"I thought he'd bowed out." The sergeant scowled.

"He came bowling in again in that yellow monstrosity of his, and he's coming on here, to support his client, he says. Apparently she met him the night she claims she was cheated of her money and told him the story."

"Just the sort of thing that would happen to Crook," said the sergeant.

"And then," pursued D. C. Kite, "there was that thing the girl said."

"You must have forgotten to tell me that."

"She asked this chap—Nikki she called him, though that's not the name on his driving license—why did he want her out of the way that August night. And Crook chipped in with something about Mrs. Gale and Number Twenty-eight."

"Any idea what he was talking about?"

"I'll tell you one thing, Sarge. This chap Nikki did."

The sergeant pondered. "Who was that woman who came forward with a yarn about Mrs. Brown meeting a young chap in her bar? Not Mrs. Gale, I take it?"

"You'll be able to ask Mr. Crook when he comes along."

"If it should be the same one," the sergeant brooded.

"Bit of a bow at a venture," Kite offered.

"They have their moments. It was an archer drawing a bow at a venture who got King Agag in the joints of his harness and another who brought down the Norman invader of the second generation, William the Second, with an arrow through his eye. If there's any chance of identification, and she'll be careful enough, publicans' wives always are, it would be a help. We can't hold the chap without bringing a charge, and even Crook won't suggest that the girl's statement unsupported is enough. As for the child—how old do you say she is, six?—Counsel's only got to say to the jury, 'I suggest to you, gentlemen of the jury, that the young lady slipped and my client made an instinctive effort to prevent her falling,' and they'll all give him the benefit of the doubt, if doubt there be. All the same," he added reflectively, "if he was really there to follow Rafe Roister's tour, it's funny he never got as far as the hotel, or even within shouting distance of him."

Elsie Farmer was washing up the teacups, preparatory to going along to the bar to make sure all was in order for opening time, when the side bell rang.

"Let it ring," counseled Fred. "We're not open yet."

Publicans had as much right to their rest periods as anyone else.

But Elsie was a woman and knew you can't offer this sort of challenge to fate. A ring at the door, the sound of a telephone bell pealing, even an unexpected turn in what looked like a straight road, may change the whole course of your life.

"Who wants it changed?" Fred said. But Elsie knew men

were the unenterprising sex. All the same, when she had opened the door and found a policeman outside, she almost wished she'd listened to Fred. You'd think even a copper would have the tact to keep away just before opening time.

"Sure you've come to the right place?" she asked tartly, hoping Fred 'ud keep his distance. Fred mistrusted bluebottles even in a just cause. Licensed Nosey Parkers.

"Mrs. Farmer?" said the bobby. "We'd like you to come down to the station. We'd like you to help us with an identity parade. There's a young chap there who's said to have frequented your bar . . ."

"I can't know every young chap who comes into my bar," Elsie protested.

"If you don't recognize him, you've only to say so. No one's going to twist your arm," the policeman urged. "It won't take you long. I've got the car."

"I'll have to tell Fred," said Elsie reluctantly. "Don't expect him to be pleased, though. He knows all about it being the duty of the citizen to aid the police, but Fred was never special struck on duty."

Fred was good and sick. "Have to come around opening time, don't you?" he said.

"We never close," quoth the policeman solemnly.

"Who is this chap, anyway?"

"That's what we hope your wife will be able to tell us."

Oh, there's no doubt about it, the police are maddening at times.

At the station a number of young men stood in a line. There was nothing particularly unusual about any of them, except the one who'd got himself up like Robin Hood—chestnut suit, green waistcoat, green suede boots with red heels and laces. Almost worth the journey to see him, Elsie thought appreciatively.

"Stand where you like," Nikki was told. He thought every eye was turned on him. That's British justice for you.

Elsie walked slowly down the line, scanning each face, betraying nothing. At the end she turned. Cheek to expect her to remember one chap out of the many who drank at the Pumpkin and Pie. And yet—and yet—she had her doubts, and in circumstances like these you have to be dead sure. One of the men put up his hand and rubbed his chin.

Elsie walked back down the line and touched his shoulder.

"You're sure?" the policeman urged. He looked a shade dubious. The police don't always get as good a press as they'd like, and he wasn't much of a one for second thoughts. His own private life was largely controlled by them.

"I'm sure," she said as they moved away. The other chaps were told they could go. Nikki was fuming. "He's got more hair on his face than he had when he came to meet Mrs. Brown, but I couldn't mistake that ring. I did mention it at the time."

When the police, armed with a search warrant, turned over Nikki's pad, they found one unusual article. At the back of a drawer they unearthed a pair of black nylon stockings still in their cellophane envelope.

"Is that what the chaps are wearing these days?" they said, and they wouldn't believe him when he said something about always having a spare pair for a girl friend. Nylons laddered too easy.

"Your girl friend's got big legs, hasn't she?" they suggested. "Can't be complimented to find you've bought her the biggest size on the market."

And, challenged, he couldn't produce the girl.

Crook and Hugh Wheeler sat in the bar of the Come and Get It, drinking beer.

"You'd think he'd have too much sense to go round flashing a dirty great ring," said Hugh rather scornfully.

"It's vanity," said Crook. "Gets 'em all in the end. Remember that chap who kept drowning wives in baths? Got away with it once or twice and thought he could get away with it forever. And there was a case in the last century—fellow shot his common-law wife as she was getting out of her pony carriage or gig and buried her in the moat. Gave out she'd left him, no one specially surprised, she was a bit older and a whole lot genteeler, as they'd have said in those days, she had the money and wouldn't part, he couldn't marry her because he had a wife already, and everything would have worked out just fine if he hadn't got overconfident, and that's when chaps become careless. Bank queried his signature once or twice, but he explained he'd hurt his hand and practiced harder than ever. But he was a randy sort of chap, gift to the village maidens, and presently it was noticed that some of them were wearing geegaws known to have belonged to the late Harriet. A bit of a tightwad, she'd never have gone off and left those behind. So they dug and they found. The Moat Murder, it was called." He looked sideways at his companion, but it was obvious Hugh had never heard of it.

"Those kids are convinced he was trying to push Jan overboard," he observed.

"Wouldn't surprise me at all," said Crook, "but they won't bring it up in court, any more than Nikki will have to defend himself on a charge of swindling Sugar out of her hard-won earnings. The police are like the mills of God, they grind slowly, but they grind exceeding small. Any minute now they'll come up with the discovery that that ring figured in some insurance claim after a house had been broken into, and let Master Nikki laugh that one off. And," he added thoughtfully, "they may trace him back to Harrogate, where he could have met the lady. Or his buddy may lose his head and sing, that often happens where death steps into the picture, even if you can scale it down to

246

manslaughter. They'll cook that couple's goose, it's only a question of time."

Hugh's face was iron-hard. He could work himself to a frazzle on behalf of the underprivileged, the homeless, meth drinkers, the aged, but he hadn't a grain of compassion to spare for Nikki and his mate. Crook even wondered, if capital punishment had been restored, if Hugh would have organized a protest on moral grounds.

Hugh wasn't thinking about Nikki at all. "That Mrs. Banks," he broke out. "She's an astonishing woman. I believe that if it weren't for the children, she'd have got rid of Jan. Publicity is so harmful to the young. Only they'd raise such a rumpus even she wouldn't dare."

"It wouldn't be the end of the world if she did," said Crook coolly. "A girl like that isn't going to spend the next ten years acting nursemaid to other people's children. She'll have other ideas. Besides, they'll be going to school soon. Roy Banks will see to that."

"She's got no family," protested Hugh.

"Only the whole world. I should koko. My dear fellow, that girl's Mr. Right will turn up O.K., if he hasn't arrived already without knowing it. There's one that was never born to die in a single bed."

And catching the barman's eye, he ordered a refill for the pair of them.